Dark Streets, Bright Lights

F. L. RICHARDS
AND
STEVE BRUNNER

Authors' Note

While the events in this book are real, the names of persons and establishments mentioned or described in it have been changed. As much as possible, verbatim dialogue is used. Otherwise, it has been contextually reconstructed but in no way affects, alters or compromises the images and impressions which the authors wish to convey.

Other works by F. L. Richards

Non Fiction (Autobiographical)

Crossroads ... Journey to Wholeness

Poetic Trilogy

In the House of the Father

The Looking Glass

Voice of a Different Heart

Available at: www.flrichardscrossroads.com

Dedication

They stirred us from complacency, challenged us to abandon comfort and compelled us to view life from a very different perspective. Forever committed to our minds and hearts, this book is dedicated to:

Annie	Jorge
Antonio	King Pin
Big José	Lady Peacock
Elder David	Roberto
Emily	Younger David
Jay	Zeus

Acknowledgments

With grateful appreciation, we would like to thank the following people:

Hal, for inspiring the writing of this book.

Barbara and Rafael, for a treasured friendship of nineteen years and for being a very important part of our life in Puerto Rico.

Anna, always "Mommy," for gifting us with her loving nature, the strength of an indomitable spirit and the wisdom of many lessons about the generosity of the heart, the contagiousness of joy and the importance of respect for all people. May she rest in peace.

José, for giving us permission to use photographs of himself and his little Manuel.

Zeus, for his assistance with language translation.

Pam, a special friend, for sharing her gifts and talents in the formatting and editing of this book.

Prologue

Puerto Rico is affectionately called Isla Del Encanto, Enchanted Island. Its lushness, intense sun, inviting waters and prolific flora, home to the indigenous tree frog, the coquí, are testaments to its captivating beauty and charm. The geography of the island exudes a charisma that is inescapable and the distinctiveness of its cultural character entices and intoxicates those caught in the web of this tropical paradise. This is how it was for Steve and me during our very first vacation in the summer of 1987.

We became immersed in this euphoric atmosphere and were drawn back, again and again, to savor more of what had been our first taste of delight. That initial swallow of sweetness, however, took on a different flavor during what evolved as an uninterrupted era of almost thirteen years. It changed to one that was bittersweet as we became wrapped up in the lives of many who, under normal circumstances, would have remained unknown to us. Some worked the streets; others just worked. All tried to make life more bearable in a common goal of survival. It wasn't easy for them, especially those who chose to make something of their lives which extended beyond the immediate, the here and now. The others could not think outside the perimeter of the present because that was all they knew; that was all that mattered to them.

The bugarón, more commonly referred to as boogies, are those we would call male prostitutes. Not exclusively Hispanic, they span the spectrum of age and appearance. Those who are younger, good looking, charming and alluringly sensual have an easier time making connections with gay men who frequent the bars, yet the ones who lack these qualities seem to survive. An ability to speak English is helpful but often not a requirement. The universal language of sex for money needs no translation. Facial expression, body language and gesture are easily understood and help to insure that happy hour will result in a happy ending. Steve and I quickly came to know who they were because of their predictable patterns of behavior. Always having been a people watcher, I found the machinations of cruising both fascinating and unsettling. It took Steve somewhat longer to learn to pay attention to the details I observed very early in our visits to the island.

Although we tried to shield ourselves from the web of seduction, we did not remain exempt from the teasing of those we came to call 'the boys of the street.' The chiseled, ripped bodies and monuments of idolatry of some eventually confronted and taunted us as they attempted to lure us into a psychology that was completely alien to the way we lived. Most had stories that were memorized from their retelling and purported a sense of motivation which would make for a better future, yet the substance of their individual scenarios blended like the tightly knit weave of a tapestry pattern. By their own admission, all but one denied being gay. Some had girl friends, wives, children and were just trying to get by. A few of them had ambitions in various careers. This current method of employment was a conduit through which respective goals would be realized in weeks, months or years to come. They were quite adept at conjuring images of lives which helped them to rationalize their present circumstances. This is what they shared in order to create confidence and trust before they made the next move.

At first, we believed what we heard because of their persuasive tone. We soon learned that they shared a common gift — tongues that dripped with honey coated sincerity. It is unfair to say that they were all like this. A few said it the way it was. Dysfunctional family life, drug dependency and/or very easy money catapulted them into an arena with no boundaries or authority figures and made their concept of time a 'live for the moment' ideology. Most worked solo, but there were some we heard of who paired up and catered to men who were into that kind of play.

The bugarón were not the only ones with whom we became acquainted. There was another group, a small circle of men and women whose lives also had been filled with a fair degree of adversity, but they made a conscious choice to use different methods and techniques to meet the challenges of daily life. Unlike the 'boys of the street', they could not be characterized by a common description of personality, behavior or the way in which they interacted with us. These qualities were unique in source and substance and, with the passing of time, they became our friends.

Steve and I never could have imagined that we would come to find ourselves inside the bubble of such an unlikely togetherness or how these individuals, each and together, would affect us from opposing perspectives. On the one hand, there was the calculated and unyielding pursuit of some to engage us in what we thought to be bizarre. On the other, we sensed the evolution of a seeming extended family. Our hope for all of them was two-fold. We longed for them to come to understand the meaning of unconditional kindness and generosity of spirit. More importantly, we wanted the gifts of self-worth and dignity to be found, once again, by those who had abandoned them and strengthened in others for whom they were shrouded abstractions as circumstances dictated. These were strange concepts which would be learned by some.....for the very first time in their lives.

Dark Streets, Bright Lights is more their story than it is ours. Steve and I were merely supporting characters who, through events and scenarios listened to as well as witnessed first hand, became part of their lives during a decade plus. Although there were many who crossed our path and have been part of personal journals, notes and snippets of writing, the ones remembered in this book most deeply and profoundly affected us.

Like so many who come from a different reality than theirs, we might have sat in judgment of need and want, the aberrant behavior of some and the varying degrees of turmoil visible in all. We chose another route which Steve's brother, Hal, during a visit to us, called "the ministry of the street." That is what inspired this writing of our experiences among the hustlers, homeless and hopefuls who found their way to our hearts.

Chronology of events is less important than is the persona of each silhouette you will meet and try to visualize. Some of the descriptions are tender and emotional while others are blatant with no intention to be vulgar. These lives were what they were, so to write about them with compromised candor would distort the naked truth of each lived experience. In ways many and varied, they were fragile souls wanting to be looked upon with understanding and wounded spirits needing to be listened to with compassion.

*Before any of us may claim the possession
of a caring nature, we do well to consider
that it comprises more than listening ears
or an understanding heart. A truly generous
spirit takes on substance and flesh when
there is a willingness to put aside the priority
of personal pleasures and embrace the
struggle of a fellow human being.*

Dichotomy

1

Steve and I studied the thirteen month old toddler as he ambled unsteadily upon the beach. His father stood nearby and bore a smile of pride as he watched his son negotiate a path across the uneven sand. He knew the peculiarities of this particular plot because he had worked there for the past twenty three years as a provider of lounge rentals to those who searched them out. The enthusiastic little one turned to his father and began to clap as if to say, "Look at me; I can do it." All at once, down he went, chuckling as only small tykes can chuckle.

José went to him, swept him into his strong arms and began to dance across the warm tan surface.

This innocent, José Emmanuel Hidalgo Melendez, was safe and secure in a sturdy cradle of love ... his daddy's embrace.

The face of Manuel could have been any of their faces, the ones called boogies. It is a face unburdened by cares and worries. It is a face that projects joy. It is a face that knows, somehow, what love feels like. We want to believe that, once upon a time, this is what it was like for the bugarón. Surely, they had experienced the same sense of wonder and excitement as very early explorers of the world around them. There must have been moments like this one that were filled with spontaneous happiness. There had to have been someone who loved them and who, like José, taught them what it meant to

feel safe and secure. To think otherwise would be a sad commentary that it always had been different, that life wandered in an unchanging repetition from day to day, past to present. The haunting questions, What happened to them? How? Why? are answered in their individual and collective journeys. This poem sets the stage for characterizations and recollections which span a spectrum from the curious and surprising to the startling and unseemly and, ultimately, to the incredulous and surreal:

Dichotomy

The silence of night
Is broken by the whistling wind
And as the sun rises
Once again in majesty,
The waves awaken
And begin to roar.

Tucked between ocean and sea,
An oasis from our desert of reality,
Puerto Rico, the Isla Del Encanto,
Intoxicates us with delight
Inviting us to savor lushness
And appreciate the richness
Of its birth.

Interrupted, then, by so many
Who walk dark streets
In search of bright lights
Their aberrant needs and wants,
Imprisoning them in desperation
And suspending them in fantasies
Of non-existent lives,
Prompt them to forget
Who they once were.

We are moved with compassion,
Becoming sober in the faces
Of these shattered silhouettes,
Trying to find and touch
That hidden place in each,
Longing to have them remember,
Perhaps help them to heal.

Captivating serenades,
Strange music to our ears
Needing embrace in the wake of exhaustion,
The coquí make known their presence
In the hush of evening's evolution.
Like a symphony of lullabies
They soothe us, giving rest,
While those others, gone from the day,
Labor in the shadows,
Forgetting us ... for now.

In the House of the Father
F.L. Richards © 2006, 2008

Big José

2

As one travels along the Expresso Baldorioty de Castro, it is not difficult to notice luxury condominium buildings which stand as proud testaments to affluence. In the midst of absorbing the pleasant images these tall structures stimulate, others appear. They stand in humbleness yet catch the eye. Their lack of glamour is stark. Their sameness of appearance is blatant. The absence of lush landscaping is obvious and compels a mental contrast to the picturesque scenes of moments before. These are government-subsidized housing . The term is synonymous with poverty. One called Development Luis Llorenz Torres is where José lived with his mom and three younger siblings. There was no dad in the home so, at an early age, he assumed the role of principal provider for his family. José was burdened with uninvited adult responsibility long before he knew what that meant.

By the time we met him during our second vacation on the island in the summer of 1988, his teenage years were but a memory that lacked form and substance since he never had the opportunity to fully enjoy them. He had, instead, done what he could during those years so his family might survive. José was twenty three when we met him. He stood 6′ 5″ and was all legs. We thought that 'Legs' might have been a good nickname so we could distinguish him from others with the same name, but we decided to call him Big José. Our first encounter with him was at the bar we often went to during afternoon happy hour. It was at the end of a side street and faced the ocean. We had seen him there doing odd jobs for the owner. Initially, we thought he was employed as a handyman. There was no indication that he was a 'working boy' who exchanged pleasure for money. While on the job, he engaged no one in conversation. Gestures of courtesy, a smile or wave, were the only acknowledgments he extended as the bar became crowded at four o'clock each afternoon.

On the day we arrived for a week of relaxation following summer work in a school, we went to the bar. From where we were seated, we could see the entrance. He stepped inside, paused to speak to a couple of people, and proceeded to walk in our direction. He sat on the stool to my left; Steve was to my right. He spoke some English; that was not his primary way of communicating however. He was wearing orange shorts and a white tee-shirt. Not long after our introduction to each other and our buying a drink for him, his one hand became affixed to his crotch. The movement of his hand was slow and deliberate. As he sat back, he said something to me, forcing me to turn and look at him. It was impossible not to notice what he was doing.

Since I speak some Spanish, I looked at Steve in order to translate. Returning to conversation with José, we bantered about his work in the bar. Indeed, he did work there; that was not his main source of income. He pushed the high bar stool back a few inches and spread his legs. While his fingers walked up and down the target zone, he poked me and said, "No te gusta?" (You don't like it?) We never had been approached like this, so we were unsure about what to say or do.

Laughing, I slapped his arm and said, "Behave yourself." I quickly added, in the best Spanish sentences I could put together, that Steve and I were a couple and that this was not something in which we were interested. It was not until he stood up that Steve got a glimpse of what was obviously a sleeping giant.

"Yo tengo hambre," (I'm hungry) he said as he extended his hand to shake ours.

We gave him a few dollars, and he left the bar. Steve and I looked at each other and laughed. We had just been initiated into the world of hustling with this up close and personal interaction. One way or another, we were going to pay for the time he had spent with us.

During subsequent vacations, usually in August, we got to know José better. Those sexually-explicit actions and words continued, but our acquaintance with him took on a different flavor. He shared with us his family life. When he spoke about his mom, his tone was affectionate. His facial expression, one which was ordinarily sensual, became quite sad. We were fledglings, so we were still unschooled about the hustler mentality. Believing that we were helping him and his family, we continued to give him money. Those early years of getting to know him are difficult to pinpoint chronologically. Of more importance is the unfolding of his story.

We were at happy hour one afternoon during one of our annual returns to the island. We had, by that time, met others who vacationed there each year during the same week as we. That day, Steve and I had more to drink than usual. José appeared; he was wearing tight white jeans, no underwear, and a dress shirt. Clean-shaven and smiling, he saw us looking at him and he approached. We had not yet learned that to look at a hustler was an invitation for the bee to fly to the honey. He joined us for a drink.

As we began to introduce him to the guys who were sitting with us, one said, "We know José … quite well."

I guess Steve and I initially looked at him a bit too long and intensely because he was clear about his impression that he thought he would be accompanying us to our condo for what would be a sexual adventure with him. As many times as we had told him that we were a couple, the words didn't matter. He just continued trying to wear us down so we would submit to what he believed was irresistible. The head games were fun; the teasing was titillating. That's all it would ever be. It was on that day that he finally understood that our interactions with him had nothing to do with sex and that we had, no doubt, given him mixed signals. What did we know? After that day, the complexion of our conversations steered clear of anything to do with his line of work. Not surprisingly, he sat with us less frequently. His attention was on others who were a more certain source of income.

It was not until we bought a condo in June of 1997, nine years after we met José, that we saw the heart of his humanity. Being unfamiliar with areas outside of our neighborhood, he offered to drive us to a number of stores so we could purchase items of all kinds. We had established boundaries long before, so we were comfortable and confident that our acceptance of his gesture would be understood for what it was and nothing more. We waited in front of our building for a nine o'clock pick up. From around the corner, we heard a noise that sounded like a muffler gasping to survive. We thought an army tank was approaching. José pulled up to our building bearing a broad smile. We had not yet started out and we were already two bags of nerves wondering if this wreck of a car would be able to go the distance.

Once inside it, sweat began to pour down our faces. The air conditioner did not work and two of the windows could not be opened. We felt as if we were driving in a sauna on wheels! We did not say anything to him because he seemed genuinely pleased to be able to help us. Without complaint, we dragged him from store to store until the undertaking of the day was completed. Exiting the parkway was a great tension releaser. We had made it back to our neighborhood in one piece. If something happened then, we were within walking distance of our apartment. Once inside the parking lot, he pulled into a spot close to the side entrance. Steve and I experienced feelings of welcome and relief. We welcomed the silence and were relieved that the car had not expired.

During the many vacation years that had passed, we came to know others like José and were somewhat more refined in our understanding of a mentality that was predicated on engaging techniques of introduction, sob stories and fictitious self-characterizations. These were the trademarks of 'the profession' and had become easily recognizable. Miguel had aspirations of becoming an attorney. Edwin spit out the names of human bones and their functions. After all, these are things a mortician had to know! Ricardo boasted about a career in the adult film industry. Juan was a tour guide. These were but delusional impressions of desire, of what might have been, but they had no basis in fact … or reality.

These guys were always hanging around, sometimes from early afternoon to night. When did they have time for anything else? The really sad part was that they believed they were convincing, that what they said was credible and those who heard the tales would be moved by a sense of admiration and compassion by dipping into deep pockets, even if no sexual tryst followed. José was not like the others who were authors of concocted, fictional stories of ambition, but he *was* a boogie and they were all takers.

As we spent time with him away from the bar scene, José revealed another side of his personality to us. There was more to him than seductive teasing and suggestive gesture. Against the advice of many, we hired him to paint our apartment. We had heard horror stories about guys like José who were invited by tourists to their hotel rooms or condo rentals. They were robbed; some were beaten. Despite numerous admonitions, we proceeded as planned. We knew José well enough to believe he did not fit that unsettling description.

For two weeks, he appeared right on time or early. Steve prepared breakfast each morning. This gave us an opportunity to discuss the day's agenda and ensure that José had food to eat. When he worked, he was focused. This had not changed at all since the early days when he did odd jobs at the bar. During any given eight hour work day, sometimes longer, he paused infrequently either to smoke a cigarette, use the bathroom, eat lunch or enjoy a glass of soda. There was no alcohol or beer served while he worked. He was not only punctual but quite efficient. He displayed obvious pride as each part of the facelift was completed. Any irritation he felt because of my demand for perfection remained unvoiced; he simply did as he was instructed.

More than once, I caught him looking at Steve. They just smiled and rolled their eyes. Steve had gotten used to my somewhat obsessive behavior during our years together. For José, it was an education. There were several days when he stayed late because he did not want to leave a job unfinished. This was prompted, in part, by an apparent sense of self-satisfaction. Of greater importance was the fact that he just did not want to hear my mouth.

At the onset, we gave him the option of being paid daily or weekly; he chose the former. It would provide steady help at home, at least for a while. By each day's end, he was exhausted. Unless something came up in conversation, we all but forgot he led another life. He was away from the street for now and was earning a salary that came from hard work, not horizontal relaxation. Unlike the other 'boys of the street' who had to scramble to find work during this time of the year called low season, José was assured of a steady income.

There came a time during those weeks when we left him alone while we did some errands. If others thought we were crazy for allowing him to step foot into our apartment, they became convinced we had lost our sanity for leaving him unattended. The more he saw the appearance of our apartment change, the greater seemed his motivation and effort.

There were a number of bifold louver doors which needed to be primed and painted. He tackled this job last because it was quite tedious. Working on these doors was a three day process involving priming and two coats of paint. Some areas required more because the paint had not dried evenly. This additional work was done because, as he saw me scrutinize what he was doing, he just knew that he wasn't finished. I didn't have to say a word!

The condo was completely furnished when we purchased it, but we had made some changes which were more suited to our taste. José was the recipient of a number of items which we did not want, but which were still in good condition. One was a stereo system. On the day we gave it to him, his face glowed. One would have thought he had won the lottery! His mom loved music but was unable to afford such a luxury. She owned a small radio; it was her only source of entertainment.

As we neared the completion of the massive undertaking, we sensed a change in his demeanor. The security and sanity he had enjoyed during this hiatus was about to end and he would return to what had been his life since he was seventeen years old. We wished there was more for him to do so we could prolong his having to strip away his clothes and dignity in order to support his family. We would not be returning to the island until after the holidays; that was months away. On the last day of work, he looked pensive and sad as he hugged and thanked us for everything we had done for him.

During the next days, we put the apartment together again and prepared for our trip back to the states. As we packed, Steve noticed that one of his rings was missing. We had bought a set while on a day trip to St. Thomas during our very first island vacation in 1987 and had worn them as a symbol of our life together. We looked everywhere; it was gone. We were aghast when we reached the only logical conclusion; José had taken it.

I bolted out of the apartment knowing that José would probably be at the bar. As I neared, filled with tension, I saw him standing on the corner of the side street where it was located. He saw my face; it was red with rage. I went on a tirade in Spanish because I did not want him to misunderstand anything I was saying. I think half the neighborhood heard me call him a liar after he denied taking it. I blurted that he had no heart and was just like the rest of the garbage that hung around there.

He tried to speak, but I was lashing out an irreverent litany and did not want to hear anything from him. Finally, he threw his hands up in the air and walked away while mumbling something. I returned to the condo, my anger being more intense than before I had left it. José's actions confirmed for us the stereotype about which we had been repeatedly cautioned: "You can take the hustler out of the street, but you can't take the street out of the hustler." This was a startling wake up call!

We went to the bar that evening against Steve's better judgment. He saw that I was like a tiger in a cage and needed to get out. Chris, a young

American guy who had relocated to Puerto Rico, was the bartender on duty. He saw my face and asked what was wrong. "That bastard … You won't believe what happened."

"Don't tell me," was his reaction to my irritated tone. He was aware that José had been working in our apartment. Not intending to put salt in the wound, but sensing that something was very wrong he said, with an air of castigation, "I told you to be careful!"

"You were absolutely right," Steve replied and proceeded to explain the events of the day. King Pin, the one we believed to be the daddy of the hustler den, was in earshot of our conversation. We had seen him at the bar, but we had never spoken to him. We knew of him through Chris, who had described for us his position in the hierarchy.

Unsolicited, he approached us and said, "He has the ring."

"Who?" I asked.

"José."

Chris leaned forward from behind the bar and asked him how he knew this. After my confrontation with José, King Pin claimed he heard José asking if anyone wanted to buy a gold ring. Had I squeezed the glass I was holding a bit more, it would have shattered in my hand. Steve had taken me to the bar to relax, but tension mounted to new heights as we listened to the older hustler. Of course, giving us this information would cost us a drink.

He attempted to sit beside me, but my mood was so foul at that moment I said, in an elevated voice, "Véte…tenemos que hablar con Chris ahora mismo" (Go … we have to talk to Chris right now). My statement prompted a jack-in-the-box reaction. He sprang to his feet and made quick tracks to the door, drink in hand. We had no doubt that this brief encounter would be spread throughout the ranks. It was no coincidence that José was nowhere to be found during our last two days. He would reappear once we were gone, but he knew we would return.

We arrived back in New York and had but a few days to get reorganized for a trip to Provincetown, the gay mecca of Cape Cod, Massachusetts. Our dear friends, Mike and Chad, had invited us to join them for what would be our first experience in a place completely absent of homophobia, labels and judgment. Steve and I were hopeful that the setting would also provide an oasis from the reality of the ring incident and the resulting myriad emotions which had gripped us like a vise.

On the way to meet them at their beautiful home in Cheshire, Connecticut, we agreed to avoid discussion of what had transpired on the island. Whatever enjoyment lay ahead, we needed to embrace it with unburdened spirits. The five hour drive from their home to the Cape allowed us ample time to plan the week's activities and catch up on life in general.

Unknowingly, Mike asked how our condo was shaping up. He saw my face in the rear view mirror and knew something was very wrong. Despite our earlier pledge, Steve and I summarized the fiasco. We knew we would be questioned at some point during the week. It was better done and over with before the festivities began.

Our vacation was incredible. The quaintness of the town attested to a New England flavor which was charming. On one of our daily walks, we came upon an artisan who created jewelry. We chose a design and had two new rings made. These looked more like bands than the nugget rings we had purchased in St. Thomas years earlier. We loved the style of these new ones. We walked through the building and found ourselves on the beach. Tranquility enveloped us as we gazed at the breathtaking view. Steve said, "Give me the rings." He held mine and handed his to me. It was if we were in a bubble of joy as each placed a ring on the other's finger and said words of recommitment. We could feel the power of love melt away misgivings. This was an unexpected, spontaneous moment that gifted us with the capacity to heal and forgive.

The week passed quickly and we were back in our apartment in New York. I was in the shower while Steve began sorting clothes for our trip to the laundry room. I heard him say something but had to turn the water down to understand what it was. I peeked out from behind the shower curtain. "Do you have your ring?" he asked.

"Which one?"

"The nugget." I extended my hand and showed it to him. His voice echoed throughout the apartment.

"Oh, my God!" He lifted his hand and opened it. On its palm lay a nugget ring.

I felt the blood rush through me; Steve's face was ghost white. "Where was it?" I asked as I quickly got out of the shower. He told me that it was inside the flap of blue briefs. Apparently, he forgot he had placed it there at some point during our time on the island. Unseen, it traveled from the island to New York to Cape Cod and back — safe and sound. We stood there, lost for words. The whole thing was incredible!

Our relief quickly turned to tears when the realization hit us. We had falsely accused José of being a thief. The accusation and my nasty, condescending barrage of an obscene litany flashed before me. I felt like the piece of crap I had judged him to be. There was no way to contact him. We had neither an address nor a phone number. We'd have to live with this until we returned to the island right after Christmas; that was five months away.

As the season approached, our usual excited anticipation was replaced with nervous anxiety. An unsettling queasiness sloshed inside me whenever I recalled how I had degraded José in public. That was a no-no. One of the traits we had come to know about 'the boys' was their machismo. It was a tough, masculine façade often covering a substance of opposite composition. José had been deeply offended. We knew the exterior bravado, but we had also seen his gentler side. We hoped the latter would prevail when we finally faced him.

More a Hispanic than an American custom, applause always accompanied landing on the island. In the past, we had eagerly participated because we were as happy as they each time we returned to our Isla Del Encanto. The conclusion of this flight was different. That gesture was muted and overshadowed by the task which lay ahead. Until we were able to speak to José, we would not be able to lift the ponderous guilt that weighed heavily upon us.

We left the suitcases packed and walked to the bar. As we rounded the corner of the side street, we saw José walking in our direction. When he caught sight of us, he quickly side-stepped and headed for the opposite side of the street. I called to him; he ignored me and stepped up his pace. We crossed the street, diagonally, in order to head off his attempt to get away from us.

It was as if the incident and resulting confrontation had happened that day. His face was tight and he tried not to look at us. I explained, as best

I could, how very sorry we were for the big mistake we had made. Steve added words, in simple English, to what we were trying to convey.

After we explained what actually had happened, his facial expression relaxed and he simply said, with a less than sincere effort, "It's O.K."

We also explained to him what had occurred later that day in the bar. We recounted the conversation with King Pin and that, after hearing his words, we believed that our suspicion was accurate. That was the moment we came to understand another aspect of the street M.O. — there was no loyalty among the ranks; it was each man for himself. Just as exaggeration was part and parcel of their lives, they did not like competition. The older one heard our conversation with Chris and became aware, unless he knew before, that José was working for us. This gave him ammunition for what had clearly been a lie. He had never heard José say anything about having a gold ring to sell. It was an intentional misrepresentation designed to stir the pot and cause trouble. With José out of the way, he could begin the whole twilight zone process, thinking he would have unhampered access to the gringos!

After that unpleasant but necessary encounter with José, his behavior toward us changed. Once cordial, he became cautiously civil. We saw him less and less and, when we did, he never asked for money or a drink. It was not until the summer of 1999, fully two years after the incident, that the José we once knew began to re-emerge.

He had been the first one we met in 1988. It was ironic that, on the day that we traveled back to Puerto Rico to begin another phase of life as permanent residents, he was the first one we saw. He embraced each of us while saying. "! Bienvenidos.. Que alegria!" (Welcome…what happiness!)

Yes, he did do other jobs for us without incident, but we sensed a change. His face did not look as full or healthy as we had remembered it. He had lost weight. His approach to work was noticeably more sluggish, and the hours he spent doing it were greatly reduced each day. He claimed he was attempting to change, but we knew well that he was telling us what he thought we wanted to hear.

During the many years of knowing him, we had engaged him in countless numbers of conversations which were designed to create, affirm and nurture some semblance of self-worth. We knew what was going on; he had been drawn into the web of addictive drug use. Perhaps it had been going on all along, but he had been adept at hiding it from us. There was no concealing it now. We began to see him, along with others, standing at 'the wall' — a small area between the bar we went to and another which was across the street. It was a cruise spot. Hungry passersby were given a glimpse of the wares for sale. On any given afternoon, José was in position. If he saw us walking down the long, narrow street, he quickly moved away.

It made us sad to consider that this young man, whose heart seemed to be in the right place, had made a choice which had little to do with reason and sensibility. By the time we moved back to the states in 2001, it was clear to us that Big José was a slave to drugs. There was nothing more we could do and were empty of the motivation to try. We wondered how he was able to provide for his mom and siblings now that his 'earnings' were being used to support a different need.

Clearly, he could no longer take care of them because he had given up on taking care of himself. He became captive in a world of unreality as the need to be numb made him oblivious to the importance of familial love and his vital role in its prosperity. We were aware of an addiction that had spiraled out of control and with each return to the island, news of his deteriorating condition disheartened us. Not too long ago, his struggle ended. With a hypodermic needle protruding from his arm, José's lifeless body was found on the beach. Rather than pondering this ghastly image, Steve and I choose to think about a time when his heart was kind, caring and a compelling sense of obligation to the mother he loved so much directed his youth.

The Davids

3

It was not our intention to remember more than one principal in each chapter. As the process of organizing and outlining recollections moved along, we found weaves in the tapestry of each journey which resulted in a decision to blend them in one body of writing. Like the commonality of the name, José, we knew a number of Davids. To avoid confusion, we refer to them as Elder and Younger.

Elder

He was in his late thirties and in outstanding physical condition. The bearer of a rock-hard, mesomorphic physique, strikingly handsome face and flawless grooming, he exemplified the extreme of macho. This guy was a head turner!

These qualities, however, were not the ones that made him stand out. Regardless of the time of day, there was an unalterable sameness in his facial expression. It was a mixture of intense and sullen. He usually sat alone, eyes down, and stared at whatever was in the glass in front of him. He always appeared to be detached from what was going on around him even at times when happy hour was raucous. Occasionally, the semblance of a smile would alter his otherwise stoic countenance. It was never prolonged, a few seconds at most. It was as if a fleeting thought amused him. To say that he was not aggressively forward is an understatement. His trance-like condition kept him wrapped up inside a remote location from which he did not often emerge.

We had heard that he was part of the street ranks, yet his behavior contradicted the boogie stereotype. The essence of attractiveness and masculinity, he was quite a piece of eye candy. These qualities provided the potential for excellent business, but he rarely spoke to anyone. Those inclined to cruise him labored to get his attention but were unsuccessful most of the time. Without eye contact, the chase was an exercise in futility and resulted in their having to keep torrid thoughts within the realm of fantasy.

The few times we witnessed an exchange with a fun seeker were on days when he was out of his shell more than in it. His posture erect, he sat with his head up. He appeared cognizant of his surroundings as well as admirers who stared at him. While the other boogies advanced quickly, he never left his seat. Body language and discrete gestures were indications that he was receptive to company. The protracted machinations of foreplay, so obvious with other hustlers, were brief and not blatantly obvious. If there was a connection, it usually occurred within minutes and was followed by a quick departure.

He walked into the bar early one afternoon. It was well before the converging of the crowd for happy hour. At most, there were four or five others besides Steve and me. He was wearing a ribbed, sleeveless muscle shirt. Black leather arm bands accentuated his mountainous muscles which flexed, then relaxed, almost as if their movement was involuntary. Veins protruded under the constricting bands and looked like they were going to burst. He was carrying a small gym bag; apparently, he had just completed a workout.

As he made his way around the interior, we saw that he was quite sweaty. He was pumped … in every sense of the word. This was not at all the same Elder David of absolute predictability we had observed in the past. Despite the fact that most stools were empty, he dropped his bag on the one next to where I was sitting then walked away. We did not turn to see where he went but continued our conversation.

We were unaware of his return until we heard the scraping of the stool legs against the wood planked floor. He exuded a 'gym' odor; it was not offensive but pronounced. Chris approached and took our glasses for refills. I glanced sideways, noting what looked like a smile on David's face. This had been noticed before, so I could not be sure if he was directing it at us or if he was finding humor in a present thought. Chris returned and placed our drinks in front of us while acknowledging and engaging David in small talk.

We both looked left and heard his voice for the first time. "How are you guys doing?" He extended his hand, first to me and then to Steve.

Chris stood there with a look of surprise then asked, "You don't know David?"

"Now we do," I chuckled.

We bought him a beer and, as Chris attempted to put the bottle on the bar, David's hand intercepted it. Extending it, he thanked us.

Steve has always been the quiet one. I, on the other hand, could speak to a wall and get an answer! This, however, was a challenge even for me. Sustaining a conversation with him was a test of endurance, even though he spoke fluent English. His responses were mono-syllabic to a few words at best. Any pause in talking prompted that downward stare we had seen before. My adaptability, usually tension-free in most situations, was tenuous. We decided to leave; that brief introduction had been enough for one day. As we pushed our stools back, David emerged from his trance, thanked us, and returned to the place in his mind from which he had escaped momentarily.

While walking to our condo, we talked about this strange guy. His personality almost defied description. For a fleeting moment, I thought of the term, shy humility. For sure, there were walls around him which seemed to be self-designed, guarded and impenetrable. It would take time, but we were eventually given a glimpse inside this enigma of a man.

As our conversations with David increased in frequency, but not length, we learned more about his stares, the sources of his protracted distraction. We came to know things about his life which placed him in his present position. His family life had not been a good one and, by innuendo, he suggested that he had spent time in jail. He did not explain anything, but his look was one which displayed unpleasant memories. We were not about to ask any questions. In this instance, less was definitely more.

Despite an oddness that clearly encased him in a remote reality, he seemed conscious enough to keep in good shape. Somewhere in the obvious confusion of his mind, he knew what was a turn-on for others. He had to have realized, too, that there would come a time when he could no longer compete with the younger ones. We wondered how he survived. Rarely had we seen him with anyone, yet he went to the gym frequently. The money had to be coming from somewhere. Maybe he had a sugar daddy who supported and allowed him to go out and do his own thing. Maybe he was a high roller and was paid for services commensurate with his raw, sensual appearance.

While only conjecture, either line of reasoning seemed plausible. The one thing about which we were certain was that his approach was different. Absent of the blatantly aggressive nature of some, his was a quiet, mysterious presence that coupled with extreme physical appeal. Those partners did the work for him.

Eventually, there came a time when he joined us for dinner at our condo having repeatedly said how hungry he was while we were at the bar for happy hour one afternoon. Before getting there, he had worked out. He asked if he could take a shower before dinner. Steve and I were working in the kitchen when he rounded the bend from the bathroom. We didn't notice him standing there until we heard his voice behind us. "Thanks, guys."

With simultaneous movement to acknowledge him, we turned. "You're welcome, David." He was standing with a towel tightly hugging his waist. We had never seen the reality of the term six pack until that evening. His physique was about as close to perfect as one could get!

I made an innocent, passing reference about his great condition. He started to turn around as if he had just received an invitation to model. As he did so, his hands gripped the flaps of the towel, unloosened them and spread them apart. The rest of his body, all of it, was in proportion to that which we first saw when he entered the kitchen. He gripped one of the breakfast bar stools, positioned it diagonally so it faced us, draped the towel over the back rest and sat on the edge of the seat — legs spread and hanging — along with what had just been exposed to us for the first time. The privacy of our home and his apparent comfortability with us must have encouraged him to emancipate his member. It was not until he began to caress it that I grabbed the towel and threw it over him.

"You better get some clothes on."

"I better … or what?"

"We're eating dinner on the terrace, and you can't sit out there like that."

"Like what?" he countered as he lifted the towel and let us see the dance of the muscle spasms.

"Exactly! Get dressed before the food gets cold."

He got the message and stood up. The rigid, straight arrow swayed back and forth as he walked. He was some piece of work... no pun intended! Despite our obvious sense of propriety, we were not certain if he understood why we had invited him. He was with us to eat dinner and he was not an item on the dessert menu. The expression, "dumb like a fox," raced through my mind. It caused pause to consider that, just maybe, he was much more in touch with himself and his actions than he had led us to believe. He exited the bedroom and helped us bring the food and drinks to the table.

As he sat, he smiled at us. "¡Buen provecho!" he announced while holding a bottle of beer.

"¡Egual!" I retorted. These phrases, invitations to enjoy a meal, were commonplace. The Elder David sensed our awkwardness as we tried to begin a conversation. We really should have been thankful because never had we heard him speak so much. Perhaps he was better able to concentrate when his head was moving in one direction!

"I'm very sorry if I embarrassed you; I didn't mean to make you uncomfortable."

We confessed that we were more than surprised by his behavior because it was completely unlike the manner in which he presented himself at the bar.

"I keep my business private." That was an interesting play on words which gave us an opening to explain our motivation for extending cordiality to him. Our reasoning prompted a response that was no great surprise. He had always been under the impression that attention given demanded attention returned. Steve quickly dispelled that myth where we were concerned.

"Before I forget, don't leave your jewelry out; you never know. If I was high, it would have been gone. Don't trust anyone."

His words were chilling and caused Steve and me to look at each other. Not wanting our concern to seem like a knee-jerk reaction, we waited until the end of the meal to make a move. Steve excused himself to use the bathroom; I knew exactly why he said this. He dashed to the bedroom to ensure that our jewelry was there. When he returned, his facial expression was one of relief. That conveyed the message that everything was accounted for.

I went to the kitchen to get dessert ready. When I brought it to the table, I had to squeeze around David's chair. He had pushed it back and was in a more relaxed position. His hand clutched his member while his legs moved in an open/close rhythm. While we were determined to maintain boundaries, it was not possible to ignore the crowning glory that made him the absolute complete package.

It was difficult for us to pretend that we were oblivious to deliberate, suggestive movements that, no doubt, were designed to make us melt. After all, we are human! To say that there was no mental or visual titillation would not be true. He made it impossible for us to pretend we did not see what, clearly, he thought to be an inescapable god of idolatry. We held our ground, enjoyed dessert and continued in benign conversation for a while longer. He saw me look at my watch.

"It must be late."

"10:30"

"I should get going."

His face reverted to one more familiar to us, the intense, sullen illusion of the bar façade he more predictably projected. No doubt, the unsuccessful attempts of his fleshy assistant caused the quick change to occur. I sprang to my feet and retrieved his gym bag from the bedroom.

As David hugged us and expressed thanks, he pressed his rock of Gibraltar against us. He was relentless! We stood in the hallway as he gave a last wave before entering the elevator.

Once back inside, I just looked at Steve and blurted, "What the hell was that?"

Steve laughed at my tone. "I have no idea."

This was a wholly different man than the one in the bar. The behavior he exhibited in that atmosphere in no way, shape or form bore the slightest resemblance to what we just witnessed. We wondered whether he was able to adjust his behavior at will, or if it was due more to his state of mind in a given situation. Was his evident laid back, sometimes coma-like presence an M.O. of calculated design? Was the appearance of things intended to foster curiosity and intrigue? The only thing about which we were certain was that he possessed a pervasively depressed nature that, like a pendulum, swayed him back and forth between two different worlds. In one, he was focused, in touch and attentive. In the other, he existed in a seeming twilight zone.

This dinner experience was nothing less than surreal. It was not because he liked being in his birthday suit. It wasn't even that he was skillful at narcissistic seduction. The real issue was that we had never met anyone with two diametrically opposing personalities, neither of which we were equipped to handle. During those hours together, we were given disconnected snippets of his life that rambled in an aimless circle of repetitiveness. When put together, however, a vague portrait could be painted. The deep, dark, painful information he shared with us made his persona not as completely weird as we originally thought. We wished we had known him longer and better. Perhaps we might have been able to offer suggestions that could have helped relieve the ponderous weight of emotional dysfunction.

We saw him less frequently after that evening. Depending upon his state of being, he'd wave or ignore us. At times when we thought it safe to do so, we bought him a beer. He would hold it up in a gesture of thanks and, before we knew it, he'd return to the outer limits. As time passed, it was clear to us that he was sinking into an abyss from which he was unlikely to return. His stare became blank. It was accompanied by eyes that were completely vacant.

In passing conversation one day, Chris mentioned that David had a sister who tried, more than once, to help him. Whether he was unwilling or too far gone to embrace her outstretched arms of love and hope is something that will remain unexplained. Eventually, he lost his ability to think and reason. His emotionally battered persona appeared consumed by a force that, like an insidious cancer, ate away until it completely debilitated and paralyzed him. He existed in a state of interior paralysis where yesterday, today and tomorrow became synonymous with nothingness.

Once in the vise of irreversible unreality, he lost the will to live. One day, he positioned himself on the ground outside what was believed to have been a randomly selected house . He injected a fatal dose of drugs and released himself from the daunting anguish that had made the prospect of living one more hour unbearable. He went to a place of quiet rest, a place where the demons of emotion no longer controlled him. A place where, at last, the torment was ended.

Younger

The physical appearance of this David was the antithesis of the Elder's always crisp look. Younger was twenty-four, tall and lanky. His thick, black hair accentuated his deep set eyes. Depending upon circumstances, his appearance spanned the spectrum from squeaky clean to a complete mess. More than occasionally, his clothing longed for a washing machine.

His posture was erect and made his height a characteristic that distinguished him from most others of his age. When he walked, there was a bounce to his step; his heels never touched the ground. While his face was youthful, it bore the tell tale signs that accompany drug addiction. He had been a user since his teen years.

David was a kid who had gone astray at an early age. He had fallen through the cracks and left untapped any real potential for a productive, successful life. Sadly, no one ever grabbed hold of and pointed him in a better direction. His persona did not boast of one who came from a professional family, yet it was possible. Drug dependency does not discriminate. It is an equal opportunity devastator!

We became acquainted with Younger shortly after our move to the island in August 1999. Until then, we had been to only two gay bars.

From passing conversations, we were aware that there was another in the neighborhood but, because of less than flattering descriptions and characterizations we had heard from friends, we never had the desire to investigate this place that catered to a much older crowd and 'crawled with boogies.' Our impressions were about to change.

During the summer months, it was always a good idea to get on and off the beach before noon. The sun was punishing during the afternoon hours and, depending upon the humidity index, there were times when the simple, involuntary task of breathing became a labor of concerted effort.

By ten o'clock on one of numerous sun drenched mornings, we ventured to the sand and surf. The beach was already a sea of lounges, sand chairs, blankets, towels and umbrellas. There was not a spot to be had in our usual locale. We walked along the shore hoping the effort would not prove fruitless. By the time we scoped out a few square feet of space, we were perpendicular to the side street which led to what was sometimes called the second home of the geriatrics. The phraseology seemed cruel, but the image was rather cute and intriguing.

A two-storied condominium building was the background to where we plopped down. There were no palm trees under which to seek shelter. My hope was that the shadow cast by the building would provide a minimal amount of shade. Such a concern was never part of Steve's thinking since he always has tolerated heat and sweat better than I.

I thought to myself, *Surely this won't take long once the blazing sun takes hold of him.* Wrong! He flipped one side to the other never opening his eyes. Eventually, he rolled over and asked me what time it was.

"Time to go," I said with a tone that made it clear I was not enjoying myself.

"Whenever you're ready," was his nonchalant response.

We walked along the side street and came upon the bar which, until now, existed only in a forum of imagery. It was early afternoon. We were hot, sweaty and parched. We decided that this might be a good time to test the waters. The blinding sun made it difficult for us to adjust our vision once inside the dimly lit bar. The place was empty; we were delighted. We took seats near the door, giving us a full view of the interior.

As we introduced ourselves to Joey, the bartender, we heard the sound of a door slam. Out from the bathroom walked a young man. We had an unobstructed view since we were the only ones there. As he walked to a stool not far from ours, I made a conscious effort not to laugh. It wasn't intended to mock him but the appropriateness of the adage, "It's what's up front that counts," raced through my mind. His jeans were packed, the instruments strategically positioned in a collective grouping that demanded notice.

"Steve, what will you have?" Joey inquired.

"A beer for me."

"And you, Frank?"

"I'm not in the mood for beer."

"Do you like vodka?" the young man interjected.

"Yes, why?"

"Try a Madres."

"What's that?"

"Vodka, O.J. and cranberry juice."

"Sounds good!" I had found a new, favorite drink. The addition of cranberry juice gave it so much more flavor.

Steve asked the guy if he wanted a drink. He ordered a beer. Before taking a sip, he walked over, patted our backs and returned to his stool to continue talking to Joey.

Steve was always uncomfortable in new situations like this one. Out came the cigarettes. Before he had it near his mouth, the youth was there — lighter in hand.

"What a smooth operator," I said after Steve thanked him.

He returned, picked up his glass and repositioned himself on the stool next to Steve's. He asked our names; he told us his was David. He was curious about how long we would be staying on the island.

Steve told him that we lived there.

The conversation continued and we saw that he was obviously high, not from alcohol, so it was difficult to follow his train of thought once he got on a roll. He went from moments of being lucid and clear to ones in which he became almost stupefied; the result was an inaudible mumble.

This was another first for us. We had never seen anyone so drugged up. He saw us looking at him curiously and began to explain to us about the drug issue he did not have. He emphasized that he had control over it and that he could stop whenever he wanted. There were others who were functional addicts; they were able to balance a drug habit with some sense of daily responsibility. These few had real jobs with obvious, clearly defined boundaries; David believed he was like them. He had no clue that what he did for a living was an alien reality and that his motivation for work was drugs … nothing more. He was a charmer. This quality, combined with what emerged as a youthful, naive innocence, made it difficult to feel anything but compassion and a compelling need to help him.

Gradually, the layers of the onion peeled off one by one. We came to understand his zaniness as well as an affectionate nature which we wanted to believe was more the core of his being than was his altered state of thinking and acting when he was under the influence. He seemed adept at living within a world of comfortable chaos and believed that his life was no different than that of others. He just went about its living in a different way. He could not see how conflicted it really was. Unlike the usual dull numbness of David the Elder, there was an occasional sharpness in the Younger's tone and wit which rallied when the drugs didn't. We didn't see this too often; it was refreshing when it made an appearance.

As one month became another, we got to know him quite well. We had heard how he got started in this business, but we wanted to see if he would verify what was, for us, both startling and shocking. We were at the beach one afternoon and preparing to return home. We heard a voice behind us. Younger approached and asked if we were going to stop for a beer. He joined us.

This was one of his good days; he was on point! I seized the opportunity and asked him, "David, how did all of this begin for you?"

"I was seventeen." He paused, then tried to divert my attention away from what was obviously painful for him to speak about.

I persisted, "I don't mean your age. What made you decide to make money on the street? And how did you get into drugs?"

His face grew pale. "My father."

"Excuse me," I said in disbelief.

"My father, I said."

Steve and I became paralyzed in place and I regretted the line of questioning. He went on to tell us about episodes of cocaine use with his father and stopped short of giving any other information. We could never confirm if David had been introduced to hustling by his father, but we had a strong suspicion that they, at one time, were a team. This thought was absolutely surreal!

If our instincts were true, how could a parent do this, even if the teamwork had not actually happened? Here was a young kid who, at one time, probably spoke, thought, and acted like others of the same age. Like them, he undoubtedly envisioned what he wanted to be when he grew up. He'd never be a rocket scientist, for sure, but he might have been spared from this ignominious existence. At that moment, my heart screamed in pain for him.

The look on Steve's face, eyes welled up with tears, added his unspoken sentiments to mine. Everyone was on overload, so we decided to return home. We hugged him tightly before we left; this was the first time we embraced David. Steve placed the palm of his hand on David's cheek, almost forcing eye contact, and said, "You are a very special guy; don't ever forget that."

David made no response; he probably did not know what to say. We turned to leave and, as we opened the door, we heard David's voice. "When will I see you guys again?"

"Soon," Steve sighed, not being able to speak with a louder voice. The talk that day was a catalyst in our relationship with David but caused us to become two emotional messes. We thought about our own children and grandchildren (we were very young grandpas!). That made the depth of concern and anger more intense.

We saw the Younger nearly every day whether in the street, at the beach, in a store or at the bar if we happened by. A box of cereal or varieties of junk food, clutched unashamedly, were his sources of sustenance on any given day. We frequently took him home with us so we could get him away from his life as a boogie, even if only for a few hours. The routine was the same. Steve prepared food so he'd have a hot meal and I waited for him to strip away his clothing so I could get them washed.

He loved our shower. The opportunities to take one were rare, so he took full advantage of these moments of luxury. Invariably, I'd find David in various 'states of being' when I returned from the laundry room. He loved to prance around in his birthday suit. He knew the ground rules, so any awakening was kept in perspective.

I vividly remember entering the bathroom one day after he took a shower. I wanted to add his towel and face cloth to the pile of laundry. The room reeked with a nauseating odor. His socks were tucked inside his sneakers. I was reeling and found it difficult to touch them. The floor of the tub was black. I managed to get out of there quickly after creating a cloud with room spray. What I had eaten earlier was close to revisiting the outside world.

Whenever I went to the laundry room with his clothing, I always prayed that no one else would be there. I made sure the fan was on and the windows were opened wide before I began the process of washing clothing that usually was an unsightly mess.

David became our 'adopted son,' an expression which we said figuratively and with humor. He took it literally. We treated and cared for him like a human being not an object. At first, he didn't understand why we were doing things for him. Like the Elder, his life had been guided by a give and take mentality. Slowly, he became more comfortable with our approach — one which was, in all likelihood, alien to him.

The most emotional time we ever spent with David the Younger was Christmas of 2000, just weeks before we moved back to the states. He, as well as others of the street and some who had become our friends, gathered at our condo to celebrate what would be our last holiday as residents of the island. Steve and I were in the company of hustlers, a drag queen and friends who knew them and had no problem with our choice of guests.

David appeared at the door wearing pants, an ironed, white shirt and shoes. His hair was brushed and flowing. For a moment we thought we were looking at a totally different person. He entered, embraced us and wished us a Merry Christmas. We stared at him as he stood and studied the holiday décor — the tree, nativity and some statuary which was special to us. He had seen all of this during recent weeks but, on this day, his attention to detail made it seem as if he were making a conscious, deliberate effort to commit the images to memory and create a mental photo album. He arrived earlier than the others, so this moment became his gift to us.

"You look great," Steve said, his voice cracking and eyes pooling with tears.

"You are making me red."

We had heard these words whenever we gave him a compliment, words of encouragement or praise that was designed to affirm him. It was as if he didn't believe he deserved to hear kind, tender sentiments or be shown unconditional affection.

He helped me set the table and made sure that each piece of silverware was in its correct position. One by one, the others arrived. Their reactions to seeing David dressed up were no less visible and voiced than had been ours.

I offered a prayer of thanks after the ten of us took our seats at the table. I looked at each one, mentioned his name, and spoke about these hearts Steve and I had come to know. I prayed that God would guide, protect and strengthen them. While most looked at me as I prayed, David's eyes looked down, almost in a posture of unworthy humility and embarrassment.

This group was ravenous; we were glad we made plenty of food. David sat right next to Steve — no surprise! Steve went to light a cigarette and, as if an instant replay of the first encounter with David at the bar, he reached over, extended the lighter and smiled.

At times, the Christmas music playing in the background was drowned out by animated discussion and laughter. If it is the medicine for the soul, then some healing happened at our table, no matter how momentary. One thing is for sure; our guests experienced something that day which was a faded memory. It had been years, too many to count for some, since they enjoyed Christmas Day in the company of others and were surrounded by love and peace.

Steve and I knew that this gathering was a bandage on a festering wound for the majority of them and that it would not be a cause for them to take stock of their lives and make noticeable changes in them. If only for a few hours they, especially David, were able to retreat from the dark streets of fragmentation and briefly enter into an atmosphere of bright lights and celebration, a world which did not remind them of that to which they would return all too soon.

Without being asked, David began to clear the table and bring dishes to the sink; he rolled up his sleeves and began washing them. Others took the cue and helped as well. We gathered in the living room having decided to wait a while before dessert would be served. I went to the bedroom to get another camera; the first had already been used up. I returned to see Steve sitting on the couch. David was right next to him; his head was resting on Steve's shoulder. This was a moment of closeness which David needed to feel and which Steve willingly embraced. Of all the photos taken that day, this one stands out and tugs at our heart strings each time we look at it.

We returned to the table to complete the meal. Realizing the day was almost at an end, the tenor of their demeanor became noticeably somber. David had been the first to arrive and the last to leave. Who knows how long it had been since he celebrated Christmas, or if it would happen ever again.

Steve and I had never experienced a holiday like this one. Traditionally, we had been with our families in New York within a safe haven of comfort and complacency. While we always prayed for those who were less fortunate, the words, while sincere and heartfelt, rang hollow — until this day. They took on flesh and substance in the presence of each humanity gathered in our home. What an epiphany!

It was a matter of weeks until our apartment was reduced to an empty shell, the myriad boxes and furniture having been picked up for transport to the states. David never returned to our apartment after that Christmas Day despite invitations extended to him. He was not happy that we were moving, so some distancing made it easier not to confront the reality.

Each time we saw him during those last weeks, his sad eyes spoke more than any words. Saying goodbye to him was gut-wrenching, especially for Steve. Although there existed a very special bond between them, we both grew to love 'our kid' with feelings of parental attachment. How we wished we could have scooped him up and removed him completely from what was an erratic, unstable, worthless existence. Had it been within the realm of even the most remote possibility, it would have been done there and then!

On the day we all had dreaded, David the Younger was more lucid than usual. It was reminiscent of Christmas day. Maybe this was his parting gift to us, an image we could be proud of. We embraced him one last time outside the bar where we had first met him on that sultry afternoon almost two years earlier. We did not dare utter trite words or espouse false hopes. Drenched in tears, we simply told him that we loved him very much and would think about him often. That was real! This was the last time we saw David.

We returned to the island in January of 2004. It had been fully three years since settling in Florida. Just as we had first met Big José in 1988 and were greeted by him on the day we became island residents in 1999, we were filled with excited anticipation hoping that David would be the one to greet us this time. We wondered if anyone after us had tried to help him. Maybe his family intervened and persuaded him to seek help so he could heal and move forward with his life. We wanted so to find him in better shape than when last we saw him. We raced to 'the old folks' bar. David was not there. One hour later, no David. This was strange because he was a daily fixture in that place.

Finally, I asked Joey if he had stopped by earlier. He looked at Steve and me in a way that made our hearts sink, then he told us what had happened. David had been implicated in a crime and was placed in prison. During that time, he became ill and needed surgery. Joey stopped short. He could barely say the words, "David died."

Daggers pierced our hearts; we could not contain our emotions. We left the bar in tears. Once we were in the privacy of our apartment, we held each other and cried for what seemed like hours. This news was unbelievable. He was only twenty-eight years old. It was impossible for us to make sense of what Joey had told us. Our complete state of physical and emotional exhaustion forced us to rest. Maybe when we awoke, we would realize it had all been a bad dream.

The new day brought with it more of the same emotion we experienced the day before. It was no dream. 'Our kid' was gone forever. We needed to get out of the apartment. If we stayed indoors, we knew we would sink more; we were already drenched in grief and depression. We got on the bus and went to the old city. It was crowded, but we saw no one. It was noisy,

but we heard nothing. David's smiling face was the only image before us. That was all we longed to see.

The morning sun made the Cathedral of San Juan Bautista look extraordinarily beautiful. As we got closer, we heard the organ playing. A deep, resonant voice echoed into the street as the Responsorial Psalm was chanted. We moved across to a small tree-lined park and sat close to each other while absorbing the sacred moment. We remained there until this funeral mass, which was being celebrated for a noted Spanish author, was concluded. No one in that church knew that someone else was being grieved at the same moment as they participated in this Mass of Christian Burial for their family member, friend, colleague. That someone was not one of affluence, reputation or status. That someone had done nothing on a grand scale to make him well known. That someone was not encircled by the deep love and sadness of many. That someone was David. As we had tried to be present to him in life, we were one with him now. If nothing else had been done for him, we were comforted by our intention. The prayers, the music, the singing, the mass, were for this young one whose life had been splintered, whose spirit had been battered and whose heart longed to be loved. All of it was for David. There was no coincidence in our decision to go to the old city, nor was there a randomness in our coming upon the usually quiet cathedral. We were supposed to be there. David was there also. The three of us were together again.

We returned to Florida with an emptiness that escaped description. While praying one morning, words and images came to me. I felt David near and began to write. Another tangible way to memorialize him had been found:

* Elegy for David

Dressed in white,
The silent thief lurked near him
Making day and night indistinguishable.
Aware of its power,
With paralyzing presence,
He played the game anyway.

Existing only for today,
Believing there may be nothing beyond,
He struggled, in delusional stupor,
Clinging to a fast-fading image
Of what he might have been
But could no longer grasp.

Abandoning dignity,
Remnants of his spirit,
Now fractured and scattered,
Became his sole possessions
And slowly dissolved, then,
Into nothingness.

Long gone is a time
When he felt the sun
Give warmth to his face
Or quiet to his soul.
Iron bars suffocated him
And brought more captivity.

Innocence, dreaming,
All that invited a future of promise
Vanished in a magician's trick,
And his life, battered and beaten down
In the turbulent storm,
No longer source of wrenching pain.

Escaping the clutches
Of control and manipulation
And bars of lamenting confinement,
He has found an undimming light
And rests in that peace
For which he searched.

In the House of the Father
F.L. Richards ©2006, 2008
* Title adapted for text.

In addition to the words of this nostalgic lamentation read often, especially by Steve, we have been fortunate enough to memorialize David in a setting quite similar to the one where we sat across from the cathedral in the old city and became lost in sacred liturgy. The place is close to our home, a prayer garden outside the doors of the church we attended for some years. It is a tranquil spot that fosters a quieting of the spirit and an opening of the heart of reflective meditation. Engraved remembrance bricks line the perimeter of this garden filled with trees, plants and flowers. His is set next to those of family members and a dear friend of Steve's. The sentiment is brief but, oh, so true:

David
Always Remembered
Steve and Frank

Whenever we go there, we are comforted because we can see his name and allow thoughts of him to flow wherever they will. He is never far from us because we can never let him go. David, forever 'our kid'.

King Pin

4

The one we called King Pin was a hustler who looked fifty something, even though he wanted everyone to believe he was far from becoming acquainted with that decade of life. His worn face and monkish, Friar Tuck hairstyle were obvious contradictions to the fabrication. Although not uncommon for many people to fib about their age, his ability to prevaricate was an inherent part of an unflattering make up.

He was a tough guy whose personality reeked an air of arrogance. It was outstripped only by a facial expression that bore an insidious, sinister smirk. From all we had seen and heard, King Pin was the head of a small group sarcastically referred to as 'the boogie brigade.' Big José and the two Davids knew him but were not part of his collection of sex toys.

This seeming head honcho routinely made rounds during happy hour. After completing two, sometimes three tours of inspection, he returned to the waiting wolves outside. One by one, they sauntered in and began eye-balling prospective clients. He knew his drones well and had to have used instinct to create matches that might be lucrative for them and him. He scrutinized their interactions from a distance as they put method and technique to work with the money suppliers. A look or gesture from him indicated whether pursuit should be continued or abandoned. Sometimes, a backup was sent in when an initial attempt at connection seemed unlikely.

His role was like that of a madam, a coordinator of those in the 'service' industry. Unlike his female counterpart, King Pin had no office, desk, chair, telephone or appointment book. Blatantly different, also, were the ladies of the night, who primped and prepared to engage in the fetishes and fantasies of their Johns. His group would be had … as is. In most cases, it was not a pretty sight. This, no doubt, contributed to their being labeled 'the dregs.' There were a few who were better looking and understood the relevance of hygiene to sales potential. These were swooped up quickly. The rest of them found a more difficult challenge. Their ability to charm, entice and excite had to be twice as effective, or they just waited until a prospect was too drunk to care.

As a rule, the boys were not visible at night. King Pin, on the other hand, thrived on leftovers. They were the ones who tarried long after happy hour came and went. They were more vulnerable, less inhibited and well on their way to becoming inebriated.

There was little that could dissuade Steve from the lure of surf and sand. I was delighted when clouds blocked the sun. There was less of a chance I would return home looking like a lobster. On days when the elements were tentative, there was no urgency to escape before the ordinarily intense afternoon rays took control.

Tornado already had opened its doors for business one afternoon as we passed and made our way down steps which placed our feet on unusually cool sand. The sky quickly deteriorated from patches of blue and intermittent clouds to a completely overcast dome. The breeze became more intense as we settled not far from the landing. The ocean began to speak loudly as waves, more intimidating than usual, smacked the beach. This was not going to be a lengthy venture!

When the sky morphed from slate gray to a darker hue and cannons from the heavens pierced our ears with repeated thunderous roars, that was it for me. It took no effort to convince Steve that it might be a good idea to pack up and get home before the sky opened. As if my words had been overheard, the rain came down in buckets. We had no choice but to duck inside the bar.

By the time we walked from the entrance to an area that was protected by a side wall, Chris had placed two beers on the counter. We must have been a sight for sore eyes because he could not restrain himself from laughing. I asked for a napkin so I could wipe my glasses and see what was so funny. He could not believe that we had gone to the beach despite a forecast which made our outing one that defied common sense.

I looked at Steve for an explanation because Chris was absolutely correct.

"A little is better than nothing." When Steve said this, the three of us just cracked up. There were no other customers, so we were able to catch up with Chris. It had been a while since we had the luxury of extended conversation with him. He usually was quite busy, especially when alone on duty.

Chris was preparing for a trip to Philadelphia. It had been more than a year since he had seen his family. In the midst of telling us about his upcoming vacation, we heard someone cough. I gazed to the left, nudged Steve's leg with mine and mumbled, "Oh, shit!"

"Stay calm," was Steve's rejoinder, said almost inaudibly.

It was King Pin. If the ring incident had not occurred when Big José painted our condo, we never would have had any contact with him. His concocted tale about having overheard José attempt to sell a gold ring on the same day Steve discovered his missing gave King Pin a plausible excuse to intrude on our conversation with Chris. This unsuccessful beach outing was the second time that circumstances brought us face to face with him.

Steve and Chris were conversing when he approached and sat next to me. *Wonderful!*

"Buenas tardes!", he said as he extended his hand to shake ours.

"Eguál," I answered even though there was nothing good about this afternoon nor did I really care how he was enjoying it. I was more than annoyed at this point.

The deluge was holding us hostage and we were a captive audience to this man who was the last person on earth we wanted to see. Since his elevator did not go all the way to the top floor, we knew his potential for a quick temper. We had gotten a glimpse of it on the day I blurted the imperative, "Véte!" (Go!) as he made the accusation about Big José. We had two options. We could ignore him and remain tense or respond to what we were certain would be an attempt by him to engage us in small talk. We chose the latter.

"Dáme un cigarillo."

"Perdón?"

"Un cigarillo."

I heard him ask for a cigarette the first time but was not impressed by his tone or lack of manners. I half smiled and said, "Por favor." He needed to understand that 'please' was the operative word.

Steve was beside himself. He kept hitting my leg as if to say, "What the hell are you doing? Just give it to him."

I knew that this was not the best time to stand on ceremony, but I did not want to give King Pin the impression that he was going to get anything by barking orders at us. Steve reached into the pack and handed one to him. He went to grab the lighter; I snatched it and looked at him.

"Que quieres?" I knew he wanted the lighter before asking the question. He pointed to it.

"No entiendo la lengua del mano." (I don't understand hand language) I was really begging the point!

"Please … the lighter." I released my grip and slid it over to him.

"Grácias." He actually said thank you without prompting.

Chris found it all amusing and had been chuckling during the bantering. He said something to King Pin in Spanish which I did not completely understand. "I told him not to mess with you two. You take no bullshit."

Sweet Jesus, I thought, *why would Chris say such a thing to this lunatic?* Steve and I wanted to crawl under the counter.

Since the rain was unrelenting, the issue of what to talk about became the concern of the moment. I thought back to our initial conversations with Big José and the two Davids and decided to ask him where he lived. That was general enough … and safe.

Two other guys entered the bar under the shield of large umbrellas as he said, "Rio Peidras."

"Where is that?" As King Pin began to tell us about his town, Chris moved toward the newcomers leaving us without a buffer.

Now, it was just the three of us. *How cozy!*

Like José, he lived with his mother in a government subsidized housing development. They were very poor. His mother was elderly and not a well woman. He did what he could to help her. King Pin continued to talk about his family situation while Chris became engrossed in conversation with the others. The hustler seized the moment and cradled his member in an obvious attempt to let us see what, undoubtedly, he thought we would find irresistible. To say that he was not shy is an understatement!

Steve, oblivious to the show, seemed mesmerized by the churning ocean and excited waves. He was unaware that other excitement was brewing right next to us. As quickly as the weather had changed and nature began to dump buckets of rain, King Pin's manhood rose as if it had been enticed by a snake charmer.

As discreetly as possible, I elbowed Steve. When he turned to me, King Pin gripped the counter with his free hand and tilted the stool back so Steve could view his meal ticket. Despite the steady but gradually lessening rainfall, we had to get out of the bar! When I called to Chris while holding money in my hand, King Pin returned the stool to its original position. We had learned that a tip never should be left on the counter when a boogie was present. More likely than not, the bartender would not be the recipient. This whole time King Pin remained in touch with himself like white on rice.

"What's the hurry? It's still raining," Chris said.

"We have something to do and we're hungry," Steve said, his tone and facial expression making Chris aware of what was more the truth of the matter. When King Pin heard a reference to food, he said he was hungry. Five dollars was a small ransom to pay so we could escape the insanity.

"Grácias, Papi," he said as he leaned over and kissed me on the neck. An uncomfortable shiver ran up and down my spine. At least Steve was not taken off guard and quickly extended his hand as Kin Pin moved toward him. He ignored Steve's gesture and gave him equal treatment.

As we walked home, I told Steve never to suggest a beach venture when there was any chance of rain, no matter how improbable. This was an experience neither of us wanted to repeat ever again.

The street psychology was based on the expression, "If, at first, you don't succeed, try, try again." King Pin was a faithful follower of this philosophy. On days when business was booming, he was busy and ignored us. If, however, the crowd was sparse or there was a lull in the action, he found an excuse to talk to us.

If a stool was available, he sat. Otherwise, he stood behind us. With each uninvited, unsolicited conversation, he revealed more about himself with a voice that became noticeably less gruff. Gradually, he came to understand that polite request was more effective than harsh demand. He learned to wait until he was offered a cigarette or a drink. This was a huge accomplishment for one who was so rough around the edges.

We were not too surprised to learn that he had been on the street since he was fifteen years old. That was when he sold his joy toy for the first time. It was also when he first experimented with drugs. Hearing this sad revelation gave Steve and me a greater insight about his evident lack of responsibility, dignity and honesty. The absence of these traits was replaced, instead, by a keen instinct to survive.

Providing pleasure to others with his very healthy endowment allowed him to make very easy money. He had little education to boast of, so there was not too much on which he could rely in terms of intellect. He chose a path that was based on no more than animal instinct. It was devoid of an ability to analyze and lacked an understanding of consequence. There was no other explanation for his blatant boldness as he unashamedly strutted around the bar while rigorously manipulating the fruits of his labor. We had come to know the strategies and the methods employed by the boogies, but his were the most extreme. His bag of tricks was filled with words, gestures and actions all well rehearsed.

It is ironic that another unforgettable encounter occurred on an afternoon when rain kept the usual crowd away. King Pin, like all of those in his line of work, hated days like this one. Business came to a virtual halt. Since that stormy day months earlier, Chris never omitted an opportunity to tease us about what we later had described to him. He brought drinks to us and gave notice that King Pin was hanging around outside. We hadn't seen him, so we thought he had gone elsewhere to conduct business.

"Hola, amigos," we heard from behind. We had risen the ladder to a position of being referred to as friends. By now, it should have been abundantly clear to King Pin that we were not a source of income upon which he would be able to depend. That unchanging posture did not prevent him from continuing attempts to bait and reel us in.

As we turned to acknowledge his greeting, he stood back. It was impossible not to notice that his one hand was securely cupped around a portion of his crotch leaving the remaining part of his extension in full view. He looked like a bull that needed an explosive release in order to calm down. We had become well-acquainted with his strange personality and brash behavior, so this display of virility received no reaction from us. By the time he sat next to me, it was a down and out situation. The zipper of his jeans was down and the primary tool of his trade was out.

Oh … my … God! I thought as I caught sight of it in my peripheral vision. I dared not look at him directly for fear that it would have been misinterpreted as a show of interest.

Steve had all he could do not to choke on a mouthful of beer. Until this moment, we never realized that the name "King Pin" had multiple meanings. Fully extended and rigid, he positioned his other hand beneath it and slapped it on his open palm.

I jokingly commented, "You will hurt yourself."

"He is strong; he like it," was his rejoinder which, of course, made the reasoning logical … to him. One of the policia touristica entered and began a slow strut around the periphery. King Pin squirmed in his seat as he frantically stuffed his fully tuned instrument into its carrying case. Luckily, the officer paused to speak to someone before he rounded the far end where we were seated.

I nudged Steve so we could take advantage of a quick exit; we trailed behind the uniform. This unexpected visit was most fortuitous. King Pin certainly lived on the edge! We were amazed at the lengths he would go to in order to sell himself. Added to the list of missing links in his personality was an evident lack of discretion.

It was Father's Day, 1998. Steve and I were overwhelmed with melancholy because this was the first time we were not with our children. Memories of past celebrations tugged at our heartstrings. We treated ourselves to an early dinner and arrived for cocktails well before the start of happy hour. A cruise ship was scheduled to dock that afternoon and the beach and bars in our neighborhood would be assaulted by hoards of gay men. Chris and Nick, a part-timer, skated around in an effort to prepare for the onslaught while the barback attended to making sure supplies were plentiful.

"Happy Dad's Day," Chris said excitedly. Noting the absence of smiles as we thanked him, he asked what was wrong.

"We miss our kids." We had to make a concerted effort to remain composed.

"I'll be right back… have two orders at the other end. What do you want?"

Chris and Nick worked well together. No one had to wait very long before being served. All were happy campers, especially the two providing libations. Not only were beverages flowing, but so were very generous tips.

Steve moved bills to Chris when he returned with our drinks.

"No," Chris said as he pushed them back to Steve and pointed to King Pin, who was standing at the opposite end of the bar.

We were in no mood to entertain idiocy; Steve became irritated. "What, now?"

"These are from him."

"What are you talking about?"

"He's buying this round."

"You have to be kidding!"

"He paid for them already."

I asked Chris to get King Pin's attention. When he looked in our direction, we held up our glasses in a gesture of appreciation.

We had been speaking to a guy who we saw at happy hour from time to time. He was a very casual acquaintance; we didn't even know his name.

He eyeballed us as if he expected an explanation for what he had observed. Obviously, he knew the street scene; maybe he knew King Pin. We asked no questions and tried to enjoy our cocktails, but he was determined to get an answer.

Sensing his curiosity as well as evident suspicion, and being keenly aware of the predisposition of some people for juicy, exaggerated gossip, we attempted to dispel any food for fantasy which might result from nothing more than what had been a benign overture. Our simplistic reasoning did not satisfy him, but sparked further inquiry about the nature of our acquaintance with King Pin. His rolling eyes and terse remarks were aimed at hammering home what was an inherent part of street life ... boogies don't do something for nothing.

Steve's displeasure with the accusatory tone was marked by an angry retaliation to the less than discreet innuendo being leveled by this guy who was becoming annoying. Steve's elevated voice and emphatic response prompted the guy to make a quick exit. We knew, with certainty, that this incident would be passed along to others and become fuel for further commentary and conjecture.

Surprisingly, the beach became far more the main attraction than the bar as taxi after taxi unloaded groups of seafarers already well immersed in a mood of festiveness. Despite our dislike for excessive campy behavior, the singing, dancing about and boisterous merriment of the clamorous cruise queens distracted us from the gloominess we felt on that special day. In comparison to the ship's capacity, those on the beach and inside Tornado represented but a handful of vacation goers. We could only imagine how the ship rocked and rolled with dizziness when the hilarity of the entire complement gripped it. These thoughts were interrupted by repetitive tapping on the backrests of our stools which caused us to turn simultaneously. We thought someone standing in the row behind us was trying to gain access to the counter.

King Pin stood there smiling. "Happy Father's Day!" were the first words we heard.

"How do you know we have children?" I asked.

"Chris." He lowered his hand but steered clear of his entertainment center. Instead, he reached into his pocket, then placed a clenched fist between us; he opened it slowly. On his palm lay two pieces of jewelry. One was a chain, the other a bracelet. He handed one to each of us and repeated his initial greeting, "Happy Father's Day."

My attempt to graciously decline our acceptance of them was unsuccessful. He cupped his hands around ours and said, "Take them… they are for you. You look sad before… now you are happy."

We were at a complete loss for words. *What is going on with this bullish boogie?* I wondered as Steve's eyes conveyed the same puzzlement.

Chris moved toward us when King Pin called to him. He said something to Chris in Spanish which he translated for us. Kin Pin saw us earlier and asked Chris what was wrong. Chris explained the cause of our somberness. He left the bar and went to one of the local souvenir shops to buy the items he had given us moments before. As he spoke, the expression on Chris' face reminded us of the one displayed earlier. We knew that, at some point, we would have to put things in perspective again.

We bought a drink for King Pin and tried to have a conversation amid the increasingly raucous gathering. It was an exercise in futility. As difficult as it was to understand him under ordinary circumstances, it was an impossibility at this moment. He kissed each of us on the cheek and indicated he was going to leave.

I thanked him, again, for the drinks and told him that it was not as much the gifts as his behavior that made us happy.

"Un placér!" (A pleasure) he answered as each of us got another peck.

This was too much to absorb in one day — drinks, gifts and an approach to us that was entirely uncharacteristic of one whose train, we were convinced, was completely derailed.

Once King Pin left, it did not take Chris long to return to us. "Get ready," I quickly said to Steve. The look on his face was telling. "You, too?" I blurted, knowing that commentary from him was imminent.

"Me, too … what?"

"You have that look!"

"What look?"

"You saw what happened!"

"Let me see what he gave you."

We placed the necklace and bracelet on the counter. Chris picked them up as if intent on studying their silver composition.

"You guys hit the jackpot today!"

"What do you mean?" Steve interjected.

"He bought you drinks and gave you gifts. What did he say?"

"Happy Father's Day."

I chided Chris for having discussed our personal business with King Pin. As if I had not said a word, he asked, "That's all he said?"

As we had done earlier, we engaged in a repeat performance of clarification. Chris knew the street mentality as well as we, so his continued digging came as no surprise to us. It was nothing less than unsettling.

"I never saw this before," he chuckled. "You two must have been really good to him!"

"Don't go there!" I interrupted with evident irritability.

"These guys are takers; you know that."

"That's why we're confused," Steve continued as he tried to make Chris understand that we could think of nothing that might explain King Pin's actions.

"Nothing?" Chris shot back.

This had become fruitless bantering. There seemed no way for us to convince Chris that what we were saying was the truth. His was a stereotypical view, a generic characterization that lumped together 'the boys of the street' and any, like we, who interacted with them. It was a mental picture that represented an oversimplified opinion which came from the experience of working in a gay bar. We could have debated the shallowness of his misguided perceptions as he defended what he believed was irrefutable proof that he was correct, but we realized the interchange had gone far beyond the point of rational conversation.

He was unrelenting in his attempt to get us to admit that we had 'entertained' King Pin and paid him well. He was unshakable in his belief that the drinks and gifts were an insurance policy which would yield future dividends. Although we had known Chris for years, we both wanted to knock his ass on the floor. Father's Day had evolved into a strange mix of somberness and sincerity, skepticism and sarcasm, snippets and skits that were entertaining. It was a day of unexpected kindness as well as unsolicited criticism and judgment. We were glad when it was ended but knew it was one we would never forget.

After that day, King Pin became routinely absent from the bar, the beach, the neighborhood. Months passed with no sign of him. We knew his mother's health was poor and thought he might have decided to 'work' closer to home. More unsettling was the unpleasant news that his misdeeds had caught up with him and he would not be around for quite a while.

How ironic a twist that this boogie who, for years, was a source of irritation that made us recoil with repugnance, would now give us reason to be concerned about him! We had never observed a redemptive quality in him. His speech, mannerisms and behavior were extreme. They were outrageous to the point of being egregious, so why did we even care where he was and how he was faring?

Although we knew him for many years, it is accurate to say that our analysis of him never extended beyond the arena of the street. Unlike Big José and the Davids, who let us enter other parts of who they were, King Pin wore the same mask of appearance because that was the only method of survival he knew. We never extended the same kindnesses to him as we did to the others. Steve never cooked a meal for him. I never washed his clothes, although there were numerous times when he remained in our neck of the woods for days without returning to Rio Piedras.

All that we had come to understand about him existed within a dysfunctional mentality which he unashamedly wore as a brash, bold, unflattering mantle of identity. Then came that Father's Day. Why did he care if we were sad? What prompted him to go out of his way in a completely uncharacteristic display of generosity and kindness? Steve and I do not believe he had an ulterior motive or think that the 'give and take' philosophy of the street bore any relationship to his buying our drinks and giving us gifts. He owed us no consideration at all; so why did he do it? Maybe our repeated expectation of courtesy and good manners had made an impression. Maybe our unyielding resistance to his sexual overtures and the seductive web he tried to weave was key even though repeated rejection is usually not followed by the atypical behavior he demonstrated.

Perhaps he saw in Steve and me bits and pieces of qualities that made us different from others he invited down the dark streets of his strange world. We will never know what caused the momentary metamorphosis because we never saw him again. Maybe it was better that way. We could remember him for those brief moments in which the hardness of his impervious shell melted away and revealed a softer interior and not the surreal images of the existence he embraced so long ago.

Father's Day has never been the same for us. What gives definition to its wholeness is the sum of the parts that comprise this yearly celebration. King Pin is an inseparable piece of that portrait. It defies reason to think that he, the zaniest, most irritating and vulgar of all we met, would give us reason to pause and remember him.

King Pin was his title, one that described the appearance of things. We were convinced there was nothing more to him until we saw, first hand, that somewhere deep inside was the substance of another self. As fast and fleeting as had been our witness to it, we knew it existed. It was real. It was concrete. It was tangible. On each return of that special day, when Steve and I are remembered by our children in ways which make the reality of love so powerful, we, too, pause to remember. Our thoughts are not about King Pin, the boogie, the one whose exterior was bold, brazen and boisterous. It is another always with him, albeit obscured, who conjures heart-warming images and memories … all because of a few extraordinary minutes. It is one more caring and tender. His name is Juan Carlo.

The You We Did Not Know

The brittle spirit relaxed that day
And the covering that made façade believable
Was stripped away by conscience long asleep.
From its uneasy rest, it rose with awkwardness
As if on the road of a novel, pristine course
Then yawned and stretched, perhaps with some relief.

It was you but not the one we knew,
The one whose voice spewed vulgar intonations,
In whose eyes resided the bitterness of anger
And whose comportment screamed opposition
To the mandate of decency and dignity,
The garbage cast aside by unresting hands
That could not abate spontaneous compulsion
To arouse what slept, then flail mammoth flesh.

But in that special moment when the 'you'
That was synonymous with calculated maneuver,
Unseemly machination, designed manipulation
Was put aside, even as brief as was the passing,
You exposed the core in nakedness before us,
A vision unknown, unexpected, most welcome.
Another self, in blatant contradiction
To the one more apparent and familiar,
Revealed what was thought an obscure heart
Abandoned to darkness, forgotten in time.

F. L. Richards ©2009

Jorge

5

The words 'high season' ring as a sweet melody in the ears of those who are fortunate enough to escape the unforgiving winter weather of the north. The expanse of beach that hugged the two adjacent neighborhood bars became a sea of lounges, sand chairs and towels from November to early April each year. The population, almost exclusively gay men, converged there from morning until late afternoon in order to absorb every moment of the tropical climate.

Clad in Speedos and thongs, the 'bodies beautiful' unashamedly strutted along the water's edge as if on a modeling runway. The air was thick not only because of the heat and humidity but also as a result of the inflated egos and overpowering narcissism that permeated the atmosphere.

In the midst of it all were pockets of older men. While a few were in terrific shape, most could do no more than look at the younger ones and try to remember a time long gone.

Steve and I fit into neither group. We were not young nor were we at that point in life when hair begins to thin and bellies begin to sag. Like many beach lovers, Steve could bask for what seemed like hours. While he embraced the sun and surf with gusto, my mission was different. I spent as much time as possible with him, but once I began to feel as if I were beginning to roast, I was forced to retreat to the shade of the palm trees. That usually took no more than half an hour. On very rare occasions, a cooler breeze cut the intensity of the rays and allowed me to remain with him a bit longer.

We had just returned from a holiday visit with our families in New York. Days later we greeted 1999, the final year of the decade. The rising of the new year sun reflected off the lagoon as we gazed upon its stillness while eating breakfast on the terrace. I knew it was going to be a beach day.

By the time we walked the short distance that put us face to face with the ocean, we were dripping in sweat. This was one of those days when it seemed as though there was not a breath of air to be had. I was already agitated before we stepped foot on the sand. It was about 9:30 a.m. and the bodies were out in force.

Those using lounges or chairs fared better than others, like us, for whom towels were good enough. The sand was so hot, they provided no buffer. I was miserable and it had been just minutes since our arrival. Steve oiled himself; I made a perfunctory effort to do the same knowing, with certainty, it would not be long before I would escape nature's prison.

While we always enjoyed being together, it was at times like this that I had no qualms about a parting of the ways. I pushed myself and managed about twenty minutes. I was fried! Steve was in his own world as he listened to opera music. I got his attention and pointed to Buena Vista; he knew what that meant. I picked up my towel and make tracks to the rear of the beach. I scoped out a large tree, positioned my towel so that shade completely encircled me and leaned back against the deck wall.

Having found relief from the sweltering sun, I attempted to read the book I brought along, but my eyes burned from the sweat that ran down my face like a waterfall. Steve had turned and was lying on his stomach; we had a clear view of each other. I got his attention again and pointed to my watch.

He mouthed, "I'll be there soon."

Yeah, I thought, *so will Christmas!*

The beach became more and more crowded despite the scorching heat. I saw a young man zigzag through the human blanket; he walked in my direction. Standing right next to me, he dried off and placed his towel on the cool, refreshing sand. Once he sat, he brushed his long, dark hair and flipped it into a ponytail. His skin was bronze and gave accent to his large, deep set eyes. His physique was not grotesquely muscular but had good definition.

"My name is Jorge," he said with a deep, distinct voice. His grip was like a vise as he shook my hand.

"I'm Frank."

He added, "The sun is too hot for me and I love the beach." His deep tan highlighted snow-white teeth and created an obvious contrast to his evenly tanned body.

"I'm not a beach person; I can't tolerate the sun for very long."

"Why do you come, then?" he shot back.

I pointed to where Steve was lying.

"Is that a friend of yours?"

"He's my partner."

"How long have you been together?"

"Many years," was my vaguely specific answer.

"That's great! How long are you going to be here?"

"Not much longer; it's too hot."

"I don't mean at the beach… in P.R.?"

"We own a condo and stay for months at a time."

His facial reaction to my last comment was the first inkling that Jorge might be a beach lover for other reasons. He went on to tell me that he had arrived from the states just days ago and was staying with his grandmother while he looked for work and an apartment. He did not get along with his family but loved Abuela (grandma).

He lifted his waist pouch and placed his brush inside it. I could see a card that looked like a piece of a boarding pass. It seemed to bear veracity to what he had just told me. He stood up, stretched and flexed his muscles. "I'm going for another swim … you and your friend want to join me?"

"No thanks; we're not staying much longer." I was finally able to do some reading when he left. Within what seemed like minutes, I felt a presence standing over me; sweat was dripping on the pages. I thought Jorge had returned. It was Steve; he looked like a cherry.

He asked who the dark haired guy was. As I was relating the conversation to him, I noticed Jorge standing at the water's edge. His legs were spread and his hands were on his waist. He bobbed back and forth, side to side and provided onlookers with a view of his athletic maneuvering. Steve had no choice but to squeeze his towel between Jorge's and mine. This was a rare happening. In the bar, I was a shield for Steve. He never sat next to an unoccupied stool. That was my job.

Jorge negotiated a path back to his towel. Before drying off, he extended his hand to Steve. "You must be his partner."

"Yeah … I'm Steve."

"Jorge. It's good to meet you."

"You, too."

Steve had always been a person of few words when placed in a new social situation. His inability to speak Spanish was a plausible excuse. Jorge spoke fluent English, so Steve's cover was gone. He must have felt comfortable because rather than burying his face in a book, he was quite eager to remain in the loop of conversation. Jorge's soft yet masculine voice and laid back, non-aggressive approach made this possible for Steve.

The bar deck was at the top of steps literally feet away from where we were sitting. Steve really enjoyed speaking to Jorge and invited him to join us for a beer. While there was no breeze at sea level, it was quite comfortable on the deck and there was no sun!

Between gulps of his first beer, Jorge thanked us and wanted to know what made us decide to buy a condo in Puerto Rico. We told him a bit of our history that included well over a decade of an ever-increasing affection for the island. By this time, Steve's granddaughter, Alexis, had passed her seventh birthday; my little ones, Frances and Mary, were approaching their third. His reaction to our making passing references to them was a photo moment.

"You two don't look like you have kids that old… and grandchildren, wow!" He begged the point on the first part of his compliment; the second was more palatable. Whether he was sincere or beginning to butter the bread, we were flattered. Jorge's low-keyed manner was quite engaging and made conversation flow easily.

By the time we decided to return home, we had been chatting for nearly two hours. There would be no happy hour today. We already had enjoyed it for a good part of the afternoon. Jorge rose first; his waist was at eye level. The white Speedo he was wearing did him justice! His thick, muscular thighs looked like weapons. They were not unlike the manhood with which he had been endowed and unashamedly paraded on the sandy turf.

After that day, we saw him whenever we went to the beach. He always spent some time speaking to us, but it became evident that he was acquainted with a number of older gents as well. Jorge migrated from one lounge chair to another, greeted them with a prolonged hug and spent time in conversation.

Once in a while, we saw money pass from their hands to his. This became a predictable conclusion to his visit at any given site. It appeared as though he needed to do very little to make a buck. Some were so captivated by his attractiveness, they almost fell off their lounges while making room for him to sit with them. Many of the gay men we have met are overly concerned with appearance. Even if theirs was fading due to age, just having Jorge next to them provided a definite ego boost. One in particular, a guy in his late sixties, took a more that noticeable liking to Jorge. It did not take long before the two became exclusive beach companions.

Watching him rub suntan oil on Jorge's back was like viewing soft porn. His face looked as if he were visually undressing the very athletic body. Whenever Jorge coated the older guy's back, his movement was slow and deliberate. Audible moans came from the senior. That's when Jorge's hands began to glide up, down and all around. It was like watching foreplay. Even if Steve and I were a distance away, we could pinpoint exactly where the two were located.

After a while, the only ones to react were those who had never seen the show before. Beyond these few, little notice was given to what had become commonplace. Many oiled themselves before lying in the sun, but there was something about Jorge and his tourist friend that almost demanded attention. There was, no doubt, some exhibitionism going on but it remained within a zone of safety. Nonetheless, it was alluringly seductive.

Touching became frequent and neither seemed embarrassed by the arousal which resulted. More often than not, members stood at attention as they rose and ambled to the ocean for a swim. Jorge sometimes fell behind the other and was the recipient of many looks, winks and smiles. If his purpose was to advertise himself, he was a walking billboard!

Whenever Jorge's companion happened to turn and see what was going on behind his back, he shot a nasty look or vulgar caveat to those who gawked at Jorge. If he acknowledged them, there was hell to pay! We don't know if Jorge realized that he was being objectified. For the tourist, this hot, young guy was a trophy which no one else was going to get near.

During the eight weeks of the vacationer's stay, we had no interaction with Jorge other than a discreet wink or wave from him when he thought the gesture would escape notice by the sentinel. Clearly, this guy was under the impression that the young beach idol was attached to him at the hip. His possessive, jealous nature resulted in their arriving, remaining and leaving … together. We were sure that Jorge was being well-compensated but wondered if he thought surrendered freedom was too high a price to pay.

As one week melted to the next, the novelty seemed to wane. His attention to the traveler was not as focused or overly indulgent as at the onset. There were times when Jorge managed to separate from him and take extended tours along the beach front. He was careful to walk an adequate distance so he could meander up the sandy terrain and camouflage himself in the thick crowd. The calculated maneuver allowed him to speak to others he knew. Although he was an exclusive companion, it was important not to burn any bridges behind him.

Not until the fun and games ended and the tourist returned to wherever he called home was Jorge able, once again, to shower his attention and charisma on those he had abandoned. There was not much time remaining until the island would exhale a sigh of relief. The months of winter vacations were nearly ended.

While the seasons of the year are distinct in the north, they are less so on the island. There are changes, however, which make one aware of the differences. With the advent of spring, the temperature begins its hike up the thermometer and is accompanied by days of increasing humidity. The beaches are quiet except for the unchanging sounds and rhythms of ocean waves. Other than locals and an occasional pocket of tourists, the electricity in the atmosphere is gone.

This is true of the bars as well. Happy hour, once pulsing with activity, becomes a more subdued afternoon gathering. When we did not see Jorge for what seemed like months, we thought that he, like the others who depended upon beach and bar trade, had found it necessary to spread out and explore other locales in order to compensate for the marked decrease in business opportunities in our neighborhood. It was uncommon but not unheard of that a tourist invited a boogie to return to the states with him for an extended period of time. We thought this might have been an opportunity presented to and accepted by Jorge. Either of these two lines of reasoning made sense. Having seen him in action, we were more inclined to lean toward the latter thinking.

As harsh as the sun can sometimes be, the ocean wind is capable of creating its own havoc. There is little else to compare with becoming a sand mummy on days when it seems that, from nowhere, gusts hammer unrelentingly. Without a lounge or beach chair to create a minimal amount of elevation between frantic swirls of sand and oiled bodies, there is no escaping the magnetic attraction of one to the other. This was our experience one day.

Early in the morning, we could see how excitedly the water danced on the lagoon, so we knew it was going to be a breezy day. We had no idea that we would be in the middle of a sand storm once on the beach. Minutes after we applied a thick layer of suntan oil and stretched out on beach towels, what had been a refreshing breeze morphed into a forceful wind. Within seconds, we were dressed in grainy, tan coats. We were covered head to foot and so were our towels. They were no longer visible under the dense layer of sand that buried them.

Steve was a trooper and was certain the squall would pass, but the stinging continued until it became unbearable. He realized that this force of nature was not going anywhere soon. We walked to the water so we could take off the body armor. It was freezing! We bobbed up and down a few times and managed to dislodge most of the sand. Had it not been for our beach bag, we never would have been able to locate our towels. With effort, we dragged them a distance away from each other and shook them out. I grabbed the bag and we moved toward the rear of the beach. Steve saw that I was not a happy camper and suggested we take cover on the bar deck, have a beer and continue to wipe off the remnants of our beach visit.

We heard a voice coming from behind us. "Are you guys O.K.? Doesn't look like you enjoyed yourselves down there."

Jorge had been watching us wrestle with the elements. I was not amused and shot him a look.

"I didn't mean to tease you," he came back with a tone of apology.

"We're going to have a beer; you want one?" Steve quickly interjected.

"Sure. There's nothing else to do."

As we approached a table completely shielded from the wind and rays, we continued to spill more sand on the deck. My face was tight with tension. "I'm really sorry, Frank. I thought if I said something funny, you might laugh … guess not."

It was not until we sat back and relaxed that we really got a close look at him. His body tone had lost some definition. He had lost weight. Conversation, once sharp and focused, was more labored. His eyes, once full of life and energy, looked like two diluted pools of colored water. We had seen these signs before and knew what Jorge had been doing during the months of his absence. Clearly, he had become well-educated in the ways of the street. With that came his initiation into the drug culture.

Uncharacteristically, Steve initiated the conversation. "Are you okay, Jorge?"

"Yeah …Why?"

"You look tired and you've lost weight."

He lowered his head and stared at the table. Steve and I looked at each other. Had we embarrassed him or was he pausing to think of a response? He gazed at us strangely and began to speak.

"You guys know I've been looking for work since I got here. No one wants to hire someone with a record."

"Looks like you have found work," I blurted in a tone that was less than sensitive as I pointed to the beach.

Steve darted a look of displeasure in reaction to my comment. He placed his hand on Jorge's shoulder.

"Do you want to talk about it?"

"I don't mind, if you want to listen. I don't tell people my business, but you guys have been nice to me. Can I have another beer?"

I left momentarily and returned with three fresh brews.

Jorge continued the saga. "I was on the inside when I lived in the states, so I can't get past the criminal background check here. Without a good conduct certificate, no one will give me a chance."

"Did your family try to help you?" I asked.

"The first time they helped, but it happened again and they didn't want anything to do with me. When I got out, I called my grandmother. She sent a ticket to my friend's house. That's how I got here."

Jorge did not offer the details that caused the periods of confinement and we did not ask. We knew, however, that the reasons were serious enough to prevent him from accessing employment.

"I met you guys right after I got to P.R. I did try to get a job. Anything would have been okay. I just wanted to make money and help my grandmother."

"What happened?" Steve asked.

Jorge proceeded to tell us about the easy money he made just by being on the beach, especially during the eight weeks of his attachment to the tourist.

"You know who I'm talking about."

"Yes … we saw you in action."

Again, my words lacked thought and I got another irritated glance from Steve.

He looked at Jorge and smiled. "Do you want to continue?"

"At first, I sat with him and we just talked. He always gave me money — usually twenty dollars. Then he started teasing me about sex. I told him I never was with a guy. He said he would make it worth my while."

"Did you agree?"

Jorge paused, then asked if he could have another beer. The A-B-C Principle was operative — alcohol aggression, booze bravery, cocktail courage.

"One day, I went to his apartment. He put $150.00 on the table. I let him go down on me. I was there for about half an hour. That was the most money I had made in a long time. It was easy, too easy, so I did it more and more. I was never into sex with guys, but I had to eat!"

"So did he," I quickly added.

We all burst into laughter. It lightened what was becoming a very intense discussion.

"Jorge, you have to know how attractive you are."

"Now I do … then I didn't give it a thought. Let's be real. He wanted something and I needed money. The whole thing just worked. He couldn't get enough of me and wanted me to move back to the states with him."

Steve, always kind and gentle, explained to Jorge that his life might have been better. "He might have been able to help you find work so you could get on your feet."

"That wasn't his plan. He said I wouldn't have to work and I don't think I'd be on my feet too much."

Laughter erupted again and made for an easier flow of conversation.

"I would have been his sex toy. I knew I couldn't do that. Having a good time here is one thing. I don't want to feel like anyone owns me."

Steve and Jorge could have continued drinking, but I had reached my limit.

"Have you eaten today?" I asked.

"No, not since last night. I'm starving."

"Come to our place and have lunch with us."

"Thanks. You guys are wonderful."

The conversation at the bar revealed to us Jorge's money-making exploits, but it steered clear of the issue which caused us to have greater concern. He had not addressed Steve's query about the loss of weight and an apparent decline of energy. Once we began eating, I brought up these observations again, hoping Jorge would explain what was happening to him.

His response did not surprise us as much as his willingness to speak about a very personal subject. "Some of the guys I've met like to party — weed, coke, H — you name it — they have it. At first, it made me less nervous and let me get into their scenes. Then, I started to like it. The more I did with them, the more they paid me."

Jorge spoke with candor as he explained who he had become … and why. This no holds barred exposé provided Steve and me with a greater understanding of the psychology of the street. The innuendos, suggestive comments and overt actions we had witnessed in the past could be seen from a different perspective. In Jorge's case, it wasn't about drugs for the sake of getting high. It wasn't about the willing stripping of dignity. It was about the desperation that results from circumstances. It was all about the need to survive by the only means he believed were available to him. He saw the tears in our eyes but could not possibly know how our hearts were wrenched. He was sure things would change for him and he would get back on track.

"How do you plan to do that?" My voice cracked as I asked this question for which there seemed no plausible answer.

"I need to get into a program, come out and stay away from here."

Steve and I had heard of others who lived in the same fantasy; it never worked. The kind of rehabilitation programs offered to guys like Jorge were short term. They lasted days, maybe one week. With no family support, they had no alternative but to return to the environment which was the source of their conflicted lives. We said nothing to Jorge about this because we did not want to discourage him. Whether his words were designed to lighten our visible upsetment or merely give lip service to a notion he already knew was less than promising, there was hope in his voice.

Unlike others who had no one on whom they could depend, he had his grandmother. She could provide a change of geography; that was an essential element in getting well. More demanding would be her ability to exact tough love when needed in order to assist him in maintaining his strength and determination. Given what we knew to be a very close relationship between them, we weren't sure whether she had the capacity to be anything more than 'abuela.'

Despite the great challenge about which he spoke with tentative resolve, Steve and I made an effort to encourage him. We had been down this road before. Speaking about self-improvement with others like Jorge was like spitting in the wind.

"When do you plan to get into a program?" Steve postured.

"As soon as I get enough money to give to my grandmother so, when I get out, I'll have something and I won't have to hang around here."

Long range vision was a daunting obstacle. Jorge spoke about the future, yet it was the here and now that needed intense attention. Either he didn't grasp that or his rationale helped him deal with the present and allow for momentary delusion about an 'if … then' equation that made no sense to us.

After that emotionally draining afternoon, we did not see Jorge. We thought that he had found the strength to follow through in getting help. We learned from others that he had been seen elsewhere. Each time, he was with a different guy, sometimes two, and looked stung out. We were hopeful that his absence from the neighborhood had been a sign of change, and it was. It was not change in a positive direction but one which resulted in his emotional descent to hell.

I usually took our dog, Peaches, for a final walk at nine o'clock each evening. It became a ponderous mission after she underwent two cancer surgeries and was slower moving. We walked in the same direction, she made the same stops and we returned by the same route. The routine could never be changed. Attempts at altering part or all of the pattern greatly agitated her. As we neared our building one night, having accomplished the purposes of a last walk, I paused so she could catch her breath. That usually made the last leg of the tour manageable for her. For some reason, she pulled in a forward motion as if to tell me it was not necessary to stop.

Instead, she decided to plop down at the entrance. I stood and waited for her to regain the steam in her engine.

I heard a voice coming from behind a fenced area of the lagoon. The distance was about fifty feet. "Frank." I looked around but saw no one. Again, I heard my name, more audible this time, and I saw a figure emerge from the shadows. It looked like Jorge, but I could not be certain. As he crossed the street and began walking in my direction, the obscure figure of moments ago took distinct shape. I was both horrified and nauseated when he approached. Indeed, it was Jorge.

My voice began to tremble. "How have you been?" I did not know what else to say, even though the mere sight of him shouted the answer.

"Look at me … that's how I've been," he slurred in a tone of sarcastic irritation. "Can you do me a favor?"

"That depends upon what it is."

"Can I take a shower upstairs? I'm sorry … I know it's late." His tone became more benign. "I haven't washed in days and my clothes are dirty."

A second request, albeit implied, had just been made.

"I have to speak to Steve … stay here."

When he attempted to bend and pet the dog, his body began to sway. I grabbed his arm and positioned him against one of the support columns of the exterior canopy.

I entered the elevator and looked at Jorge. He stood motionless, looking at the ground. I knew that Steve would not have a problem with Jorge's request, but I felt obliged to talk to him first.

"Jorge is downstairs."

"Why didn't you invite him to come up to the apartment?"

"Steve, be prepared."

"What do you mean?" he asked in a tone that revealed alarm.

"He's a mess. He doesn't look the same and he's filthy."

Instant images of the Jorge we once knew flashed through Steve's mind and caused tears to well up in his eyes.

"How bad is he?" Steve's voice was shaking. I just looked at him. That was enough of an answer.

"Is he hungry?" Steve yelled to me as I walked down the hall.

"I'm sure he is."

When I exited the lobby, Jorge was standing in the exact position where I had left him. There was one difference. His hand was affixed to his crotch and forced notice of his playmate. I steeled myself. *This is not going to be easy.* We entered the elevator and began the ascent to the eleventh floor. He was all over me — hugging, kissing my neck and thanking me repeatedly.

"Easy, tiger." I said as I tried to force a smile while moving him back from me.

"He **is** a tiger … some guys call him, 'the beast'."

By the time we entered the apartment, Steve was already preparing food and had set a place for him at the terrace table.

"Steve … my man," was Jorge's greeting; it was accompanied by more hugs, kisses and thanks. Steve looked stunned and was clearly speechless. He turned and continued working at the stove and I handed Jorge a plastic bag and a pair of shorts.

"What are these for?"

"Put your clothes in the bag and use the shorts after you shower."

Jorge went into the bathroom to do as I had requested. Steve turned to me and whispered, "Oh, my God! What has happened to him?"

I was about to say something when Jorge appeared, bag in hand. He was dressed in nothingness. All of this behavior was strange to us. He had never been forward or demonstratively affectionate. Never had he engaged in seductive machinations nor had we ever seen him in a state of complete undress. No doubt, the drugs he used enhanced his ability to feel completely uninhibited.

Steve was cooking, Jorge was showering and I hastened to the laundry room hoping that no one else would be there. I dumped his clothes in a washer and retreated to the elevator as fast as my feet could carry me. Jorge was standing in the kitchen talking to Steve when I got back. He sounded more lucid and looked infinitely better. He was wrapped in a towel and held the shorts in his hand.

"They're too big ... they keep falling off my waist. ... Okay if I sit like this?"

"Sure, enjoy the food," Steve answered as he invited Jorge to take his place at the table. We took our seats at either end and watched him consume the meal like a vacuum cleaner.

"What has happened to you, Jorge?" Steve's voice was soft and full of concern.

"I'm gonna get help real soon."

It was a dead end conversation.

"Where are you going when you leave here?"

"I know a cheap hotel ... I can get a room for about twenty dollars ... can you guys help me out?"

"Why don't you stay here? Sleep on the sofa bed, get a good rest and we'll have breakfast in the morning?"

"I would love to stay but if I don't get my fix in the morning, I won't be able to move. I need coke and H to get me going."

Steve and I had to restrain ourselves from bursting into tears. In truth, I wanted to blast him because of the condition he was in but that would have done no good and might only have served to anger him to the point of some physical retaliation. That was the last thing we needed.

He pressed on and lowered the tab to fifteen dollars. Steve reiterated more emphatically, "We can offer you the sofa bed for the night … that's all we can do to help you." We were certain he had no intention of seeking shelter. He would sleep on the beach and use the money for his A.M. wake up call.

While Steve and Jorge continued what had become idle chatter, I returned to the laundry room to collect his clothing. I returned to find Steve washing dishes. From the bathroom, running water could be heard. Jorge was standing at the sink, buck naked, and flipped his hair into that signature pony tail. I placed the bag on the floor and told him to let us know if he needed anything. As soon as I uttered those words, I wanted to pull them back. He grabbed his member and slapped it against the sink.

"He can use some attention."

"Behave yourself and get dressed."

He was sly! We refused his request for money to get a room, so he figured that he would collect for services rendered. It wasn't going to happen!

Steve and I were watching T.V. when he entered the living room. His jeans were tightly packed; notice of the contents was unavoidable. Even as we rose and walked with him to the door, Steve made a final overture of invitation to Jorge. He pressed forward and squeezed each of us with a vise-like grip. He was intent on letting us feel the power of his masculinity and the object of his seductive virility. It was a silent, last-ditch effort to win us over. After he left, the first words which came to my mind were, *Another one bites the dust.* It was a succinct analysis but an apt characterization of what had become of Jorge.

As we had done in past circumstances which bore a seamless connection to this scenario, we found it difficult to verbalize the emotions that overpowered us. Unquestionably, we were sad. When we met Jorge, he was strong, vibrant and focused. All of that was gone. Those qualities had been stolen away by an insidious, silent thief that chipped away until only a shell remained. That was what Jorge had become.

Although we were well-acquainted with the methods and techniques of those who traded sex for money, we also felt some resentment. We thought he was different; he was not. We believed that his resolve to improve was genuine; it was lip service which he knew would keep us interested in his well-being. The many times we shared with him, the countless conversations and, on this night, our efforts to give him shelter and safety were meaningless.

In truth, we had become irrelevant because a greater power than selfless generosity was at work. The immediacy of want and need had come to dominate his thinking and behavior. He wanted drug money because he needed to avoid the agonizing pain of physical debilitation. Jorge had spun a web into which he could not lure us and was forced to return to the darkness of night on a continued quest. We were certain he would find success along the way. As he released the silky fiber that would create yet another elaborate design, there awaited someone, somewhere, who would be attracted and respond to the beckoning voice from within its weave … "Come into my parlor," said the spider to the fly.

Antonio

6

On par with David the Elder, both in appearance and enigmatic personality, was another muscle guy who frequented the bar. Ruggedly handsome, he was in excellent physical condition. While white jeans and work boots were the constants of his attire, a variety of colored, tight-fitting tee shirts accented a different look whenever we saw him standing in his usual position against the deck railing of Tornado. He was never without his faithful companion, a gym bag.

Unlike David, who could be in a crowd but detach himself with his trademark downward stare, this guy stood with an air of confidence. It was difficult not to notice him since his demeanor commanded attention. There were times when a casual gaze from him became a hauntingly intense stare. He spoke to no one nor did we ever observe anyone acknowledge him. We found this both interesting and curious.

On days when we decided to go to happy hour, we always arrived early so we could claim stools that would provide an unobstructed ocean view. A mammoth fish tank flanked the interior of the oblong bar so it was important to steer clear of having to gaze at repetitious movement that could make dizzy the most sober of customers. There were occasions, however, when sitting space was limited and we were forced to look at the watery occupants.

Sometimes, we had no choice but to come face to face with 'Mr. Muscles' as we approached stools directly in front of the spot where he seemed to maintain squatter's rights. The saving grace was that there was no eye contact with his somewhat scary countenance. We had no idea whether or not a story went with the face. He was not a social mixer and his routine was predictable. He always stood with beer in hand and studied the crowd. The empty bottle was left on the rail and a quick departure followed. We did not think he was part of the street ranks since we saw him only on weekends. Often, a small towel was draped around his neck. Judging from his stunning physique, it seemed logical to assume that a workout had occurred earlier.

One Saturday afternoon, weeks after Jorge's disturbing visit, we settled in for happy hour right in front of his spot. We were fortunate to find a place to sit because the gathering place became extremely crowded. On more than one level, business was jumping. Robert, a part-time bartender, was working with Chris and Mike, an older self-proclaimed brassy queen. We had known him for years and found his personality not at all offensive but endearing. Those he knew well were always greeted with an affectionate quip. Sometimes, we were his "little cups of pudding" or "apple dumplings." More often would come the announcement, "Here are my little chick-a-dees." Mike was quite a character who was able to make happy hour more spirited than anything found in a glass.

The three were moving about without pause as drink orders were barked at them from every direction. We usually did not have too long a wait before being served. On this afternoon, however, Tornado was overflowing with customers. There was a predictable increase in numbers on weekends, but this was extraordinary!

While Steve gazed around less intently, my people-watching skills were in high gear. The boys of the street were out in force and meandered through the increasingly close quarters. Some connected quickly while others eye-balled prospective clients before making a move. It was difficult to know where to look since so much was going on at once. Now and then, I nudged Steve for a reaction to an observation. By his own admission, he never paid much attention to detail, so any commentary from me usually produced a quizzical look from him.

It took about fifteen minutes before I was able to get Robert's attention, order drinks and find out what caused the need for three bartenders. "Gay cruise … overnight stay," was his brief explanation.

As he gave each of us a beer, we heard a voice behind us then an arm slipped between us and rested on the counter. We did not turn to see who had wedged in, but continued talking to Robert. He reached into a chest, removed a bottle of beer and slid it in the direction of the waiting hand that intercepted it and quickly retreated. Because it was impossible to carry on a conversation and every bit as challenging to order a second round, our happy hour stay was cut short.

I rose first, turned quickly and literally rubbed shoulders with someone attempting to get near the bar. "Excuse me," I said spontaneously.

"Don't worry about it." A broad smile accompanied the response.

Steve was trying to get Robert's attention to ensure that a tip would find its way to his hands and not someone else's. We had learned that leaving money on the counter was a no-no! Steve was clueless about my encounter until he got up from his stool. His facial expression was a Kodak moment when the guy said hello to him. We realized whose deep voice we had heard earlier and whose arm had pressed between us to gain access to a brew. It was the guy with the gym bag, Mr. Muscles, the one we would come to know as Antonio.

From time to time, we enjoyed breakfast or lunch at Buena Vista. The café, which was adjacent to the bar area, was a popular eatery. The food was delicious and quite reasonably priced. One Saturday, a few weeks after the gay cruise happy hour experience, we decided to have lunch there and then sit on the beach. Because the day was overcast, there would be no scorching afternoon sun.

As we approached the corner of the side street that led to the bars and beach, we saw Mr. Muscles leaning against the stop sign. He greeted us as if we had been long-time friends. Although our destination was obvious, he asked what our plans were.

"Lunch and beach," I said.

"The gym was too crowded so I'm waiting for Tornado to open … guess I'll have a beer and try again later." We knew little about gyms and workouts, but we thought it odd that he would indulge before pumping up.

"The bar doesn't open for another forty-five minutes," Steve told him.

"Can I sit with you guys instead of waiting out here?"

"Sure. You can have a bite to eat with us if you're hungry."

"Thanks … I'm Antonio," he said as he practically crushed our fingers in the forceful grip of his handshake.

The cozy café had no windows so there was always a breeze. On brisker days, wind whistled through the interior and muffled the music playing in the background. This was one such time. We found a table along the front wall. It was all that separated us from the beach a few feet below.

Antonio's wavy, dark hair swayed and danced with random movement. As hard as he tried to keep it in place, its self-will took control. "I must look like a mess," he chuckled.

"Not at all," Steve countered.

Conversation came to a halt as he assaulted the mound of fries, a large salad and a huge burger. Steve often teases me about how quickly I eat. I was a snail in comparison to the speed with which Antonio devoured every morsel of food.

The silence made us uneasy so I asked him what kind of work he did.

"Construction," he said, and went on to tell us he was part of the team that was renovating Las Palmas, a large hotel resort which was not far from our condo. His voice revealed an engaging calmness so unlike the macho, intimidating bar façade we had observed. Stories about his job were a mix of light-hearted and serious snippets of what seemed to be a daunting challenge for the workforce. There were not too many weeks remaining before the deadline by which all must be in readiness for the re-opening.

It was evident that he took his job seriously because he voiced annoyance about the laziness of some co-workers. Apparently, the bosses shared his concern. Just days before, they called for a meeting with the workers to re-emphasize the urgency of completing the project before the New Year's Eve gala event. To motivate them, each would be allowed to bring a guest. The tab would be paid by the company. "That put a fire under their asses."

"Your wife must be excited," Steve said.

"I'm not married. I'll take my friend, Elisa. We have known each other for many years … she's a great lady."

The conversation shifted away from work and became centered on this special woman in his life. She had three children and was expecting a fourth; she was raising them alone. On each pay day, he gave her money. One of her neighbors sometimes let Antonio use his car to take her shopping or to the beach in our area. The neighbor and his wife were happy to watch the children and give Elisa a break from routine.

"It's wonderful that you are so concerned about her," I interjected.

"She's been a good friend and I love her kids … maybe you guys will meet her one day when we come to the beach." Antonio glanced at his watch and sprang to his feet. "I hate to leave but I have to get to the gym, then meet someone … hope we can do this again … I did all the talking and don't know anything about you two."

"We're sure we'll see you around," Steve responded.

This unexpected, very pleasant encounter was, indeed, an ice breaker. More than that, it reaffirmed a time-honored expression, "You can't judge a book by its cover."

After that lunch experience, Antonio abandoned his post and sat with us whenever he saw us at happy hour. We received regular updates about the renovation project as well as how Elisa was progressing with her pregnancy. There came a time when we met the wonderful lady friend about whom he had spoken with great affection. A beach day was planned and included lunch at our apartment.

Elisa was a hefty woman, heavy with child. Quiet at first, she seemed timid. Antonio sensed her uneasiness and redirected the conversation to one which focused on the children and the upcoming birth in January. As Elisa showed us photos of the three little ones, her face beamed with pride. All were boys and close in age … three, two and one. She rubbed her stomach and proudly announced, "This one is a girl."

We learned that each of the boys had a different father and none were involved in their lives.

"They are deadbeat dads … they don't do shit … that's why I help her as much as I can."

Elisa looked at Antonio with adoration. She rubbed his arm and said, "I don't know what I would do without him." Their approach to each other was so natural and genuine, they easily could have been a married couple. They displayed obvious inquisitiveness because they asked questions about our backgrounds and showed particular interest in wanting to know about our relationship.

While enjoying lunch, the conversation was designed to have Steve and me reveal some personal aspects of our lives. When we told them about our many years together and that we had been married and have children and grandchildren, their facial expressions became ones of confusion and curiosity. They seemed riveted to our words as we explained how we came to understand ourselves and embrace the need to live and love only as we were able.

Just as Antonio had dominated the conversation that day at Buena Vista, Steve and I felt as if we had been placed on the undraped stage of life during this gathering. Elisa glanced at her watch and realized we had been talking for hours. They had to return home and collect the boys from her neighbors because the couple had evening plans.

As she hugged and thanked us, she said, "I haven't relaxed like this in a long time; it was wonderful!"

After they left, Steve told me what Antonio had whispered in his ear when they embraced, "Thanks for making her so comfortable."

We sat and spoke about the visit, how charming Elisa was and how evident had been Antonio's indignant tone when speaking about the absence of dads in the lives of the three innocents, but we wondered if they had told us everything.

Within weeks, the stores became alive with Christmas spirit. Although the holiday season was one of excited anticipation on the island, there is no place like New York during that special time of year. We busied ourselves with preparations for travel to the Big Apple. Gazing at the mammoth tree at Rockefeller Center, enjoying the holiday extravaganza at Radio City Music Hall and peering into store windows alive with animated characters resurrected the child-like wonder in each of us.

The most important gift of Christmas, however, was our ability to be with our families. Returning to our roots was essential. We were able to step back into a reality that was, at times, difficult to remember on the island. We reconnected with those we loved, those for whom life was so different, yet a nagging ache pulled at our heart strings and compelled us to think about others for whom life was synonymous with struggle. We wondered how the special day would be spent by them. We knew that it would not resemble the festiveness we were enjoying. More likely, it would be but another day of sameness on which the glad tidings of Christmas that permeated the air with joy and celebration would see a stark contradiction to what was the substance of their lives.

Gathering with our respective families around tables filled with plenty was bittersweet. We remembered Big José, the Davids, crazy King Pin, Jorge, Antonio and Elisa. Our families did not know them, but the words of reflective prayer, spoken by each of us in two different households, made them understand how care and concern went far beyond the walls inside which everything was wonderful and comfortable.

We returned to the island and celebrated New Year's Eve with some friends, but were unable to remain with them until midnight because the predictable uproar in the neighborhood would send our pooch, Peaches, into a frenzy of howling. Alone, we raised glasses in the midst of a rite of passage. The nineteen hundreds were put to rest as the year 2000 ushered in the turn of the century. Our thoughts were not only about the thirteen years we had enjoyed together and the blessings that came from them but also about those we knew on the island who were less fortunate. We prayed that the new year might bring a measure of change and healing to the wounded spirits who had become part of our lives.

Gay tourists were not the only ones who flocked to Puerto Rico during the winter months. Our apartment became a hotel. We were never alone for very long. Family and friends took full advantage of the opportunity to shed layers of clothing and enjoy some fun in the sun. First on the list of visitors in the new year were Steve's ex wife, Michelle, and Sheila, a long-time friend of theirs. Steve and Michelle had managed to maintain a cordial relationship. That had a positive effect on her ability to accept me. It was all so cozy! The two ladies arrived during the early part of February, the most popular vacation month on the island. We spent that week showing them the sights. One afternoon, Michelle asked if there was a bar nearby; she wanted to buy us drinks.

Steve delicately explained that Tornado was a gay bar. "No problem!" was her quick response. Sheila decided to remain at the apartment and rest. The fast pace of each day had caught up with her. As we strolled down the avenue, I told them to go to the bar while I picked up a few items we needed. I gazed at the check out counter when I entered; the line of people was endless. There was another on the lower level and it was usually faster moving. Within minutes of having filled my basket, I was ready to exit through doors which led to a side street. I paused momentarily in order to redistribute my purchases so the bags would be easier to carry.

"Hey!" the voice was unmistakable; it was Antonio's. We had not seen him for months and assumed that he was spending weekends with Elisa, the boys and the new arrival. He was without his gym bag and looked different. His thick, black, wavy flow was now a crew cut.

"What's with the hair?"

"You like it?" he chuckled.

"It's different!"

He saw that the bags were cumbersome and took two from me. As we began walking to the corner, I told him that Steve and his ex-wife were waiting for me at Tornado.

"Okay, let's go."

While moving in that direction, my curiosity prompted me to ask, again about his hair cut. "A new look?" I joked.

His facial expression became serious. "I was in jail … didn't play it smart and got busted."

"What happened?"

Unwilling to divulge details at that moment, he said he would tell us about it sometime. I reiterated that Steve's ex-wife was with him and asked that he not mention anything in her presence. Steve did a double-take when he saw Antonio walk into Tornado with me.

Antonio's tense look and guarded tone morphed to a broad smile accompanied by a cordial exchange when he was introduced to Michelle.

I felt as if I were with Dr. Jekyll and Mr. Hyde! At that moment, I had no idea that the figurative analogy would prove to have basis in fact.

Quick pleasantries were passed, then Antonio sauntered over to 'his spot' with a beer we bought for him. Then, a middle-aged guy walked into the tomb-like place. Two o'clock in the afternoon was usually a quiet time at Tornado. He stood not far from where we were seated. He ordered a drink, spoke to Chris briefly, then walked over to Antonio. As curious as Steve and I were, we refrained from looking at them and continued our conversation.

Michelle told us that she wanted to do some window shopping and would meet us back at the apartment. Once she left, we were able to view the goings-on. The man continued to the far end of the bar; Antonio trailed behind. A wave of the guy's hand prompted Chris to excuse himself and bring a second round of drinks to them.

He returned to us, bearing a weird look on his face. "That's an interesting situation," he said with a smug tone.

"What do you mean?" Steve queried.

"Nothing … forget I said that." His comment made us all the more inquisitive, but he was unwilling to offer details. He was more interested to know more about what he thought was a strange relationship between Steve and Michelle. We heard bar stools scrape against the planked floor and saw the two walk in our direction. It was impossible not to notice the protruding outline in the man's slacks and Antonio's packed, white jeans. Obviously, their manhoods had been introduced to each other, if only through conversation, and had assumed postures of excited anticipation at the prospect of becoming better acquainted.

"Wow!" was all Steve could say.

I was unsure if his exclamation came from what was right in front of us or by the realization that Antonio might be into construction of a different kind.

As they passed, Antonio placed his hands on our shoulders. "See you on the weekend?"

"Sure," I answered, hoping Antonio would note my peculiar smile. Once they left, I could not resist telling Steve the thought that had raced through my mind. "I don't know who's going to have more fun."

So uncharacteristic of displaying a spontaneous sense of humor, Steve followed with, "It looks like an even match to me."

It was a fast trip to the airport that Saturday morning. Although we had a enjoyed being with Michelle and Sheila, we had forgotten New York's fast pace. We were exhausted and looked forward to becoming reacquainted with peace and quiet. We spent most of the day catching up on chores and enjoying a much needed nap.

By the time we arrived at Tornado, happy hour had come and gone; pockets of stragglers were all that remained. Antonio must have seen us enter because he was standing directly in front of us before we moved up the few steps which led to the interior. Earlier, Steve and I had agreed that we would refrain from commentary or questions should we see him there. Based on my conversation with him as well as our observations days earlier, this was a more challenging pact for me to honor. Steve was noticeably more relaxed because we had accomplished a return to normalcy and we no longer needed to be concerned about what we said and how we behaved in our own home.

Antonio pointed to a remote side table. "Can we sit there?" He and Steve moved in that direction while I went to the counter to get drinks.

"My little rose blossom," was Mike's greeting. His voice echoed throughout the place. "Where's my other flower?" he added as my face became as red as a tomato. I pointed to where Antonio and Steve were seated.

When I returned with our drinks, Antonio piped up, "He's some piece of work!"

I thought, *Look who's talking!*

He saw Steve staring at his hair. "You like it?"

"The question is, Do *you* like it?" Steve darted back.

As Antonio rubbed the mound of stubs briskly, he responded, "It's easy to take care of, but I had no choice about getting it cut. ... Did Frank tell you what happened?"

Steve nodded affirmatively.

Antonio began to explain the circumstances which led to what looked like a lawn mower had plowed across his head. Just about a week after we had lunch together, he and two co-workers were talking during a morning break. One asked if he knew where to get some cocaine and weed. Antonio admitted having tried both but was quick to add that neither had a good effect. One made him racy; the other put him to sleep.

"If I had been smart, I would have said 'no' and left it at that." The two gave him money so the purchase could be made during their lunch break. Antonio told us of two locations which were notorious drug dens; one was along the ocean on a road that led to the old city. The other, closer to the area in which he worked, was identified by the name of a bus stop. A turn down a side street brought buyers to obscure back roads which seemed to meander to nowhere. We had heard about these places, but this was the first time anyone shared the experience of going to one of them. His description was chilling.

"So I walked over to 'the stop' to do the deed. It didn't take long to find someone who would sell. I was in and out in a few minutes. I felt a hand on my shoulder. Two cops were casing the place and must have seen me. They found the stuff and cuffed me. I lost my job, apartment, hair … everything. Now I gotta make money however I can."

I glanced toward the door and saw the guy who left with Antonio on the day we had drinks with Michelle.

Steve caught what became my protracted stare. "What are you looking at?" he asked. I drew their attention to the entrance.

"Isn't that the gentleman you were with the other day?"

Antonio's complexion became crimson. "Can we finish these beers and get out of here?"

"What's wrong?"

"Let's just go!" His tone was emphatic.

Before we were able to make the hasty departure Antonio had demanded, the gentleman walked past us and smiled at him. With a stoic expression, Antonio returned a hand wave.

"We're going to prepare supper. Come and eat with us," Steve postured.

"Good … I gotta get away from here," was his response to Steve's invitation.

We were perplexed by how on edge the sight of the man made Antonio. It certainly did not appear that way days ago.

As beautiful as had been the rising of the sun that morning, it was breathtaking to stand on the terrace with Antonio and watch a gradually fading glow give accent to lights which dotted both sides of the waterway and looked like a path that led to the illuminated harbor in the distance.

"This is so beautiful," he sighed. It was as if he embraced the imagery of the present moment as a way of distracting himself from what had unsettled him at Tornado. He returned with me to Steve's domain, the kitchen, and sat on a breakfast stool.

"Pew!"

I turned with a start thinking he did not find the aroma appealing. His nose was buried in the sleeve of his shirt.

"I didn't realize how bad I smell … and look at these jeans." This was a déjà vous moment! He asked if he could take a shower before supper.

"Do you want me to wash your clothes while you freshen up?" I asked.

"Thanks!"

Remembering Jorge's ploy to remain wrapped in a towel, I grabbed two pairs of shorts and handed them to Antonio.

"Why two?"

"One is larger than the other. Pick the one that is more comfortable." I was not as lucky as when I was able to skate in and out of the laundry room the night Jorge visited us. I had to wait for a machine to become available. All the while, I wondered what was going on upstairs.

Returning about twenty minutes later, I heard talking as I opened the apartment door. Antonio had reclaimed his seat in the kitchen and was holding my shorts in his hand. It was obvious that Steve's were tight-fitting yet he chose to wear them.

Shirtless and barefooted, he leaned back and sighed, "This is so fucking nice!"

"Glad you're comfortable," Steve replied. Whether he positioned himself unknowingly or intentionally, there was no was to escape notice of the snug shorts behind which rested a mountain of flesh. With every passing moment, what had been our suspicion became validated.

He looked at his ever-stretching shorts and asked, "Is it okay to sit outside like this?"

What a loaded question that was! I told him that we often sit without shirts, even though I knew that was not the point of the question. Once we began eating, I told Antonio that he looked quite a bit more relaxed than earlier.

"Yeah … thanks for getting me out of there."

Steve took my lead and made a further comment about how unsettled he seemed at the bar. "What happened that made you want to leave so quickly?"

For the duration of the meal, Antonio did most of the talking. This was a good thing for two reasons. This man of apparent mystery revealed more about himself. Also, the uninterrupted talking distracted him from focusing on his pride and joy. He explained that he had time remaining on his gym membership after being released from jail. That is when he met and became friends with Sergio. They worked out together a number of times and, one day, he invited Antonio to his condo for a drink and a bite to ear.

"I was in no position to refuse." He went on to give us a blow by blow description of the visit. Sergio told him to get comfortable on the couch while he made drinks and sandwiches. He placed them on the coffee table and sat close to Antonio. Then, he reached into a drawer and lifted out a mirror on which were lines of cocaine and an envelope containing a number of joints.

"At first, I said 'no' when Sergio asked if I wanted anything. He made more drinks and I finally gave in … I had nowhere to go, so what the hell." Antonio paused deliberately as if he realized that his admission contradicted an earlier claim that the racy/lethargic combination did not agree with him.

During the momentary hiatus, I could not help considering how Antonio's visit bore an uncanny resemblance to others before him. The request to take a shower, my trip to the laundry room, Steve's preparation of a meal and the teasy display of manhood … this was a replica of what we had experienced a number of times. It was as if strategy and method were memorized text from a manual of standard operating procedures for boogies. Oh, if those kitchen stools could speak, the stories they would tell!

Steve was never an analyst of behavior so I was certain he had not put the pieces together. He brought me back from my mental bantering when he asked Antonio what happened next.

"I popped a rod like I never had before."

"Sweet Jesus!" I yelled.

Antonio's face became beet red and he quickly apologized for what he thought was an offensive description. Steve and I laughed, then I explained how my comment was reserved for unexpected, surprising or startling statements; his was all of these.

"Should I go on?" Antonio asked me with a sheepish tone.

"Only if you want to."

"Are you guys sure you want to hear the rest?"

"We'll let you know when we've heard enough."

The lines and weed made Antonio horny. Sergio's eyes became fixed on the increasing protrusion in Antonio's jeans. He began to massage his own crotch, then reached over and grabbed Antonio's extension. "It was weird," Antonio interjected, "but I was hot and had to get off." He shared the steamy details of how that happened... three times. His serious tone gave way to a chuckle when he said how easy it was to make one hundred dollars that day.

He alleged that the idea of sex with another man initially freaked him out, but the drinks, lines and weed had 'opened him'. "He got me into things I never heard of ... the action turned me on ... that was the weirdest part." Antonio pushed his chair back, slouched slightly and extended his opened legs under the terrace table. If the shorts were snug before, the material had now been stretched to the limit.

Since Antonio avoided an answer at Tornado, Steve restated the question. "Is Sergio the guy you left the bar with the other day?"

"Yeah."

"If your first experience with him was so strange, why did you go with him again ... and why did you want to leave in such a hurry when you saw him today?"

"I'm not gay, but I like messing around. Sometimes that scares me. Today, I just did not want to deal with him."

His response did not sit well with me since he admitted liking the adventure of same-sex play. Had he acknowledged Sergio more cordially, he would have made some money yet he wanted to remain in our company. It didn't make sense.

Antonio brushed his hand across his crotch a few times, then gripped and squeezed his member. His shorts rose and fell in a cadenced rhythm. Perhaps he thought that a change in venue would be of benefit and he would add us to his list of playmates. It was time to explain our position to him.

He looked annoyed as he listened to our 'no can do' reasoning. Was his irritation caused by our negative reaction to his advances or by the realization that he passed up a sure hit with Sergio?

It was nearly eleven o'clock when I remembered that I had not taken Peaches for a walk. She was fast asleep so I did not disturb her. Of greater importance was the need to retrieve Antonio's clothes from the laundry room. I knew that Steve would be uncomfortable if I left them alone, so I asked him to get them while I cleaned up.

The at-attention soldier helped me clear the table. Even as I worked at the sink, he stood beside me and grabbed himself almost as if he had not heard us just minutes earlier. He seemed determined to get a rise out of me. I realized there had been no mention of his lady friend during the meal and seized the opportunity to derail his intentional maneuvering.

"How is Elisa?"

"Okay."

"And the children?"

"They're fine."

His answers were not only short but vague. It was as if talk of her would have distracted him from his present mind set. For sure, his thoughts were moving in a direction that had nothing to do with her.

Steve returned moments later and handed him a pile of neatly folded clothing. Antonio placed them on the breakfast bar, removed the shorts and handed them to Steve. Undoubtedly, he thought that if we saw his Goliath, we just might entertain some play time.

"Antonio, get dressed. It's late." As soon as I said this, the soldier began to relax. Once dressed, he approached and kissed each of us on the cheek.

"Thanks ... the food was great," he said matter of factly. We stood in the hallway until the elevator doors closed behind him. Although his descriptions were detailed, we had many questions that were left unanswered. If anyone could enlighten us, it was Chris. His past comment, "That's an interesting situation," was the key that might provide explanations.

Steve and I believe that things happen for a reason. Although we went to happy hour during the next days, we did not see Chris. Since the staff worked on a rotating schedule, we assumed he was off or had taken some vacation time. Robert seemed to be working more hours and with greater regularity. There was a new face behind the bar as well. Robert introduced us to Carlos, the new part-timer.

"Business must be good," I joked.

"What do you mean?"

"The boss has added another bartender."

"He's replacing Chris."

Steve and I looked at each other with disbelief. Chris had worked at Tornado for years and was the most popular staff member.

"What happened to him?"

"He moved back to the states to live with his family … Carlos will do well here."

With Chris gone, there was no hope that we would be able to lock together the pieces of the puzzle. Just as we finished speaking to Robert, Antonio and Sergio walked into the bar together. If we were confused before, we were completely baffled now. He introduced Sergio to us and told him he'd join him in a few minutes.

Antonio saw our evident bewilderment and said, "Before you guys say anything, let me talk."

Just as he had ignored our reasoning nights before, I could not resist the opportunity to return the favor. "What the hell is going on with you?"

He told us that Sergio was opening a business in Ponce, a substantial distance from San Juan, and he was going to work for him.

Steve piped up. "Where will you live?"

"He has a house … I'll stay with him."

"Are you happy about this?"

"Happy … what's that? I have to survive."

We were dumfounded by his revelation. We understood his need to survive, but could not grasp why he chose this as an option. Having met Elisa, we knew how close they were and how greatly she depended upon him for help with the children.

"What about Elisa and the kids?" I asked with a tone of alarm.

"I'll send her money. She'll be okay."

"That's it? What about helping her on weekends … who will do that?"

"I have to do what I have to do."

"She must be very sad."

"I didn't tell her yet … I'm going to see her today. I have to go … thanks for everything."

He hugged each of us and walked away. We were distraught, more for Elisa than for Antonio. How could he cast her aside like an old shoe? How could he tell us that she would be okay when he knew how much she needed his support? How could he turn away from the children he adored? Antonio was the only one who could answer these questions as he abandoned the uncertainties of yesterday and knowingly entered a 'friends with benefits' situation even though he had characterized it as strange, even weird. Once again, the here and now was of utmost importance because it provided an immediate fix. Although Antonio assured us that he would keep in touch, we never saw him again.

Roberto

7

In September of 1998, the island of Puerto Rico felt the rage of an unleashed beast of nature which was accompanied by the fury of what sounded like a piercing locomotive whistle:

"Hurricane Georges was the second major hurricane of the 1998 Atlantic hurricane season. When it made landfall over Fajardo, Puerto Rico on September 21st, sustained winds were recorded at nearly 120 miles per hour. It brought a ten foot storm surge along with twenty foot waves on top of it. The hurricane spawned two tornadoes and dropped immense precipitation in the mountain regions, amounting to a maximum of 30.51 inches. Over 22,000 people were given refuge in 139 shelters in cities throughout the island. Georges was the first hurricane to cross the entire island since the San Ciprian hurricane in 1932. 72,605 homes were damaged and 28,005 were destroyed. Tens of thousands were left homeless. 96% of the population were left with no power; loss of water was experienced by 75%. Georges caused $1.9 billion in damage to Puerto Rico."*

* Hurricane Georges — Wikipedia, the free encyclopedia

We had owned our condo for more than a year, but were in New York when this uninvited Goliath of an interloper visited hell and havoc upon the place we had come to call our second home. Glued to the television, news casts were our only source of information. The images we observed were horrific. It took a number of days before phone service was restored. Just hearing Barbara's voice put us at ease. She was our neighbor, dear friend and rental agent. While the building swayed in the face of the forceful, punishing winds and drenching rain, no damage had occurred to the structure or our apartment. She did not think it was a wise idea to return to the island within days of our phone conversation, but tickets had already been purchased. We needed to see for ourselves what our neck of the woods looked like.

The trip from the airport to our condo was an epiphany. As we gazed out the windows of the cab, what had occurred became real. There were broken windows, shredded awnings and felled trees everywhere. Our hearts sank at the sight of numerous homes which had no roofs. We were depressed by the unsightly images of destruction; the blatant results of hours of brutal battering.

After unpacking, we walked along the avenue. Although a few shops remained boarded up, business appeared to have regained a semblance of normalcy. This was a refreshing sight after what we had observed on the Baldorioty de Castro. As we approached Tornado, we saw Joe standing at the entrance; it seemed strange that the doors were closed. He was the senior bartender whose ordinarily intense facial expression and serious nature made him the least endearing of all who worked there.

On this day, he was very different. Sullenness was replaced by somberness and his face looked tired, drawn and sad. We knew something was very wrong. As he described the ruins which lay behind the doors of what had become a tomb, his predictable matter-of-fact manner of speaking became a tone of lamentation. The interior and upstairs quarters had been destroyed in the turbulence. Although rebuilding and renovation were planned, the process would take months, maybe longer, to accomplish.

Tornado had been a place of welcome where we had gotten to know island residents, tourists and some of the 'working boys' we never thought would become a part of our lives. Joe had never been a great conversationalist, even when at his best, so we did not spend too much time speaking to him.

Saddened, we returned to our apartment to consider other options for afternoon socializing. Although we had heard about the bar where we first met David the Younger, we had not as yet ventured inside because of the images evoked by its nickname, the Wrinkle Room. If we wanted to enjoy happy hour, one option remained; it was Buena Vista, the bar across the road from Tornado. Other than its eatery, we never liked the atmosphere there. The crowd was much younger and raucous. Especially during Sunday afternoon Tea Dance, it was impossible to carry on a conversation. The addition of strategically placed mini bar stations made mobility a daunting challenge. These obstacles dissuaded us from going there on weekends. More importantly, we could not adjust to the sharp contrast after eleven years of experiences at Tornado.

It took some time, but Hurricane Georges became a distant memory. The island regained a steady, strong pulse and there was talk of a new owner who planned to have Tornado up and running as quickly as possible. Nothing happened quickly in Puerto Rico, so the meaning of his well-intentioned desire was open to interpretation.

One Friday evening, we decided to go to Buena Vista for a nightcap. The crowd was sizeable, but nothing like the hoards that usually squeezed in for happy hour. As we walked inside, someone waved at me from a distance. Realizing I was not who he thought I was, he approached and apologized, adding that he had forgotten his glasses. From where he was standing, I looked like someone he had met days earlier. He extended his hand to each of us, introduced himself as Roberto and asked if he could join us.

Despite a pronounced accent, he had some facility with the English language. With deliberate pauses, it was as if he had to consciously think about how to put his words together so we would understand him. He misused tenses and modifiers, but we caught the context of his questions and statements.

If either of us asked him to repeat a word or phrase, he laughed because he knew we were confused. His approach was one of boyish innocence that complemented his very youthful appearance. We were quite surprised when he told us he was thirty-five; he looked many years younger. Our visible reactions prompted him to reach for his driver's license.

I noted the area in which he lived and asked him about it. That inquiry resulted in our learning quite a bit about him, more than we needed to know. He lived with his mom and dad. He was married at one time and had a daughter and son. He did odd jobs during the week, which included part-time employment at his brother-in-law's construction company. This was the best we could grab from his labored attempt at carrying on a conversation.

Unsolicited, he told us he was gay and did not flinch as he announced, "I am a boogie."

Years earlier, such a declaration from a complete stranger would have made us very uneasy, but we had become well-schooled in the physical and personality extremes of those who worked the streets. Had Roberto chosen not to share this tidbit of information, we never would have suspected he was a hustler.

"I am not like the other ones."

"How so?" I asked.

"What is that?"

He did not know what I was asking him. As much as I did not want to expose my flawed use of Spanish, I was getting a headache from the effort necessary to talk to him. When I rephrased the question, he began to babble so quickly that I had no clue about the explanation of what made him different from others in the sex for money business. Not wanting to embarrass myself by admitting that his words escaped my understanding, I said that Steve did not speak Spanish so he would have to try his best in English.

The three of us laughed when he said, "Now we are all the same."

Steve poked me in the side; that was always a signal that it was time to leave. It was late and I was drained. I had felt like a dentist pulling teeth in order to put bits and pieces of disconnected ideas together into sentences that made some sense.

"I will see you again?"

We made no response, just smiled as we shook his hand and moved away from the counter. Little did Roberto know that words were not necessary to create an impression of him. He lived with an intact family. He had a driver's license. He paid for his own drinks. He did not exhibit the stereotypical approach of others we had come to know. There were no sexual innuendos or blatant gestures aimed at seduction. There was no attempt at exaggeration when he spoke about his sexuality and how he made money. He did not boast of grandiose, future ambitions. This analysis, however, was based upon an initial encounter of brief duration.

Perhaps his methods were different and the result of intentional design. If so, they were unquestionably unique. In time, we would come to know more about him and draw conclusions that were based upon fact rather than speculation. A case of mistaken identity brought us face to face with Roberto and would take Steve and me in a direction unlike any we had experienced.

During the next months, we saw Roberto infrequently since he usually did not travel to our neighborhood during the week. If we happened to see him at Buena Vista, he was always engaged in conversation with someone; he was quite popular. He would acknowledge us, but that was the extent of interaction. The few times he sat with us were the results of unsuccessful attempts at connecting with potential clients; that didn't happen often. We were prepared for what we thought would be the sooner rather than later surfacing of his street mentality. So far, there were no indications that it would be imminent. Instead, his behavior was consistently charming and very polite. Also, he revealed more and more of an appealing sense of humor that was irresistibly engaging.

Although life had evolved in ways quite different than we expected, Steve and I loved the island. Each return to it was accompanied by feelings of heightened excitement and anticipation. We began serious talk about the possibility of relocating there permanently. We once had asked Joe, the sullen presence at Tornado, what he thought about the idea. Since he was a transplant from the states, we thought he might shed some additional light on our discussion.

He was not aggressively enthusiastic. "Vacationing and living here are two very different things." He was a negative person to begin with, so we were not sure if his comment was a jaded reaction which was rooted in a 'cup half empty' approach to life or a realistic estimate that was the result of discussions with others who had made the same inquiry.

We also spoke to Don, a friend who had retired from the field of education and moved to Puerto Rico years earlier. He was content there but looked forward to trips back to the states to visit family, friends and colleagues. This was a common ailment from which many suffered and sought relief — island fever. Every so often, it was necessary for them to get away from the routine of life on a body of land that measured thirty by one hundred miles. We did not grasp this reasoning because we always experienced a nagging emptiness each time we left our Isla Del Encanto.

The situation was becoming a bit confusing. There was one person, however, whose opinion was valued. Barbara had always demonstrated an ability to analyze the entire picture of a situation at other times when we sought her counsel. She knew the pros and cons of mainland and island living and we were confident that she would be able to provide us with candid objectivity. She knew our histories and had met some of our family members during the years since 1990 when we first met her. She was aware that Steve's parents were no longer with us, but that my dad was still living and had celebrated his eightieth birthday. She encouraged us to carefully consider this before making a final decision. She spoke from the first-hand experience of caring for an aging mother whom we had come to refer to as "Mommy."

Finances were another issue. Until now, our condo was self-sustaining. Barbara handled all aspects of rentals including the payment of monthly bills. There was always a positive cash flow that allowed us to maintain the New York co-op with relative ease. Full time residence on the island would negate future rental income and result in our having to support two homes. This major factor caused us to do a reality check. While the intrigue of the island had completely captivated us, the dollars and cents of survival was a factor to be seriously analyzed.

What we thought would be a no-brainer became a daunting situation. We understood all that Barbara shared with us, but there was a personal issue which rose above all other considerations. Open heart surgery had left Steve incapable of enduring cold weather. For him, the move was a necessity in order to escape a climate that had become intolerable during the months of winter. Eventually, everything fell into place. I was reassured by family members that dad would be fine. Steve's daughter and granddaughter showed eagerness in wanting to rent the New York co-op. When it became clear that no obstacles remained, a final decision was made. A new chapter in our life together was about to begin in a place nestled between ocean and sea, fifteen hundred miles from our roots.

Having laid the groundwork with our families during our '98 holiday visit, we returned to the island eager to share the good news. Barbara, Rafael and "Mommy" were delighted as were other building residents with whom we had become acquainted. All voiced excitement and encouragement about what, indeed, was a life-altering decision.

While shopping soon after our arrival, we met Don. While he usually did not display much emotion, our words were music to his ears. It was he who told us about the reopening of Tornado. This was wonderful news! What we thought would take an eternity had been accomplished in months.

As we walked down the side street later that afternoon, we could hear music drifting from what had been a battlefield. The interior bore a new look. The oblong counter and mammoth fish tank were gone. A new design placed a much smaller counter area against the side wall that was adjacent to the entrance, now festooned with tropical flora. The restructuring created a huge amount of space for tables as well as a stage-like platform that became a focal point. Although different in appearance, one thing remained unchanged. Its charm was still very much alive and was the drawing card that brought back many who, like we, had an unspoken loyalty to this wonderful gathering place.

In early February Steve's brother, Hal, came for a week's vacation. Some years older, he is quiet and reserved … a true gentleman in every sense of the word. I had come to know of his deep spirituality and involvement in the affairs of the church he attended in New York. Likewise, he was aware of my prior ministry as a deacon in the Roman Catholic church. While he was aware of the nature of Steve's and my relationship, he never voiced criticism or judgment. He is one of those rare people who truly understands the nature of unconditional love.

It had taken some years, but we had become close. With the deepening of our friendship had come an ever-increasing mutual affection. Despite this, initial feelings of anxiety gripped me because I could not predict what his reaction might be should we encounter any of 'the boys' in our travels. Surely, I thought, Tornado would be off limits.

Steve knew his brother well and did not share my evident nervousness. A few days after Hal's arrival, Steve postured happy hour to him while describing the gay bar; he was immediately agreeable. Even as we walked down the avenue, my stomach did pancake flips. I did not want anything to negatively affect what had begun as a perfect week together.

When I saw that Mike was on duty, I broke into a sweat. "My little cupcakes," was his less than discrete greeting.

Whether Hal found the salutation cute or ridiculous, he smiled as Steve introduced them. We were not seated very long when Roberto and someone we knew walked into the bar. We had met George while visiting Chad and Mike in New England years earlier. When Steve invited George and Roberto to join us, I thought I'd pass out. Although our encounters with Roberto had always been pleasant, the nature of who he was and what he did on weekend visits to our neighborhood were issues I hoped would not surface.

Hal had always been a great conversationalist; this served us well during our time with them. As much was shared, Roberto remained true to his courteous nature and nothing was revealed other than a commendable effort in trying to be part of the conversation. Before leaving us, George extended his hand to shake ours. Roberto rose from his seat and hugged each of us.

"It was so good to meet you," were Hal's words that accompanied a broad smile.

That was the moment I was finally able to relax. It wasn't because Roberto and George were leaving but because of the genuinely positive reaction displayed by Hal.

The next day, we arose early because a trip to Old San Juan was planned. Hal lived life with great joy. New experiences were embraced by him with gusto. His excitement was clearly evident as he spoke about the opportunity to step back into history. Although Steve and I had gone to the old city numerous times, Hal's anticipation of a wonderful day was contagious and filled us with renewed eagerness.

Steve packaged a gift he had bought for his granddaughter. It was the wrong size and needed to be exchanged. He hoped he could remember the location of the store since the sales receipt contained no information other than its name.

We hurried through a light breakfast and made our way to the bus stop. As we approached, we saw Roberto and George standing there. They, too, were going to spend the day surrounded by myriad cultural and historical sights. There were times when one could eat a three course meal while waiting for a bus, but on this day that was not the case. We had just greeted one another and there it was.

The ride from our neighborhood to Old San Juan was about twenty minutes. During the course of travel, Steve mentioned the exchange he needed to make and said he was not sure if he remembered where the store was situated.

"What is the name?" Roberto asked.

Steve removed the receipt from the bag and handed it to him.

"I know the place. I will show you."

The congested, narrow streets were a challenge to negotiate. Because numbers of cruise ships docked close by, some were almost impassable. We were forced to walk single file as we maneuvered from one side street to another. Bumper to bumper traffic caused us to stop frequently and assess how best to get to the other side of an intersection.

Roberto led the pack and assumed the role of tour guide. Steve and I were most willing to allow him to take charge of what was one big mess. He paused at churches, monuments and a number of stores which provided Hal with a rich sense of what made the area so interesting and enticing. Roberto really labored when trying to explain the sights to him. Despite his lack of good facility with the English language, Hal seemed to understand him and absorbed his every word.

We rounded yet another corner, then Roberto pointed and said, "It is there."

We had no clue where "there" was until we walked more than halfway down the street and were standing at the entrance. Steve and I took care of business while Hal remained outside with Roberto and George. As we exited, we saw the three of them engaged in conversation and laughter.

"Roberto would like to continue showing me around," Hal said.

George spontaneously interjected that he was agreeable and added that he was enjoying himself.

This was a great relief for Steve and me. While we had some familiarity with the city, Roberto knew it well so we seized the opportunity to ensure that Hal's first experience would be truly memorable.

The highlight of the day was a visit to the fortress, El Morro. As we neared the expansive grounds which led to the arched entrance, Hal stopped. He appeared awestruck at the very sight of the imposing structure. On that day, we spent more time than ever inside those walls of Spanish history. Not a square foot was left unexplored. Roberto's face was aglow as Hal voiced his amazement at everything he saw. Clearly, it was a source of pride for the young Puerto Rican to hear Hal's reactions and observe how engrossed he was in the present moment.

The day passed all too quickly, though we had been there for many hours. As we began our return to the bus stop, Steve asked George if he and

Roberto had dinner plans. Our time together would continue. They agreed to join us for a meal at our condo.

As if the day had not been exciting enough, the ride home became a harrowing experience. It was cut short by the crashing sound of a car as it made contact with the side of the bus. We were halfway between the city and the area in which we lived. Although the driver assured us that another bus would be coming soon, Steve and I had long ago learned the relativity of time on the island.

The packed bus emptied and the street became a sea of people. Some began to walk, others appeared content to wait and the rest of us searched for available taxis. Our location did not lend itself to quick access. Cabs which darted by us were already occupied with those who seized them while in the city. We were tired and hungry so the last thing we needed was a situation which would test our patience, especially mine.

"Just stay calm," were Hal's words as I went on a tirade about the predicament.

I had no choice but to chuckle. I had heard these words numerous times during family gatherings but, at this moment, they were a much needed stress reducer. News about the accident must have gotten back to the city because, as if from nowhere, one empty cab after another appeared. We were on our way once again.

Unlike Steve who is a master in the kitchen, I do not have great culinary talent. One of the few dishes in my limited repertoire is pasta with meatballs and sausage. A favorite of Hal's, I prepared a pot the day before so that when we returned from the city trip we could enjoy a "heat and eat" meal. There was an ample quantity to feed the ravenous group with plenty for leftovers.

We sat together around the table on our terrace and enjoyed the evening as much as the hours of our guided tour. While our encounters with all of the other boys of the street had a different flavor and complexion, this experience with Roberto validated our impressions of him ... appearance and substance were truly the same.

During Hal's remaining days with us, we did not see George and Roberto again, but he did witness Steve and me in action as one or another of the boys crossed our path at the bar or our apartment. Steve decided it was time to explain to him who these guys were and the cause of our willingness to help them.

Characteristic of Hal's personality, he was tender and affirming. "You two have the ministry of the street." His statement was an epiphany. Neither of us equated generous spirits and listening hearts with what he viewed as a spiritual calling. His beautifully stated observation was the inspiration from which *Dark Streets, Bright Lights* was conceived.

The remainder of Hal's visit with us flew by as quickly as had our day in Old San Juan. We hated to see him leave because his presence brought immeasurable joy, peace and love to our home. We do not think he realized the extent to which he had ministered to us!

It was not until George returned to New England that we saw Roberto again. He was at Tornado dressed in the mantle of his weekend identity. Although he was with someone, he found time to come over to us and reiterate what a wonderful day had been our city trip. During this chance meeting, we told him that we would be traveling to New York and would not return to the island until August.

His reaction was unexpected. "That is so long I won't see you."

It occurred to us that we had not told him about the move. Now was as good a time as any to let him know about it.

"Que alegria!" (What happiness!) was the quick response that came from his more perky voice.

"I will see you more?"

"Definitely," Steve answered. There was some sadness in this moment because we had come to like Roberto and knew we would miss him during the next six months.

On a warm, bright morning in late July, a caravan of cars followed ours to the post office in order to mail thirty eight cartons filled with our life in New York. Days later our friend, Tony, led us across the Triborough Bridge so our car could be processed for transport to the island.

On August 10th, we arrived. The Big Apple would always hold a special place in our hearts but, from this moment on, only the past tense would be used when referring to it. We were now residents of Puerto Rico.

The process of unpacking and organizing was tedious. Barbara and Rafael had done a commendable job in lining up the boxes as they arrived. Things needed to get done quickly because the living room looked like a warehouse and we never did well with clutter.

We were aware that our car would not arrive for days, which made the reality of having to walk everywhere while lugging heavy bags of groceries and housewares an unpleasant prospect. On one such trip, days after settling in, we met Roberto. We rarely had ventured outside of our neighborhood nor had we ever used public transportation for any purpose other than trips to the old city. We asked him which bus went from our area to Plaza las

Americas. It was a popular shopping mall but a distance away from where we lived.

"Why do you go there?"

"We need a vacuum cleaner."

"What is that?"

I did not know the Spanish translation and was forced to demonstrate. There I stood and moved my arms back and forth while trying to imitate the motor's sound. Passersby must have thought I was nuts!

"Don't take the bus. I can use my friend car. When do you go?"

"Yesterday," I joked. My intention was to make him understand the immediacy of our need. His blank stare was a clear indication that he missed the humor in my comment.

"Tomorrow," Steve said. "We want to go tomorrow."

"I see you in the morning … early."

We accepted his kind offer with tentative confidence. There was no guarantee that his friend's car would be available. Also, it was the weekend. If Roberto connected with someone, it was unlikely that we would see him. Barbara gave us the travel information we needed so that, one way or the other, our goal would be realized.

By eight o'clock the next morning, Steve and I were dressed and in the midst of preparing breakfast when we heard a knock at the door.

"I am here. Are you ready?" Roberto asked as he peered through the bars of the exterior *rejas* (gate) and waited for me to unlock it. The aroma of bacon and eggs wafted into the hallway causing him to inhale deeply, then release an approving sigh. "It smell good," he remarked when he entered the kitchen and greeted Steve.

"Are you hungry?" Steve asked, noting that Roberto's eyes were fixed on the mountain of scrambled eggs and crisp bacon which lay neatly arranged on a platter.

"Very … I get up early and drink coffee."

"Good! There is plenty."

"What is plenty?"

"Mucho."

"Steve, you say you don't speak Spanish."

This lighthearted bantering set the tone for the day. Plaza las Americas was an expansive mall that sprawled in all directions. Multi-leveled, it was reminiscent of those in New York but was more upscale than any we had ever seen.

Roberto must have sensed our quick pace. "Go slow. We no have to rush."

I explained that we were concerned about his returning the car so his friend would not be stranded too long. That was not an issue. He owned a second vehicle and had told Roberto that he could return the car early the next morning. We explored the mall from one end to the other and were most impressed by the elegance of its décor. We waited until our venture was nearly completed before we made our purchase.

As we meandered through a sea of cars in the parking area, I erupted into laughter. Steve and Roberto looked at me as if I were crazy! Thoughts of Big José's jalopy, the sauna on wheels, flooded my mind. A newer model, this car had air conditioning and windows that functioned. It provided a smooth, quiet ride so unlike the ghastly noises and bumpiness that made José's more like an artillery tank. Steve caught the humor in my analogy while Roberto pieced together my labored attempt at translation.

We arrived home in the latter part of the afternoon. Roberto lived quite a distance away but had mentioned earlier that his friend lived in our area. Rather than having him drive to his home and get up at the crack of dawn the next morning, we invited him to stay for dinner and sleep on the sofa bed.

As soon as he agreed, Steve rose and went to the kitchen. Within minutes, the conversation in which Roberto and I were engaged became muffled by the deafening sound of ice crushing in a blender. Soon after, Steve appeared. "Piña Coladas, anyone?"

We gathered around the table on the terrace and enjoyed the refreshing afternoon breeze while sipping the libations. Actually, I sipped; they guzzled as if they were drinking soda! The second batch was better than the first. Before any of us got to the point of immobility, I suggested that we prepare something to eat.

Roberto asked if he could take a shower even though his appearance did not indicate the need for one. Steve and I wondered if this was the moment when Roberto would assume his weekend personality and allow all that comprised it to pop out.

Our concern proved to be unfounded. He emerged from the bathroom with a towel wrapped tightly around his waist; it never left that position. There occurred no behavior or comment which might have caused an uncomfortable situation. He collected his neatly folded clothing from the breakfast bar and returned to the bathroom. When he joined us outside, he was fully dressed. This was truly unique!

During prior conversations, he often mentioned his family. This seemed a perfect opportunity to learn more about them. We knew that he had been working with his dad and brother-in-law on a project to renovate their home, so I inquired about its progress. Roberto's parents lived modestly. As a result, the work was proceeding slowly. An additional bathroom had been completed, but it would take time before a new family room was constructed. He spoke of his parents with deep affection; it was evident that he enjoyed a close relationship with them.

Although his children did not live with him, he saw them frequently and helped support them as best he could. His tender description of family life seemed inconsistent with his other persona. I asked him why it was necessary to sell himself for sex.

"I have to help my parents and kids."

"Do your mom and dad ask you about the money you make on weekends?"

"I tell them I have a job here."

"That is true. You do have a job!" My attempt at humor did not produce a chuckle, not even the slightest hint of a smile. It seemed painful for Roberto to speak about his family and his weekend endeavors in the same context. It was as if he made a conscious effort to disassociate one from the other.

"Do they know you are gay?" Steve asked.

"No. I don't say the truth … they will die if they know." Tears welled up in Roberto's eyes. The mere thought of what might be the consequences was almost unspeakable. It was evident that Roberto was in touch with himself in ways that were a stark contrast to any of the other boogies we had met. He cared less about himself and more about his parents' perceptions of a son on whom the sun rose and set. Clearly, he was the golden nugget in the family. To destroy that image was a prospect he could not bear to consider.

He was confident that, one day, he would abandon his weekend life of random trysts that filled his pockets and settle into one more peaceful and predictable. This resolve did not meet our ears as hollow, delusional images but revealed a strong desire to embrace what he believed was within his grasp. We so wanted to share that belief!

The next morning, Steve and I awakened to the alluring aroma of coffee. Roberto was dressed, the sofa bed was put away and he was ready to leave. "I have to take the car to my friend."

Responsibility. Priority. He not only knew these words but his behavior was testament to the value he placed on them.

"Thank you for making coffee," Steve said.

"No … thanks to you for everything. I am so comfortable here."

"We are happy; you are always welcome to visit us."

He hugged and kissed each of us on the cheek. It was not an offensive gesture but an indication of sincere appreciation.

"I will see you soon?"

It was as if our voices blended in a single response — "Definitely!"

From that bright summer day in 1999 until our move back to the states in January 2001, we spent a great amount of time with Roberto. Dinners, sleep-overs and beach days allowed Steve and I to observe changes in his weekend routine. There appeared to be a correlation between the prosperity of his brother-in-law's construction business and his need to engage in a manhunt. Numbers of weekends were spent with us; he never went to the bars. We gave him money from time to time because we knew, with certainty, it would be used for an unselfish purpose. On one occasion, he told us that he had spoken to his parents about returning to school. He wanted to become a chef.

"What do they think?" Steve asked.

"Oh, they are happy … then I will cook for them and my mom will rest."

"What do you think?" I followed.

"I can do it. I love to cook. I study every day! I will study English and speak better."

Steve and I hugged him, hoping he would feel the confidence and hope that surged through us. We never thought that, after so many years of having been exposed to the psychology of the street, there would emerge any whose sincerity and enthusiasm gave us cause to believe that there was a light at the end of the tunnel. He was the one among many who possessed the emotional capacity and physical capability to detach himself from a sordid past and thrust forward to embrace a newness in life that could gift him with a stronger sense of self and a greater measure of success.

Roberto was the only 'boy' to whom we gave our phone number after leaving Puerto Rico and resettling in Florida. From time to time, he called and updated us about the happenings in his life. School continued to be an abstract reality that was dependent upon his ability to save money for tuition. His claim of focusing on this essential condition was a part of every conversation and became repetitiously predictable.

Sadly, weekend jaunts to the bars continued and there developed a new dimension to his money making potential. He began to take advantage of opportunities to visit the states and stay in the homes of tourists with whom he had become acquainted during their island vacations. From what

Steve and I knew and understood about these invitations, there were big bucks to be had!

During one conversation, he mentioned a desire to visit us in Florida. We were agreeable not only because we knew him well but also because we thought that a separation from weekend work on the island, albeit brief, might increase his motivation to get on with life sooner rather than later.

Our reunion occurred in September 2004, almost four years after we left Puerto Rico. His youthful appearance remained untouched by passing years. His charming manner was no less endearing than we remembered it and his sense of humor was as sharp as ever. The good manners and courteousness that distinguished him from others were unchanged.

Two other things remained unaltered as well. One was his ability to communicate in English. It had been one thing to spend hours or a weekend with him. It was quite another to live under the same roof for ten days. His commendable effort abated my anticipated stress and prevented Steve from being reduced to an outside observer. We concluded that this hiatus allowed him to be less distracted by the ever-present need to make money. He seemed more attentive to what he was hearing and more capable of conversation in which Steve and I understood him … at the same time.

The second issue was that he loved the beach as much as Steve. While I had been able to retreat to the shade of palm trees in Puerto Rico, the beach not far from our home in Florida was absent of protection for sun haters like me. This resulted in my looking like Nanouk of the North. My sand chair was crowned with a detachable umbrella. My head was covered with a cap. My tee shirt remained on and an extra towel blanketed my legs. I was quite a sight!

Each day, Roberto planted himself right next to Steve in the kitchen. He always gave assistance as he observed culinary talent in action. One day, he offered to prepare a typical Puerto Rican dinner. Steve grabbed the suggestion with quick approval. Roberto was an enthusiastic cook.

"What about school?" Steve inquired as he assumed the role of assistant to the chef.

"Someday, I will go."

"Someday." Steve repeated as he patted Roberto on the back.

"How did you learn how to cook?"

"When I was small, I watch my grandmother. She was my first teacher."

The chicken with rice and beans was a more tasty dish than any we had enjoyed on the island. His talent was unquestionable! Conversation during that meal provided a natural segue to addressing ongoing part-time work in which he continued to be engaged. This was the first time that our comments were somewhat sharper and much more candid. He was wasting precious time in a life that was going nowhere fast. He had been given a wonderful talent that was being ignored. He was choosing to leave untapped the potential for success.

His facial expression clearly revealed his understanding. This was one of those tough love talks in which the nuts and bolts of reality superseded our concern about his feelings. We had spit in the wind many times before but hoped that, this time, it would be different.

The days passed all too quickly and it was time for Roberto to return to the sameness of a life from which he had escaped for ten days. Our good-byes at the airport were very emotional, a clear indication of the affection we had developed for him.

"I will see you soon?" he asked as he wiped tears from his eyes. This was the first time we could not answer that question with any degree of certainty.

"We hope so," was the only response that could be conveyed with truth because we did not want to make a promise we might not be able to keep.

At first communication continued, but phone calls became less frequent, of shorter duration and eventually dissolved into nothingness. Although Roberto's cell phone was no longer in service, he had our phone number. We were an ocean apart wondering and worrying about him.

During subsequent visits to the island in 2005 and 2008, we searched for him; he was nowhere to be found. No one had seen him in quite a while. We could not imagine what had happened to him. Had he changed his ways? Had he met someone who lifted him from the ambiguity of leading two lives? Had something terrible occurred?

We could not bear the thought that circumstances might have sent him into a downward spiral. We were consumed with a nagging emptiness prompted by the unknown. There emerged no answers and resulted in a more than occasional tug at our heart strings. We were left with a photo album of mental images. That is all we had to keep Roberto close in thought.

While Steve and I hold sacred all that makes us uniquely individual, there is a seamless connection between us about what we call the core of life's journey:

> There are no coincidences, only purpose and plan. We are
> exactly where we are supposed to be at any given time.

These beliefs resonated with truth during our most recent visit to our Isla Del Encanto. On the morning of January 24, 2009, I awoke with eagerness knowing that, within a few hours, we would be joined by Steve's son and daughter-in-law, Kirk and Theresa, for a week of fun in the sun. She was especially excited since this was her first trip to Puerto Rico. At 4:30 a.m., our phone rang. I answered with trepidation thinking that something happened to my dad, who just celebrated his ninety-first birthday in July.

"I have some bad news," were Kirk's somber words. While their flight from New York to Ft. Lauderdale would arrive as scheduled at 9:40 a.m., the connecting flight to Puerto Rico, on which we were to travel with them, was cancelled. Known for his sense of humor, I thought Kirk was joking. It quickly became evident that what he said was true. A mechanical malfunction was the cause of the aborted flight.

A surge of mixed emotions gripped me. I was relieved that the problem had been detected before we were thirty thousand feet in the air, yet I was angry because we would have to scramble to make a new reservation. I recited a litany that was far from sacred! Kirk and Theresa were already booked on the later and only other flight that day. It would not depart until 8:10 p.m.

Steve and I were now in limbo. I quickly ended my conversation with him and called the airline. Luckily, there remained a few unreserved seats. It was not yet 5:30 a.m. and my nerves were shot! I called Kirk and made arrangements to pick them up when they arrived in Florida. I woke Steve and shared the not-so-glad tidings; he sprang out of bed like a jack-in-the-box and added more to the irreverent litany I spewed earlier.

This radical change in our itinerary had a number of consequences. Rather than arriving on the island at 2:30 p.m., we would not touch down until nearly midnight and then have to disturb Barbara and Rafael in order to get the keys to our condo rental. There was no food in the house, so an unanticipated shopping venture needed to be undertaken. Most irritating was the reality that an entire day of our vacation was lost.

Kirk and Theresa were remarkably positive about the situation, and this calmed our nerves considerably. After stopping for breakfast en route to our home, we picked up some food and beverage to sustain us during the long hours of waiting which lay ahead. Once back at the ranch, we saw a blinking light on our phone's answering machine.

"What now?" I blurted in a foul tone, wondering if yet another obstacle would interfere with our revised travel plans.

"I am looking for Frank and Steve. It is Roberto. Please call me." Steve and I stood motionless and speechless. We were in a complete state of shock. Kirk and Theresa stared at us with perplexed looks.

I retrieved the number and dialed it. "This is Roberto's father. He is not here now." I explained who I was and that Roberto had left a message. Thankfully, his dad understood me. He said he would have Roberto call me when he returned from the supermarket.

Within twenty minutes, we heard his voice. "Que alegria! (What happiness!) were his first words to us in more than four years.

"For us, too!" I responded with equal excitement. He'd found our phone number while doing a long overdue cleaning and reorganization of his bedroom closet. When I told him that we would arrive in Puerto Rico that very evening, he repeated the exclamation again.

Plans were made to see him the next day. I told him that he would be meeting Kirk, Theresa and dear friends from Arroyo, Andrea and David, so he must avoid discussing the bars and his weekend activities. I was puzzled by his laughter and comment, "I don't do that anymore."

"What do you mean?"

"I will tell you tomorrow."

Not only did this brief exchange arouse my curiosity but his correct use of English was more pronounced. "Nos vemos, pronto." (We will see you soon).

What had been a vague response four years earlier was soon to become a concrete reality. A potentially disastrous day had become a happy mistake. Plan and purpose … there was no other explanation! That night, we landed in Puerto Rico at eleven thirty. By the time we were given keys to the apartment by Rafael and bought some items at a bodega, it was well past three o'clock. Although we were exhausted from what had seemed like a day without end, Steve and I were filled with anticipation about seeing Roberto again.

Andrea and David speak very little English, so past practice placed me in the role of interpreter. I was prepared for the inevitable stress which always accompanied my feeble efforts to keep Steve engaged in conversation. He became anxious when he realized that he would be alone with them while I went to meet Roberto at the bus stop closest to the condo. Thank God Kirk and Theresa were with us or Steve would have been a basket case.

Roberto's face had matured but hints of youthfulness were still obvious. More noticeable was his improved use of English. He spoke with fluency and did not make many grammatical or usage errors. I asked how the marked change had occurred. "I want to tell you and Steve at the same time … I have a surprise for you."

At that moment, I had no idea what an understatement Roberto had just made. As we exited the elevator, we heard laughter coming from the apartment. It was apparent that Steve survived the ordeal. Hugs, kisses and introductions set the stage for what was to be an awesome afternoon.

Steve and I sat in amazement at Roberto's effortless ability to keep everyone involved in discussion. Every so often, Theresa interjected a Spanish phrase which Andrea found both admirable and cute. As Roberto spoke, Steve looked at me a number of times. He, too, heard the difference in Roberto's communication skills.

Curiosity got the best of him. "Your English is very good. What happened?" he asked.

"Do you remember when I said I wanted to be a chef?"

"Yes … you were saving money for school."

"I'm doing it." Roberto reached into his travel bag and handed a document to Steve. I looked on as he began studying what was a transcript of credits from the Universal Career Community College of Humacao, reflecting a grade point average of 3.25.

He explained that his family was helping him so that he could complete the remaining course requirements. Roberto beamed as he was showered with words of congratulations and encouragement. Andrea, a teacher, added an expression we have heard often — "Very good, very well, very fine." This always had resulted in laughter but, on this day, the endearing comment was more than a cute remark or trite reaction. It was a heartfelt affirmation of a job well done.

| 798 | UNIVERSAL CAREER COMMUNITY COLLEGE RECINTO DE humacao

|NOMBRE
|NUMERO S.S.
|CURSO   ARTES CULINARIAS   ·
|TOTAL CREDITOS   :54   FECHA DE COMIENZO :01-11-2006   FECHA DE GRADUACION:12-19-2006   PROMEDIO GENERAL   :

CODIGO DEL CURSO	TITULO DEL CURSO	NUMERO DE CREDITOS	TERMINO	NOTA	PUNTOS DE HONOR
ESPA 100	DESTREZAS DE COMUNICACION EN ESPAÑOL	3	1	A	12
ENGL 100	DESTREZAS DE COMUNICACION EN INGLES	3	1	B	9
REHU 205	ADMINISTRACION, LIDERATO Y RELACIONES HUMANAS EN LAS OCUPACIONES TECNICAS	3	1	B	9
ARCU 900	HISTORIA DE LA COCINA, HIGIENE, SANEAMIENTO	3	1	B	9
ARCU 905	INTRUDUCCION A LA PREPARACION DE ALIMENTOS, CALDOS Y SALSA	3	1	B	9
ARCU 908	DESARROLLO DE RECETAS Y ELABORACION DE MENUS	3	1	B	9
ARCU 810	TABLAJERIA BASICA Y EMBUTIDOS	3	2	A	12
ARCU 910	MANEJO DE LOS VEGETALES, PASTAS Y PRINCIPIOS DE NUTRICION	3	2	B	9
ARCU 915	COCINA MEDITERANEA	3	2	A	12
ARCU 920	ADMINISTRACION DE RESTAURANTES Y CONTROL DE COSTOS	3	2	B	9
ARCU 925	APERITIVOS Y ENTREMESES INTERNACIONALES (FRIOS Y CALIENTES)	3			0
ARCU 927	COCINA VEGETARIANA Y ORGANICA	3			0
ARCU 930	COCINA CARIBEÑA Y ORIENTAL	3			0
ARCU 935	COCINA NORTEAMERICANA	3	2	B	9
ARCU 940	COCINA REGIONAL EUROPEA	3	2	B	9
ARCU 945	REPOSTERIA FINA Y PANADERIA COMECIAL	3			0
ARCU 950	PRACTICA EXTERNA	6			0

|EL ESTUDIANTE ARRIBA NOMBRADO ( ) HA (✓) NO HA COMPLETADO LOS REQUISITOS DEL CURSO ARTES CULINARIAS

_______________________   02-7-07
 FIRMA REGISTRADOR (A)   FECHA

|LEYENDA: A =Excelente   W =Baja ||Equivalencia en Créditos "Quater Hours"|
| B =Bueno   I =Incompleto |
| C =Satisfactorio K =Covalidado || 1 Crédito Teoría   = 20 Hrs
| D =Deficiente   T =Transferido|| 1 Crédito Laboratorio= 20 Hrs
| F =Fracaso || 1 Crédito Práctica   = 30 Hrs

No one in the room, except for Steve and I, knew what a monumental accomplishment this was. They met him that day, totally unaware of a background that had become heavy baggage. We were so proud of what was tangible evidence of his recognizing that the fullness of life extended beyond today, the here and now, the bubble of the present tense. He finally had grasped that there was a more dignified mantle of identity to be embraced than the one he had chosen to wear each weekend for many years. Above all else, it was abundantly clear that the concepts of self-respect, worthiness and perseverance were no longer abstract but real, concrete, attainable and had become welded to the core of a new self-image.

Before returning to Las Piedras and Arroyo, the seven of us went out for a mid-afternoon meal. It was not only a celebration of family and friends but also a tribute to Roberto. His accomplishment was testament to the veracity of the words he uttered years earlier, when a case of mistaken identity brought us face to for the first time … "I am not like the others."

The unexpected chain of events which occurred on the day of travel were, indeed, part of a plan that had a greater purpose. If the original flight to the island had not been cancelled, we would have been unaware of Roberto's attempt to contact us. Our week with Kirk and Theresa, most enjoyable as it was, would have been quite different in complexion.

Like the other 'boys of the street' —Big José, the Davids, King Pin, Jorge and Antonio — this once self-proclaimed boogie would have remained in the realm of yesteryear's memories. Roberto's presence would have been one of many in a convolution of mental images glimpsed by us in the rising and setting of the sun over an island that, for them, was anything but enchanted. His voice would have blended with theirs in a cacophony of sounds heard in the crashing of waves against the sandy shore. Sidewalks and cobblestones would have remained, forever, bearers of a past that rests in the silence of absence.

Happily and thankfully, these predictable scenarios that occur with each revisiting were dulled because Roberto had emerged from the shadows. He shattered the stereotype, broke the mold and proved that change was possible.

These were the bugarón, the boogies, the boys of the street, the hustlers. Whatever term might describe them, Steve and I never forgot that they were human beings. We were tireless in our efforts, sometimes to the point of emotional exhaustion, to look beyond the façade of appearance and touch the substance, the hidden interior of what made them tick.

Roberto is the success story, but what about the others? They were more than what they did, more than the sexual frolic they believed was the only route on which they could travel. As strange as it may sound, each was a gift to Steve and me at different times and under different circumstances during our many years in a place that, initially, was an escape from our own deserts of reality. How ironic that our plan and purpose was superseded by a greater need!

We are certain that our impact on them was minimal, but there is some degree of comfort and satisfaction in knowing that we did not ignore and leave unattended those in obvious, dire need of attention. Whatever morsels of kindness, understanding and encouragement they were cognizant enough to embrace were momentary, fleeting and absent of the emotional glue that creates a lasting bond.

For us to ponder walking in their shoes is an inconceivable notion. To reflect on their emptiness eludes understanding. To believe that their lot in life was justly deserved is a shallow rationale that would have supported assumptions but offered no answers. It would have been a far easier task for us to have stood back and criticized those in the street ranks. Instead, we came to recognize and understand that there was more to each of them than met the eye. We witnessed how they struggled in the face of adversity made worse by the attitudes and behaviors of many who characterized them as useless, worthless garbage.

From all Steve and I learned about them, each and together, we believe that these words capture the essence of what they felt but never were able to articulate:

You do not know me because you have chosen to see the mantle, the bindings, the armor that preserves me. You dare not look beyond the superficial to mind and spirit, heart and soul. Do not be quick to exact judgment upon what repulses your reality and nauseates your gut because, when all is stripped to the core, I am one created just like you.

Perception

8

According to Webster, perceptions are based upon observation, a conceptualizing of mental images and a capacity for comprehension. While we may not be conscious of such a bookish explanation, perceptions are a part of our lives everyday. We look at ourselves and others. We exist in various environments. We see and hear things that may cause bells to ring and whistles to blow. Our emotions may be stronger in some situations than in others.

Regardless the stimulus, much about life is based upon perception. There exists no formulary by which it is governed. Rather, it is a matter that falls within the realm of individuality. Two people may gaze upon the same painting and be moved to react in completely different ways. A song heard by a group may tap into different emotions and result in opposing interpretations of meaning. A class may analyze and dissect a piece of poetry and come away with myriad reactions which seek to uncover the depth of the writer's purpose. And so it goes with most of what comprises this thing we call our lived experience. Underpinning all of it is who we are as individuals … our individuality.

About it, Steve and I believe:

> *One of the great gifts of life, individuality is part*
> *of the mantle of identity worn by each person. It*
> *cannot be bought or should the acceptance of any*
> *condition ever define the essence of its nature.*
> *It is within us, just waiting to be recognized and*
> *embraced. That is when the characteristics of*
> *day and night, physical and emotional, become*
> *crisp, distinguishable and no longer blend in*
> *the sameness of monotonous repetition. That*
> *is when courage stares at the face of adversity*
> *with defiance. That is when new possibilities are*
> *perceived with increased resolve and a greater*
> *awareness of a purpose which urges us forward.*

It is far too easy an analysis to say that this personal credo is no more than common sense or a generic formula easily understood and attainable. To do that would trivialize its implications as well as validate how closed eyes cannot see nor closed hearts feel the pain of others in whose lives the promise is an abstract, intangible, obtuse illusion. If Steve and I had stood on the "I can ... so you should be able to" principle, we never would have ventured outside the bounds of convenience and safety. We would have resisted vulnerability and recoiled, no doubt, from others whose perceptions about life were alien, even absurd.

By now, it is clear that the bugarón (except for Roberto) had no clue about the gift of individuality. They had forgotten who they once were and became unable to resurrect and reclaim what they believed was dead. Bandages placed over oozing, festering wounds aptly describe what Steve and I were for them. The coverings were powerless to stop the pain caused by a more formidable adversary. They lived within the grip of a vise controlled by a sinister thief that squeezed away the minutes, hours and days of what had become a naked reality stripped of dignity and a limbo-like existence devoid of self-worth.

Those few who became like extended family walked upon roads no less filled with twists, turns and detours. In contrast to those in the street ranks, they never completely lost their vision of self or their hopes and dreams for a better future even though the 'how' of accomplishment seemed daunting at times.

What really set them apart from the others was a keen understanding that the horse goes before the cart, not the reverse. As a result of this insight, they were able to muster enough strength to fight against the foes of failure, defeat and surrender. They may have lost a battle along the way but refused to lose the war on the battlefield of life. They did not submit to any person or circumstance which might have irreversibly diminished them nor would they allow their perceptions of purpose and plan, although murky at times, to become distorted images of what was beyond their grasp.

From the comedic to the serious and intense, their personalities represented a garden of flowers that withstood the elements with varying degrees of success. Some tended to wilt more easily than others but managed to regain enough stamina to stand tall once again. The rising and falling of their emotional stems is what intrigued us the most. While the boogies worked the streets, this group just worked.

Emily

9

The summer of 1993 was an unforgettable one. For six weeks, I supervised and Steve taught a program for immigrant children in an unairconditioned school building in our district. It was a daily test of endurance as we fought the sweltering heat which was accompanied by humidity that could be cut with a knife.

With increasing anticipation, we counted the days until our escape from the sauna that was New York. Our annual week on the island was sure to be an oasis where we would find relief, relaxation and refreshment. How wrong we were! Record temperatures and an obvious absence of anything that remotely resembled air flow made us feel as if we had jumped from the frying pan into the fire.

Although happy hour was a late afternoon activity, the sun remained unrelentingly brutal as we walked to Tornado on the afternoon of our arrival. The daily battle of the vocal chords was in full swing, the collective noise streaming out from the close quarters. There was a strange newness, however, which almost muted the markedly elevated decibel level and sounded like a record stuck in one position. A staccato-like laugh, we could not imagine who was the bearer of the repetitive honking that was unlike any human sound we had ever heard.

She stood behind the bar with a posture of confidence; her appearance commanded notice. It did not seem an intentional display of ego, self-confidence or bravado but a natural part of how she presented herself. She was an energetic, vivacious, stunningly beautiful woman of ebony composition. Her movement was effortless, as if she were well-schooled in the workings of the interior.

Bearing an engaging smile that revealed perfect, snow-white teeth — a dazzling contrast to her complexion — and eyes that gleamed with an enticing sparkle, she approached us and said, "I'm Emily. What can I get for you?"

When she returned with our drinks, she did not hurry off but remained for a few minutes to chat with us. Her voice had an intriguing accent. More evident, however, was her impeccable grooming. With skin unmarred by the slightest blemish and hair and makeup that looked like works of art, she was dressed to kill! As if her voice and laughter were not sufficient attention getters, her appearance was the icing on the cake. There were many compliments showered upon Emily on that first day of employment. We were taken by what was the absolute of natural beauty and charm. Others, more focused on appearance, wished they owned her outfit!

At first, it seemed strange to us that she would take such measures for a work shift. We thought it was a conscious choice so she would make a good impression. We quickly came to realize that this was not the case. She possessed an innate ability for looking the part of one for whom life was wonderful.

With each conversation, we learned bits and pieces about this unique woman and came to realize that a positive attitude about life did not always reflect its reality. Her catharsis was conversation. She had the gift of gab that made everyone feel special.

Steve and I loved to hear her speak. Her accent was pronounced but not easily identifiable. We knew she was from one of the islands but could not pinpoint the exact location. When she told us that she was from St. Kitts, my heart pounded. That was the birthplace of my maternal grandmother. Emily was the first person of common origin I knew. Steve, aware of my background, was clearly thrilled that she was able to answer my many questions. We have always believed that this remote connection contributed to her developing a genuine liking for us.

We quickly learned her work schedule and made it a point to stop in during early afternoon shifts when there was no crowd. While she passed pleasantries with others and was careful not to neglect their beverage requests, she rooted herself near us. Our talks were always informative, enlightening and very entertaining. She asked lots of questions about our backgrounds, family and the history of our life together. When we told her about prior marriages, children and Steve's seven-month-old granddaughter, Alexis, she was visibly taken aback.

She saw our puzzled reactions and quickly interjected. "You look too young to be a grandfather!" Steve loved hearing those words.

Recounting the circumstances under which we met, became friends and found love brought tears to her eyes. We apologized because we thought our descriptions had caused her to become sad.

She quickly responded, "No! It's wonderful. I wish it had been that way for me." Her wistful response spoke volumes. It expressed a longing for what might have been more than a sadness about what was obviously lacking in her life.

This conversation gave us another glimpse of the developing portrait of Emily. We had witnessed her fun-loving approach and hilarious sense of humor. We now would become privy to deeper places within her — the seat of emotion, the chamber of seriousness and the heart of one we liked more and more.

It did not take us long to realize why we went out of our way to speak to her as often as possible during our brief island stays. She was a breath of freshness. She was articulate. She represented a reconnection to a normalcy that eluded us when dealing with 'the boys of the street' or when conversations during happy hour permeated the atmosphere with the smell of sex. We looked to Emily for some balance and found it.

Emily got to know her customers well. It took little time for her to establish a loyal following. The queens loved her! She understood the scene and was well-equipped to deal with the zaniness that was inherent in a gay bar. Like we, she seemed intent on stepping back every so often and conducting a reality check. We were quite surprised the first time we observed this.

By her own admission, she did not discuss personal issues at work. Steve and I were exceptions to that rule because she felt very comfortable with us. We thought we knew a great deal, but one afternoon during the latter part of that week, she gave us a huge surprise.

A small group of people were huddled outside the bar. This was not uncommon, so we paid little attention to the goings on. As we got closer, there was Emily in the center of the tight circle. When she saw us, she waved in a gesture of invitation. She was not, however, the main attraction. She held the hand of a little boy who looked to be no more that five years old. In a stroller was a younger one who could not have reached his second birthday.

It was just about four o'clock. By the time we walked to where she was standing, the group had dispersed and converged on the bar's entrance. She saw our looks of complete astonishment and belted out her trademark laugh. It was both contagious and infectious, and our spontaneous chuckles erupted into full-blown belly laughs. The little ones were amused and began to giggle, too. After settling down enough to speak, she unveiled another piece of herself. These were her sons.

Steve reached into his pocket and handed Emily some money. "Buy ice cream for the boys."

Her face glowed with gratitude, almost as if this were a kindness of extraordinary measure. As she hugged us for the very first time, she said she would explain things another day. The embraces were not perfunctory or the result of obligation for what Steve had done. Each of us felt the emotion of genuine appreciation wrap around us. This was, indeed, an epiphany!

The person of Emily, seen from one perspective until now, revealed more of an interior about which we were unaware but eager to learn. What was emerging was a more complex substance than the appearance of things had exposed. As we enjoyed cocktails that afternoon, a soothing, mild breeze caressed us in much the same way as we had felt moments before. It was a perfect analogy that distracted us from the thought that the week was flying by and it would soon be time to return to routine, responsibility and work. Although our acquaintance with Emily existed within a brief span of days, it was as if we had known her forever.

In the years that followed, our relationship with her deepened. We watched Marcus and Antony grow from little ones who were completely dependent upon mom, to boys whose individual personalities were taking shape. They were well-spoken and very polite. Marcus, the older boy, excelled in school. Little Antony was preparing to enter kindergarten during our trip in 1996.

This was a vacation of celebration for Steve and me. We both took an early retirement incentive and were no longer constricted by the girdle of time and the frustrations of an education system that had been intent on stripping its ranks of their enthusiasm, motivation and joy.

Emily knew we were educators and was quick to tell us how hard she had worked with Antony to get him ready for the world of learning. He knew colors, numbers, shapes, the alphabet and letter sounds. We could not imagine it any other way. As much as she adored the boys, she was a tough task master. They had no choice but to walk the straight line of high expectations. More by actions than words, she demonstrated a keen understanding of the concepts of priority, responsibility and sacrifice. Both mommy and daddy, she was cast in a role that tested her ability to do a juggling act so that the family machine would remain well-oiled and functioning.

We always seemed to be learning something new and different about her. She had a background in cosmetology and as a beautician. These skills served her well in securing part-time work with private clients. She met with them on days off and at any other times her work schedule permitted. Two jobs, providing care for the boys in her absence, getting involved in school and leisure activities and being two parents in one comprised her daily call to duty as she faced the demands of raising a family. She was a hustler in the best sense of the word, yet the casual observer never would have surmised that her plate was full. We never heard her complain about having to be a multi-tasker or when relating to us the events of a day when twenty-four hours were not enough.

All that contributed to our impressions were praise worthy, but they were brought into question and put to a radical test one day when a trip to the beach with Marcus and Antony became a harrowing experience. It was about 1:30. We had finished some errands and decided to stop for a beer. Emily was sitting at a side table. That she was upset was all too obvious in a facial expression that revealed a mix of panic and anger.

Not wanting to intrude but becoming alarmed by our vision of this strong woman reduced to gut-wrenching tears, we went to her. "Is there anything we can do?" Steve asked.

"I have a splitting headache," she sobbed.

I told Steve to stay with her while I went to buy Tylenol. When I returned, his face bore a somberness that made my stomach sink. "What happened?"

Once Emily began to recount the fiasco, I understood why Steve's complexion had become pale. She had taken the boys to a beach area at the far end of the main strip. Coming from the sidewalk, the jingle-jangle of bells caught her attention. The boys reacted immediately and began to hound her to buy them ice cream. She told them not to move from their blanket while she walked the less than thirty feet that distanced them from the vendor. She stood in line while keeping her eyes fixed on them.

The tourist police were out in force on the unusually crowded beach and must have observed the unsupervised boys. Two uniforms appeared while she was paying for the treats. She turned and became filled with terror when she saw them scoop up her sons. She raced back to what would quickly become a nightmare. Try as she did to explain the circumstances, her words fell upon deaf ears.

"Where are they?" I asked.

"They have them." We thought Emily was going to collapse as she choked on these words that made the situation one that went beyond the unfathomable limits of the incredulous. We never had heard of anything so preposterous, yet having come to know the reputation of some of the policia touristica, we should not have been shocked by the course of action they took.

We could not understand how they just dismissed plausible reasoning. None of it mattered! How could they not have seen her get up from the blanket and continue to visually guard them while in line, even amid a sea of faces? Emily stood out in any crowd!

"What happens now?" I asked.

Before she could get the boys back, she had to appear in a legal forum that we concluded was a division of family services. The situation would have to be explained by her. There were no guarantees that the one listening to her would exercise greater understanding and compassion than had the two who said, "We are just doing our job."

It was painful for us to witness this unsettling cycle of crying, aimless staring and labored attempts at speaking. We dared not leave Emily for fear that the reality of what was happening would leave her unable to present herself with coherency later on. Listening to an hysterical, emotionally unhinged parent would not have worked in her favor. We spoke softly to her during intermittent moments when she was able to calm herself and focus on our words of comfort and reassurance. Clearly, she had conjured images no less ghastly than those of one walking to the gallows.

Joe, the senior bartender, ordinarily sullen and standoffish, entered the bar and walked immediately to the table at which the three of us were sitting. For the first time, we observed a very different personality emerge. He was quite empathic and offered to take her to the place where culpability and consequence would be the center of discussion. Steve and I were among the few who knew that Joe had been a priest at an earlier time in his life. It was refreshing to note that he remembered some of his seminary training, even though he never put it into practice.

Since Emily had his shoulder to lean on for support, we rose from our seats and stood on either side of her. Simultaneously, we bent forward and kissed her cheeks. She reached up and pressed her hands against our faces. "Thank you so much," she sighed, trying to remain composed.

The next day, we made fast tracks to the bar hoping there was some news about the outcome of the proceedings. We were less than fifty feet away when we heard that honking which, years before, startled us. We were so happy to hear it now, we almost bumped into Joe who was exiting just as we turned to enter.

"She's okay. Thanks for staying with her yesterday."

"The boys?" Steve asked.

"They're home with her." We saw what looked like a labored attempt at cracking a smile. We knew how devastated Emily had been and how deeply we agonized for her, but never would have thought that this gruff, aloof, often sarcastically irritating man would look beyond the tip of his own nose and enter the pain of another human being.

When Emily saw us, she lifted the hinged section of the counter and stepped out from her work station. Arms outstretched and waiting, she pulled us close to her. As repeated whispers of "Thank you" flowed from her grateful heart, she released us from the clutch of a bear hug.

Despite our insistence that it was unnecessary for her to buy each of us a drink, she was adamant and refused to accept money. "It's the least I can do."

Business was slow and provided her the opportunity to recount what transpired at the hearing. She explained how encouraging Joe had been during the trip there. Whatever he said had filled her with such confidence that, by the time they entered the building and located the room in which the hearing was to take place, she was calm and focused.

An older woman sat behind a large desk and asked who the gentleman was. When Emily explained that Joe was her boss, she asked him if he wanted to remain with her; they were invited to be seated. Maintaining an obviously stoical expression, the decision maker lifted papers from the desk and began to read them. Changes in her starched, tight skin became noticeable as she filtered through the multi-paged police report. Every so often, she paused and looked at Emily. Although tears welled in her eyes, she did not lose composure. As the last page was placed to the side, the officer paused and stared at the pile.

While only momentary, Emily said it felt like forever until she began to speak. So unlike the countenance that made her heart race with concern, the voice was calm and tender. "Are you ready to take your sons home?"

A resounding, "Yes!" brought a smile to the officer's face.

"I guess you are." The boys were brought to her and the four of them were dismissed.

"She said nothing about what happened on the beach?" I asked.

"Not a word." The only conclusion that seemed plausible to us was that the officer did not believe the situation merited discussion because the two uniforms who had taken the boys might have rushed to judgment with a course of action that did not rise to the level of misconduct that warranted a formal hearing. Speculation was unimportant. The only thing that mattered was that Marcus and Antony had been reunited with Emily.

As we rose to leave, she blew a kiss to each of us and added yet another, "Thank you."

Steve and I thought nothing of what we did for her the day before. The simple gesture of kindness we extended did not cost us anything. It was done spontaneously because someone we liked very much was in distress. It was evident, however, that Emily viewed our presence and concern for her as anything but commonplace.

"What are you doing here?" Emily gasped when she saw us walk into Tornado one afternoon in June of 1997.

"School is not finished, is it?"

Steve and I looked at each other with puzzlement. "We retired last summer. Don't you remember?" Steve reminded her.

"Oh, my God, you never told me!" It was inconceivable that we neglected to share the news with her since everyone within earshot had been aware of our plans.

When we told her that this was to be a short stay she asked curiously, "Why? You have all the time in the world now that you're not working."

"We're closing on a condo we bought." I said.

"A condo ... what?" she yelled back.

"We bought a condo and came to get the paperwork finalized," Steve reiterated.

"When … where? Tell me everything!"

Her excited expression was contagious and prompted me to begin babbling about the details.

"I have news, too."

"Are you getting married?" I asked in a jocular tone.

"I should be so lucky! No. I got an apartment in one of the buildings on the avenue."

"Which one?"

"Palm Terrace," she proudly announced.

It was not one of the more luxurious edifices on the main strip. In fact, it had been an eyesore for years. Recent work to the exterior façade and lobby had made it less obtrusive and created an appearance more in keeping with others more modern and upscale.

This was a huge accomplishment for Emily. Because she could not afford a car, she had spent years depending upon a transit system that was less than reliable. That daily stress was heightened by the distance from our neighborhood to the school which Marcus and Antony attended. Neither was an issue any longer. She could walk to work within minutes and had gained the opportunity to accompany the children each morning to a local school in which they were now enrolled. Although life seemed easier for Emily, there was a hint of unspoken sadness even as she readily acknowledged how the changes had given her great relief and peace of mind.

Other than this brief conversation, we did not see Emily again until the day of our return to New York. Before heading to the airport, we stopped at Tornado to have a drink. There was little time to give her the details of what had resulted in our becoming property owners, but we told her that after our holiday visit with family and friends, we would return for a first-ever experience. We were going to be staying for three months.

"We will have plenty of time to see you," Steve said.

"That's great. I can't wait!"

"Once we get back to the island, we would like you to join us for dinner at the apartment."

"You're on!"

In the states, January 6th is a day which bears little importance other than its designation as the ending of the holiday season. In Puerto Rico, 'El Dia de los Tres Reyes' (Three Kings' Day) is celebrated with great enthusiasm, especially by families with children. Those who follow tradition provide the young with straw to place under their beds for the camels of the kings. It is gift-giving day and is accompanied by the same festiveness with which state-siders enjoy Christmas.

Steve and I had always observed this day referred to as The Epiphany, so the significance of custom was not strange to us. Dinner with Emily on that night would be a perfect way to conclude our favorite time of year. I was in the kitchen when I heard Steve remark, "You look gorgeous."

"Thank you, sweetie," was Emily's affectionate response as she entered the apartment.

I placed a platter of cheeses and crackers on the dining room table and went to greet her. Steve was right. She looked stunning in the sleek, black dress that gave accent to her shapely figure. As always, hair and makeup were perfect. She extended her hands to show us her latest creation.

Wiggling her fingers she asked, "Do you like them?" The use of different colored polishes combined to form an attractive, repetitive pattern on nails that were the longest we had ever seen. They looked like weapons! One finger on each hand was crowned with a diamond-like dot that glistened under the dining room lights.

"Your place is beautiful. I love the Christmas decorations."

Steve returned to the kitchen while I gave Emily a tour of the apartment. When we went out to the terrace, she stood against the rail and stared at the rippling waters of the lagoon. She seemed mesmerized by the reflection of lights that shimmered as if in a syncopated dance. The night was clear and provided a crisp image of the distant harbor. It was as if she had become lost in a moment of tranquility.

"This is so beautiful… what a view!" she exclaimed when she returned from the privacy of inner thoughts.

After enjoying 'pickies,' Steve presented dinner.

"Oh!" Emily said with a tone that bordered embarrassment as she observed the large steak that lay across her dish. "I don't eat meat."

Steve quickly offered to prepare something more to her liking, but she agreed to tackle what had been absent from her diet for years. Unlike the liveliness of her personality at work, she was noticeably more subdued during the meal. The difference was so glaring, I could not resist asking about it.

Emily told us she was keenly aware of the relationship between surroundings, behavior and the adaptability of one to the other. At Tornado, her purpose was not only to serve drinks but also to ensure that customers enjoyed themselves. Since she depended upon tips more than the minimal salary she earned, she recognized the importance of a light-hearted, friendly, engaging approach that insured financial benefit as well as result in a return by customers, especially tourists. "Is it wrong for me to do that?" she asked.

"No," was our simultaneous response.

Steve added, "You are there to make money. You always put your best foot forward. That is what attracts so many to Tornado. They know they will have a good time when you are on duty."

"Thanks, I needed to hear that."

"Why? Your personality and presence have been wonderful additions."

"Sometimes, my friendliness has given mixed signals."

Steve and I looked at each other with obvious confusion.

"Tornado is a gay bar," I said, "so what possibly could cause you to think this?"

We never observed anything in Emily's behavior that would prompt such a peculiar self-characterization. When she explained the basis of her comments, we understood what she meant. As she became more well known and word of her reputation spread, there occurred a subtle shift in the demographics of Tornado. Random and unnoticed by her, at first, straight men began to frequent the establishment.

"I acted like I always do. I didn't know they were straight … I can tease gay guys and know that's where it stops. Even when these others played along, I did not think anything of it. I thought they were gay. Then, one of them asked me out on a date!"

"Did you think he was kidding?" Steve interjected.

"Yes, that's why I continued joking with him."

"What happened?"

Emily moved back her chair in order to give us the full flavor of the continuing banter between them. "I told him, that might be fun, but your head is in another place. He looked down, stared at his crotch, then said something I never expected: "No, baby, my head is exactly where I want it to be. I'm not a fag; I'm a real man."

Having come to know Emily well, we were very aware of her dislike for labels and that she hated the word, 'fag'.

Emily was never one to use profanity, but his caustic comment sent her into a rage. "Then, I said, Who the hell do you think you are? Finish your drink and get the fuck out of here … and don't come back!"

She saw our reactions to the startling conclusion of the encounter and began to laugh.

"No one is going to say something like that and get away with it. Just the way he said 'fag' made my blood boil."

Clearly, Emily was protective of her customers. We were her bread and butter, but there was something more important. She was intolerant of intolerance and an arch defender of equality. I could not resist a rejoinder.

"Good for you, Emily. The world has enough homophobic assholes. We don't need them at Tornado, too!"

"It gets better," she added.

"What do you mean?"

This episode was one of a number which Emily described to us. In passing, she also mentioned two occasions when she had been propositioned. Short of supplying the details of those circumstances, she made it clear that she was offered substantial amounts of money for sex.

"No matter how difficult things are or how much I have to struggle, I could never do that. I have children and a reputation. They mean more to me than money."

"You are an incredible woman," Steve reacted with tender affirmation.

"Thank you, sweetie … You are two of the nicest people I have ever met."

"Let's have dessert and change the subject," he quickly added.

The pause in conversation, like intermission during a play, was a segue to other topics. Steve and I went to the kitchen. When we returned to the dining room with coffee and cake, Emily was not there. She had returned to the terrace and was looking at the expanse of water that connected us to the old city. I called to her, but there was no response.

I tugged at Steve's arm and he followed my lead. We stood on either side of her and cupped our arms around her shoulders. As tears glided down her cheeks she sighed, "I wish I could give my boys a better life."

"Come inside," Steve said softly. "Dessert is ready."

In the past, Emily's expression was animated when speaking about her children, but this comment bordered lamentation. Marcus, nearly ten years old, had developed a love for baseball. Often, he went to watch games in which some of his friends played. It broke Emily's heart to see him so energized after returning from one and discussion of his participation occurred. She knew she was unable to satisfy his motivation but did not want to discourage his enthusiasm. Rather than placing upon his shoulders the money issue or give a negative response to his strong desire, she used a more positive approach. "I hope it will be soon," she would say to him. "Mommy has to save more money first."

As much as she wanted to give Marcus hope that he would be part of the team one day, she knew it would not be an easy or short term accomplishment. Steve excused himself from the table while I refilled Emily's coffee cup.

"I'm sorry … You don't have to listen to my problems."

"That's what friends are for!"

"You are such dear guys!"

Steve returned and handed a white envelope to Emily. She looked confused and asked, "What is this?"

"Open it," Steve said with a broad smile. She looked inside and clutched it to her chest. Tears flowed again, but they were not ones of sadness. Steve had given Emily a check to cover the cost of registration, a uniform and a glove. "You've just saved the rest of the money," Steve chuckled.

"Don't tell Marcus where this came from." Just as we had placed our arms around her moments before, she rose from her seat, walked around the table and stood between us. One hand on each of our shoulders, she pulled us toward her. Tears wet our cheeks as she kissed us. She could not speak because she was clearly overcome with emotion. She held us close to her and shook her head, as if in a state of complete disbelief. This was a powerful moment for Steve and me. We had helped her to remove herself from a garden of Gethsemane and experience a moment of personal resurrection.

"Your coffee is getting cold," I said.

That broke the intensity of what we were all feeling and prompted her to return to her seat. Emily became quiet and appeared pensive. It reminded us of the day on which we saw her emotionally unhinged after the tourist police removed Marcus and Antony from the beach. Three Kings celebrations were supposed to be festive, so I needed to say something to bring her back to us. "Let me get you some tissues. Your makeup is all over your face." That did the trick.

She reached into her handbag, removed a small mirror and burst into laughter. "I'm a mess!"

"Not at all," Steve said as he reached across the table and gripped her hand. "You are a very together woman and an incredible mom."

The substance of that evening with Emily was reminiscent, in some ways, to others we had shared with the boys of the street. Struggle was evident. Need was clear. Our response was the same. What distinguished it, however, was the absence of a self-serving motive. This time together represented a continued but more intricate weaving of the tapestry of our friendship with her. It was a refreshing prospect because Steve and I knew that our presence was held by her with some regard. Our words and gestures of encouragement and affirmation were listened to and embraced. We were certain that the money given to her would serve a greater good.

This Three Kings Day, The Epiphany, was a commemoration unique to any Steve and I had experienced. The giving of a tangible gift to Emily fulfilled one significance of the day. Her gifts to us were so much more profound. She had reminded us about the meaning of acceptance without conditions. She gave us cause to reflect on the essence of parental love that made our own children present to us at that very moment. She confirmed our belief in a God who is always near and through whom purpose and plan take form and flesh. No dollar amount could measure the worth of these unseen treasures.

No one could have predicted the changes which would result from the vengeance of Hurricane Georges in September of 1998. Part-timers at Tornado were placed in the unenviable position of having to find other employment. Mike and Joe, older and more financially comfortable, could afford to wait it out until the business was up and running again. Emily was fortunate because she was able to make ends meet by making full time her work as a cosmetologist and beautician.

When Tornado eventually opened its doors, we thought Emily would be there. It seemed odd that we did not see her. We assumed that she was tying up loose ends with clients who had made appointments in advance.

One afternoon during the fall of 1999, weeks after we relocated to the island as permanent residents, we were en route to do some shopping. It was a crisp, invigorating autumn afternoon that made our walk along the avenue a pleasure. I glanced into the window of The Stop, a straight but gay friendly bar. Steve, unaware of my pause, continued walking.

"Steve," I yelled.

"What are you looking at?"

"It's Emily!"

He made fast tracks back to where I was standing. Through the window, we heard that honking we had come to love. She pointed to the door and buzzed us in. What a wonderful, unexpected moment of reunion this was! We never accomplished the purpose of our walk, but remained with her so we could catch up on the many months during which we had not seen each other. She was as beautiful and vivacious as ever. Immediately, she took out her wallet and showed us a picture of Marcus. There he was in his baseball uniform bearing a smile of incredible happiness. It paled by comparison, however, to the glow so apparent on Emily's face.

"I decided to tell him where the money came from."

"Why?" Steve queried.

"He is old enough to understand that it is not easy for me. I said that two dear friends gave him the gift."

"What about next season?"

"It is taken care of. After the hurricane, my beauty business did very well. I already have saved enough money."

"Speaking of the hurricane, why didn't you return to Tornado when it reopened? We never asked about you because we just assumed you would be returning. We knew you had a side business but thought you would be back. We know Mike retired and Joe is still there, but all the faces behind the bar are new ones."

Emily went on to explain that the new owner did a clean sweep and brought in his own bartenders.

"Not long ago, I stopped here for a drink. The owner offered me a job … I grabbed it."

"That's great," I said. "Now you can literally roll out of bed and walk a matter of feet to your job."

"I love it!"

"You look and sound wonderful. We are so happy for you."

"How long are you staying on the island?"

Steve and I began to chuckle. During the months of discussion and decision-making that resulted in our permanent relocation, we had not seen Emily. Her question was a clear indication that no one told her that we now lived in Puerto Rico.

"How long are we staying?" I asked Steve with a wink.

"For a while."

Emily looked confused and followed with, "What's a while?"

"I guess forever is the same as a while, isn't it, Steve?"

"Sounds right."

"A while … forever … what are you talking about?" Emily asked.

"We moved here in August," Steve said nonchalantly.

She screamed so loudly, all movement stopped. Realizing that we had been playing her along, she began to honk almost uncontrollably. This incited an uproar of laughter that lasted several minutes. Emily's unique sound was as contagious as ever! When she collected herself, the others settled down and resumed conversation or the games of pool from which they had been interrupted.

"We have to celebrate," she said.

"What do you mean?" Steve asked curiously.

"I have an idea. Have you ever taken the evening cruise that leaves from Miramar?"

"Yes. When my younger son graduated from high school, he came down for a week and we took the sunset cruise."

"Oh," she responded as if with disappointment. "… So that would not interest you."

"We would love to do it again."

"Great. We'll get together and party."

Steve and I just looked at each other. When she said 'party' she meant it. As serious and reserved as Emily had been at our Three King's dinner, we knew she could be a hell raiser!

That Tuesday evening in late October was as clear and crisp as had been the day. As instructed by Emily, we were to meet at Tornado …

6 p.m. sharp. The few friends we had invited were already there when we arrived, but there was no sign of her. Within minutes of our ordering drinks, she appeared. She was wearing really short shorts and a blouse that clearly accentuated the positive. As if her apparel was not sufficient to call attention to herself, the sneakers she wore were encased with blinking lights. Steve and I never had seen anything like these. Then again, Emily was one of a kind! We quickly finished our drinks and the six of us began the trek down the avenue and across the bridge to the small harbor from which the cruise boat was to set sail.

By the time we entered the dock area, it was about 6:45. It seemed strange that so few people were there. The boat on which we would tour the surrounding areas of San Juan was unlighted. The ticket office was dark. Those waiting were as perplexed as we. Phone reservations had been made by all and each individual or group was given a confirmation number.

Emily's face bore a look of irritation as she scouted in search of someone who worked there. Not one employee could be found. It became evident that we were going nowhere, but none had a clue as to the reason. We heard a woman near the front of the line say, "Look at this." Emily immediately approached her. She was pointing to the ticket window. In the lower right corner was loosely affixed a barely legible note written on a small scrap of paper — Tuesday cruise cancelled.

Audible displeasure, including a number of expletives, could be heard among the twenty odd who had gathered anticipating an evening of enjoyment. We knew that when Emily made the reservation, she was required to give a contact phone number before she received a confirmation number for our group of six. She polled several others and all had followed the same procedure.

"Why the fuck didn't one of these assholes call all of us?"a tourist blurted from his spot. That heightened the agitation of the small crowd.

As disappointed tour goers dispersed, we six remained so we could decide what to do so the evening would not be a complete loss. Ron, whose manner and behavior were the most campy of our friends, suggested a return to Tornado. Another, named Nick, postured a bus ride to the old city.

Emily perked up in quick opposition. "I'm not dressed for that … no way!"

Dan, yawning even as we traveled to the dock, said, "Let's call it a night."

"Call it a night?" Emily yelled with a markedly inflected tone. "It hasn't started yet!"

As we hiked back, Dan continued yawning but more audibly. He commented how the return trip seemed longer and more tedious than had been the first leg of the evening. It was later, moods were mixed, the anticipation was gone and we were moving at a much slower pace. This was not rocket science! Then, too, Dan was not the sharpest knife in the drawer.

We arrived back at our old stomping ground a bit after eight o'clock. One of the new hires with whom we had become acquainted was on duty. Eduardo, whose nickname was E.J., was a dead ringer for Antonio Bandaras. "If I were ten years younger …", Emily sighed.

"Get in line, honey," was Ron's quick-witted retort.

From behind the counter, E.J. placed his hand across his chest and bowed as if he had just received a momentous accolade. "Thank you … thank you," he responded, first looking at Emily then at Ron.

Whatever frustration we felt earlier quickly dissipated and was replaced by a mood more in keeping with the atmosphere of happy hour. E.J.'s engaging approach seemed to be magic and did the trick. It didn't hurt, either, that he was drop dead gorgeous!

E.J. observed me remove my camera from its case. "Let me take some pictures of the group."

Ron was insistent that I take a few 'poses' of E.J. By this time, he needed cups for his lips because he was drooling as he unashamedly made gaga eyes at the strapping bartender. With affected tone and intentional elevation, Ron panted, "I want an 8x10 glossy!"

Either he was smitten with E.J. or his hormones were raging with lust. Both were probably accurate descriptions of his 'junior high school crush' behavior. E.J. was a good sport and played along with Ron's unreserved comments.

Emily leaned across the table and whispered, "Don't get too excited, Ron, he's straight."

Ron's reaction was like a balloon that had been deflated. "Why did you have to spoil my fun?" he came back at her.

"That never stopped you before," Dan interjected with uncharacteristic sharpness.

At that moment E.J., carrying a tray of refills, approached and asked what all the laughter was about. "Emily just ruined my night," Ron said wistfully.

"What do you mean?" E.J. queried as he placed the drinks on the table. That question stopped Ron in his tracks. E.J. repeated his inquiry, but Ron remained speechless and stared at him.

Then Nick, our sports jock friend who was not usually appreciative of queenish behavior, startled us when he said to E.J., "Ron is hot for you and Emily let him know you are straight."

"Yes, I am," he boasted. E.J. began to flex his muscles and turn around slowly. His eyes became fixed on Ron. "You can look all you want, but the candy store is closed."

Ron was on the verge of hyperventilation and moaned, "Get me away from this torture!"

Bursting into laughter, E.J. rounded the table and stood behind his admirer. He placed his hands on Ron's shoulders and began a slow, forceful massage. "Calm down or you are going to pass out."

Ron turned and gazed up at E.J., "If I do, promise you'll catch me in your arms," he gasped. Then Ron looked at the rest of us. "I'm never going to wash this shirt again!"

We all howled as we watched E.J. roll his eyes. This scenario was far better than anything we would have experienced on a boat in the middle of nowhere.

As the night wore on, the few remaining customers seated at the counter departed. That left E.J. alone with our merry band. He pulled up a chair and sat right next to Ron. "Do squeeze in," he said. Ron really had it bad for this hunk of a man. Then, E.J. took out a deck of cards and showed us a number of tricks. He was quite adept at keeping all of us attentive and intrigued.

During the course of conversation, I asked E.J. if he was born in Puerto Rico; his accent was distinctly different. He was born in Spain and belonged to a gypsy family who, like nomads, moved from place to place and eventually made the island their home. We were being entertained by a thoroughbred Spaniard, a gypsy and a suave, seductive bartender all rolled into one person.

Ron was ready to jump out of his seat; he was literally panting. "I gotta go," he said as he rose from his seat.

E.J. put the cherry on the cake, saying, "Bye, sweetie … see you soon?" he asked in a non-offensive but very sensual tone.

Ron exhaled a loud moan, "Oh, yes!"

Once he left the bar, we had a chuckle listening to Emily and E.J. banter.

"You made him nuts."

"Guys like Ron are great for business. They love to tease and I don't mind giving them a head trip. Their tips are good."

"You gave him a 'head trip' alright," Emily honked back.

"Oh, shit, you don't think he thought I …"

"Was serious?" she interrupted. "Oh, yes he did!"

"Wow!" was all E.J. could respond.

The hours had flown by. It was nearly midnight when we realized the time. As much as Steve and I hated to see the evening come to an end, we had drunk enough and were exhausted from laughing.

E.J. rose first. "I have to clean up; I'm gonna close early. Thanks for making my shift so much fun."

That was an understatement. E.J. probably had no idea how enjoyable he had made the purpose of the evening. Although the boat ride was cancelled, it didn't matter to us. Nothing could compare with this gathering of friends, especially Emily. To what extent she might have lived up to her reputation as a hell raiser amid the party atmosphere on a cruise boat is something we never witnessed because the outing was never rescheduled. Instead, Steve and I were gifted with a welcome celebration more intimate and personal. Nothing could have been better than that!

As slow-paced as was life on the island, time seemed to slip away quickly. The holidays came and went, and the year 2000 was upon us. The Brunrich Inn, a name derived from combining ours, was open for winter visits. We rarely saw Emily or other friends because our routine was altered substantially when guests were with us.

Pockets of time during which we were able to catch our breath were rare, but we managed to go to Tornado to view a new attraction that had become a huge drawing card. The redesigning of the bar after the hurricane brought with it the introduction of nighttime entertainment on weekends. Male dancers and female celebrity impersonators drew sizeable crowds.

Once night, a well-known male stripper was in the lineup with the 'ladies.' We thought it very strange that when they took the stage, the queens hovered closely. As soon as the hunk made his way down the steps from the upper quarters and jumped on the stage, the masses backed away. At first, we could not understand their rationale, but we were about to find out.

We were seated at a table directly in front of the stage. The music, loud and rhythmic, accompanied seductive gyrations that resulted in the removal of his shirt. This guy was a mass of muscle. He eye-balled us once, twice, three times, then jumped over our table. With one hand, he lifted it and threw it on the stage. He stood facing Steve. I was directly behind him. He grabbed Steve's hand, maneuvered it between his legs and slapped it in position against his butt. He grabbed my hand, moved it in reverse direction and cupped it over his equipment. There we were, a literal captive audience as he strutted his stuff to the sound of the electrifying music.

Above the din, we heard the unmistakable sound of Emily's honking. When he released our hands, he jumped back on the stage and returned our table to its position between us. That is when we first saw her. She was sitting with a young woman. When the dancer exited the stage with an uproar of applause, there was a brief intermission. God knows, we needed one! We went to Emily's table intending to tease her about what she had found so hilarious while viewing our awkward predicament.

Before either of us could say a word, she roared, "You got a kick out of that, didn't you?"

We would have used other words to describe our reaction, but she was sitting with someone we did not know.

"It certainly was different," Steve said with deliberate diplomacy.

"Of all the guys in here, he picked on the two of you … how hysterical!"

Again, her choice of words did not quite capture the essence of the experience.

"I want you to meet someone. This is my daughter, Maggie."

"Your what?" I yelled.

"My daughter … she is eighteen."

Steve and I were speechless. All these years had passed and never had Emily spoken about her. Had she not told us that Maggie was her daughter, we would have been none the wiser. Her appearance was a stark contrast to Emily's. Light-skinned with blond hair, daughter looked nothing like mom.

Years earlier, Emily had dated a Caucasian airline pilot. This may have been the link that connected them. Emily's reference to that time in her life had been a brief, passing, 'by the way' comment which was accompanied by no details. It was not beyond the realm of possibility that he was Maggie's father.

As if physical appearance were not enough of a distinction, Maggie was quiet, soft-spoken and possessed a laugh that would blend in a crowd. She said little during the brief intermission but was more amazed by the witty exchanges between her mom and us. We remained for the second half of the show, but they did not.

"She's returning early tomorrow morning," Emily said. We did not know to what she was referring and asked no questions. There would be time for her to satisfy our curiosity … and confusion.

During the months that followed, it was virtually impossible for us to get out for afternoon socializing. We became prisoners as apartment renovations proceeded one after another. New kitchen counters, the replacement of ceiling in-lays, the addition of accent lighting, closet remodeling and a new exterior door comprised the list of projects.

In early September, we heard the sounds of hammers and electric drills for the last time. Antonio's frustration with the slowness of co-workers when Las Palmas underwent renovations made much more sense to us. Unless one actually experienced the 'mañana syndrome' in action, there were no words to aptly describe the procrastination that made us wonder if 'tomorrow' would ever come.

While we had met Emily in brief passings, we awaited an opportunity to sit with her and find out more about Maggie … and the airline pilot.

As much as we espouse a strong belief in purpose and plan, something very unexpected happened in October. A friend once had shown us pictures of a home he had bought in Florida. In passing conversation with him one day I said, "We've never been to Florida and would love to travel there sometime. Are there any hotels close to where you live?"

"When you come, stay with me," was his generous offer.

Within weeks, we were in sunny, southern Florida. We arrived on a Monday and by Friday, we were in contract to purchase a home. Steve and I had previously discussed the difficulties associated with having New York based health insurance when attempting to find participating physicians on the island; they were few and far between. Also, we had become weary, to the point of emotional exhaustion, as a result of dealing with 'the boys of the street' for so long.

We were being guided to begin yet another chapter in our life together. The new face of our condo would not be ours to enjoy for much longer. Just as the remodeling had kept us away from our friends, the myriad details of the move back across the ocean were all consuming. Whenever we passed The Stop, we were hopeful that Emily would be working. After several unsuccessful attempts to connect with her, we ventured in one afternoon to find out her work schedule.

"She's not here anymore," the bartender said.

"Do you know where she is working?" Steve asked.

"No one has seen her," was Edwin's comment that made our stomachs sink.

We asked everyone we knew if they knew where she was. We searched her out at other bars and clubs in which she might be working. We inquired about her at the condo building in which she lived. The unvarying response from all to whom we spoke was like an echo from a mountaintop ... "I don't know where she is."

We did not think it possible to shed more tears or feel greater gut-wrenching emotion than those which overwhelmed us during past years, but this sadness was pervasive. Concern, worry, alarm and speculation banged at the door of our hearts. After being so close to Emily for eight years, it was incredible to think that she vanished without a trace.

On the morning of January 18, 2001, we stood silently in the empty shell that had become our apartment. It was a bittersweet moment as we looked to newness while, at the same time, we choked on tears of lament. In truth, it was as if someone close to us had died and we were gripped by the churning that came from mourning the loss.

Annie

10

She lumbered down the narrow side street, a seeming retreat from observation, an oasis from the scrutiny of others. There was no way, however, to shield herself from the punishment of what surrounded her labored attempt to place one foot before the other. Blistering sun and thick humidity pounded unrelentingly and made the very action seem beyond her forbearance. She paused, then continued in a repetition that narrowed the distance between us even though we, too, had halted to relieve the weight of cumbersome grocery bags.

One of those I carried, slipped from my hand and hit the street with an impact that caused her to turn. She stood and watched us transfer things in order to make more even our burdens. As we neared, the vague image became more defined. We realized there was no way to escape an encounter.

Puffy, black circles accentuated her haggard appearance and bore witness to a lack of sleep. One strap of her wrinkled, stained blouse hung loosely off her shoulder and revealed a bra dingy from wear. Her hair, oily and unbrushed, resembled a bird's nest that had been tossed about in the wind. Both shoe straps were ripped and, from the side of one, a small toe protruded through a hole in the material. In one hand, she clutched a zippered bag that bulged in all directions. Judging from her presentation, it did not seem an unreasonable assumption that it contained all of her worldly possessions. The other hand gripped loosely fitting, tattered jeans as if its release would make them fall from her waist.

"Got a cigarette?" she asked, her voice low and raspy.

Steve handed one to her and lit it. She inhaled so vigorously, she began to cough as though she could not catch her breath. Then, she made a strange sound and hurled a wad of spittle on the ground. Already queasy from the mere sight of her, our stomachs convulsed when, after expectorating, she let go the band of her jeans, picked up her blouse and wiped her mouth. Her gaze became fixed on the bags of groceries which lay between us.

"Are you hungry?" Steve asked.

"Yeah … looks like you bought a lot of goodies."

"Get something to eat."

"Thanks a lot."

She stared at the ten dollars Steve had given her as if it were gold.

"This will sure help me … by the way, my name is Annie." We retrieved our weighty purchases and with an intentional increase in pace, we moved ahead of her to the corner where a right turn obscured us from her view.

There was such irony in this untoward meeting on that sultry afternoon of August 10, 1999. It was a special day for Steve and me, one on which a long-anticipated goal became a reality. It was supposed to have been a day filled with excitement and happiness about opening a new chapter of memories made. Instead, our initiation as permanent residents of the island would be remembered for coming face to face with human suffering.

There is definitely a positive side to being compulsive. Carefully labeled boxes and an inventory list made the process of setting up our new home far less tedious than had been the daunting task of sorting, packing or discarding all that had been part of our life of thirteen years in New York.

Although not frequently, we did manage to get to happy hour when we could steal away for an hour or so. One afternoon about three weeks after settling in, we made plans to go to Tornado, then treat ourselves to dinner in celebration of our new relationship with Puerto Rico as well as the completion of the myriad tasks that made our apartment appear as something more than a warehouse.

Just minutes after four o'clock, the crowd was already sizeable. We found stools at the far side of the renovated counter area which now hugged the entrance wall. The bartender, speaking to customers at the opposite end, did not take notice of us. We were unaware another was on duty. We saw someone emerge from the kitchen with two bags of ice positioned on one shoulder. The other worker lifted the hinged section of the counter and intercepted them. The ice bearer could not be seen at first. Once inside, we got a glimpse.

"What'll ya have?" she barked.

When she moved away to prepare our drinks, I looked at Steve expecting a reaction. "Do you recognize her?"

"No… should I?" was his unsurprising response.

Drinks in hand, she turned, stopped short and stared at us.

"What's going on?" Steve murmured.

"It's her," I said emphatically as if a change in tone would have made him recognize Annie. He was clearly confused until she began to speak.

"You two … you're the ones who gave me a cigarette and money."

"Yes we are," I affirmed.

"Annie?" Steve followed with a tone of complete surprise.

"It's me!"

"Oh, my God … I didn't recognize you."

"You guys must have thought I was a bag lady."

"No, you looked to us like someone who was going through a difficult time," Steve said with every ounce of diplomacy he could muster.

"Bullshit!" she laughed. "I was a total mess!"

A voice yelled from the center section … "Annie!"

"I'll be right back," she said as she moved to attend to the source of the irritated tone that had caught her attention.

Steve looked at me, still incredulous to the transformation standing before us. The darkness that had encircled her eyes no longer visible, a hint of makeup had altered the face of the tired, worn Annie we observed weeks earlier. Her hair was brushed and arranged in a flowing pony tail. The blouse, jeans and sneakers in which she was clad were new. The metamorphosis defied description!

After calming the savage beast with a libation, she returned. "Who the fuck does he think he is, yelling at me like that! I told him if he ever raised his voice to me again, I'd punch his lights out! … He saw me talking to you and got impatient. … Don't leave, I want to ask you something after I take care of a few other customers."

Her reaction, blurted with rage, sounded extreme. Frankly, it was unwarranted. Happy hour was noisy; Annie had to have realized that. Short of eye contact, the only way to get someone's attention was to yell above the chatter. We heard the guy call to her. It was not the voice of authority nor was his intonation one of demand. He simply wanted to order a drink! Having witnessed a not-so-gentle Annie, we dared not move until she asked her question.

"I want to thank you again for helping me out," she huffed. "Are you free tomorrow about noon?"

"Yes, why?" I asked quizzically.

"Meet me at McDonalds. I want to buy you lunch."

"That is not necessary."

"I think it is. You two are the only ones who helped me when I got here. Everyone else looked away. I felt like I was invisible … please, this is important to me."

"Sure, noon it is!"

While walking back to our apartment the phrase, deception of appearance, flashed through my mind. Images of the poised, well-groomed, vivacious Emily on her first day of work at Tornado were a stark contrast to those conjured by a revisiting of that unforgettable street collision with Annie weeks earlier as well as our first-hand view of a less than endearing work ethic just moments before. Just as we had come to know the deeper places of emotion within Emily that lay in silence behind outer coverings, we were about to learn from Annie how the façade of appearance was not the whole of her personhood.

When it came to punctuality, Annie seemed to be cut from the same cloth as Steve and I. We arrived at our lunch spot ten minutes early; she was already there. Trays filled with food, she led us to a single, corner table.

She began, "The person you saw on the street is not who I am."

"No need to explain yourself," Steve interrupted.

"Yes, there is! You could have ignored me and kept walking, but you didn't. Forget about the cigarette and money … just to talk to someone … I had been feeling like an outcast. You guys made me feel better even though I looked like hell."

"Look at you now … that's the good news!"

"The only good news is my friend, Maria. Thank God for her. I knew I'd have a place to stay when I got here."

In light of our first encounter with her, Annie's remark was peculiar. She appeared as one who was wandering aimlessly to nowhere in the grip of homelessness. We were also confused by her reference to 'good news' and 'Maria'. Something had happened to Annie, but these comments gave no hint about what it was.

We sat in silence as she elaborated. With Maria's assistance, she had made travel plans but an unforeseen circumstance arose on the day of Annie's arrival on the island. She was greeted by a note that was taped to Maria's mailbox that read: 'See Lourdes Rivera for keys … feel at home … back in a few days … I'll explain.' Annie followed the instructions and brought the note to Lourdes. She looked completely baffled and said, "I have no keys … Maria did not leave keys with me."

We heard Annie's girl-like, gigglish laughter for the first time. "I shouldn't have been too surprised … Maria was always a scatter brain." This was the first indication that this woman and Annie had known each other for quite some time. Then, her tone changed abruptly as she continued, "A few days became six. I had no choice but to live on the street … anything was better than being there."

"Where's there?" I asked, hoping the pieces of conversation would begin to fit together. Annie had been in the states and suddenly, she was in Puerto Rico.

"What made you come to the island … it sounds like you ran away from something."

"Not something … someone … I'm getting to that." For the remainder of our lunch date, Annie painted a picture of her life during the past year. It was so graphic and disturbing, the mere sight of food was nauseating.

From all indications, there was a time when Annie lived the American dream. She was married, the proud mother of two children. The family home was modest but comfortable. A dog completed the portrait of family life which was much like that of others she knew.

Changes in her husband's personality were benign and random at first. An intemperate response or visible impatience while doing a home project did not cause Annie to become concerned. "Everyone can have a bad day," was the rationale that prevented her from becoming overly concerned. Gradually, though, his tone of voice and the aggressiveness with which he displayed displeasure escalated.

Witnessing his unpredictable mood swings, Annie attempted to encourage him to talk about what appeared to be increasing anger. Whenever she mentioned this, his response was silence or a litany of profanity. Realizing that there was grave trouble in paradise, she offered the possibility of their going to marriage counseling. She thought he might be more inclined to agree to the suggestion if she went with him. This was the moment Annie was sure their marriage was in trouble. A crack across the mouth that caused a bloody lip was his answer to her well-intentioned motive.

Argumentation intensified with vile language or sarcastic criticism and became routinely accompanied by slaps and punches. The situation worsened to one in which Annie became the recipient of full-blown beatings. The children were exposed to more than they should have witnessed and began to act out in school.

Several conversations occurred between mom and teachers so that, together, they might help the youngsters, eleven and nine years of age. It was an exercise in futility because Annie had great reticence about divulging the truth. The children had been admonished by her not to tell anyone what was going on and given the reassurance, "Mom will take care of this."

To us, this seemed an unfair burden to place upon the shoulders of innocence. She was so overwhelmed with her own anxiety, the reality that the children were also victims escaped her thinking. We made no mention of our reactions for fear that such might be perceived as judgment and incite an outburst. Within the silent safety of our thoughts, we continued to listen to Annie's harrowing tale.

One day, a nasty altercation resulted in a fist fight. It was literally, 'the straw that broke the camel's back'. This was the first time Annie defended herself against a physical assault. Enraged by her effort to retaliate, he placed her in a head lock, dragged her to an open window and threw her out of it.

"Sweet Jesus!" I gasped. "He what?"

"He tossed me out of our bedroom window ... on the second floor ... I broke my back. The ladder ... that's what I said made me fall."

"Ladder?"

"There was a ladder outside the window. As I fell, my leg hit it and caused it to topple to the ground. Thank God it did not land on me … I'd probably be dead!"

"People believed you? What about your children?"

"I was very convincing. I knew I had to get away from that insane bastard. I was afraid he would start beating the kids. I had to protect them. Good thing they didn't see what happened … they were in school."

"What made you decide to come to Puerto Rico?

"It is far away and my best friend, Maria, lives here. I knew she would help me."

As Annie described their decades-old friendship, her characterization of Maria as a scatterbrain became clear. More importantly, she was trustworthy. Annie had no hesitation in revealing a blow by blow description to Maria because she was confident that the true nature of the incident would remain shrouded in secrecy.

Although Maria's family had relocated to the island years earlier, there remained an inseparable bond between the two childhood friends. "Maria always wanted me to come for a visit. Who knew that the circumstances would be anything other than a vacation?"

For the duration of her hospital stay and recuperation at home, Annie felt a sense of temporary safety. Someone was always there to lend a hand and the initial stages of physical therapy occurred at home. This time period allowed her to put an escape plan into motion. Her children knew of Maria from past conversations, so her eventual sharing of the plan was intentionally vague. This would prevent a pinpointing of her exact whereabouts. Her excuse for travel, plausible but fabricated, involved a visit with the children to a family member. There was no paper trail that would reveal the purchase of an airline ticket because Maria had made the arrangements and contacted Annie's cousin with the itinerary.

As expected, her husband was adamant in his opposition to her leaving the home. Her parting memory was a barrage of profanity hurled at her as she prepared to collect the kids and go to the waiting car outside her door. Samantha and Annie were first cousins and very close to each other. Once at her home, Annie confided in her the gruesome details of 'the year from hell'. Samantha was visibly aghast at Annie's surreal account and did not hesitate to state her disagreement with her cousin's plot. Nonetheless, she vowed to maintain silence.

The truth be told, Samantha was correct in recoiling from the complex prevarication Annie had conjured. We could not understand why Annie lied about the emotional and physical abuse or how she could literally let him get away with such egregious behavior. Annie was perceptive enough to understand that if the truth came out, Children's Services would have gotten involved in the mess. That image, however, was not as daunting as the prospect of worse retribution by her husband. Her tone was grave, a glaring testament that she truly feared for her life. Whatever might be the potential legal ramifications, Annie was steadfast in her belief that her course of action, albeit risky, was the only option that would guarantee immediate relief for her and the children.

A pause in the twilight zone account gave me an opportunity to speak. "How could anyone who calls himself a man degrade any woman, especially his wife?"

"A man? … He is no man … he's a poor excuse for a human being!"

"Did he ever love you?"

"There was a time … I guess … but he became a different person. I didn't recognize him anymore. I should have gotten my kids away much sooner."

Steve and I sat motionless, each wrapped up in images of Annie's haunting saga. It was nothing less than a horror story! Of all the tales of woe we had heard during our years of experiences in Puerto Rico this was, by far, the most chilling. It was beyond the limits of anything we could fathom. Situations like Annie's made for good television drama. It was incomprehensible to consider that we actually knew someone who was a human punching bag; someone who had been reduced to an emotional shell of a human being.

A worker came along and pointed to our trays. "Basura?" (garbage) he asked. I shifted them, still filled with burgers, fries and sodas, and watched as he opened a receptacle and dumped the contents. 'Basura'. This also seemed an apt description of Annie's shower experience at Maria's home. While it provided an immediate cleansing and physical relief, an emotional Goliath awaited her. For real, substantial healing to begin, progress and be sustained for the long term, Annie needed to commence the process of dislodging from her gut all that had diminished and objectified her. She would have to find the courage to look into the eyes of the fear and pain that had made her feel powerless, worthless and grievously wounded her self-image.

We were not sure if she was capable of attending to the myriad components that rendered her weak and fragile. Good intentions and voiced resolve were commendable, but lip service absent of action is useless. There was one thing, however, about which we were certain. We had been drawn into Annie's suffering and would remain close and help her in whatever ways feasible.

Comparisons between Annie and Emily were inevitable and did not take long to surface. Emily had been the essence of charm and polish. Overtly friendly and willing to engage customers in conversation, she possessed a charisma perfectly suited to her job. Annie, on the other hand, came with baggage that weighed heavily upon her. She was burdened with the scars of abuse that barely had begun to heal. Consequently, she emerged aloof and apathetic as she went about the business of each day. Beyond listening to drink requests or acknowledging a tip, there was little communication with most happy hour goers.

Walls up and defense mechanisms at the ready, it was as if she expected an incident to occur at any given moment. An unseen force compelled her to keep fists clenched inside figurative boxing gloves. Truly, she was caught between a rock and a hard place. She wanted, needed to do well, but working in a bar where virtually all customers were male was a challenge. A sharp tone and abrupt service did not endear her to most who frequented Tornado.

Unaware of any plausible reason that would explain her often bizarre behavior, more than occasional temper flair-ups from customers provoked nasty outbursts from her. Each time we witnessed one of these unsettling verbal battles, it seemed as if Annie's husband was sitting on the other side of the counter and his was the face that became the object of her unleashed beast. Emotional purging was essential, but displacing pent up anger, bitterness and resentment upon the shoulders of others was an impediment to Annie's ability to regain emotional healthiness and became a stumbling block to her effectiveness at work.

One afternoon, it became clear that her pugnacious nature had caught up with her. It was damp and rainy, so happy hour was absent of the majority of its faithful followers. Steve and I had evening plans that would prevent us from remaining there for the duration. Once Annie began to speak to us, we were thankful that the socializing would be brief.

"The boss spoke to me yesterday. He told me if I don't shape up, he would have to let me go."

"Shape up?" Steve repeated. "What did he mean?"

"He got some complaints that I was nasty to customers."

"What do you think about that?" Steve continued, hoping Annie would admit that the concerns discussed with her were valid.

"What do I think about that? … It's bullshit! This is who I am … this is how I work."

"Is it?" Steve smiled. "That's not the Annie we've come to know."

"I don't want to talk about it now. I'm off tomorrow … wanna do lunch?"

"Why don't you come to our apartment this time … how's twelve-thirty?"

"That works fine for me."

Annie's was a perfect exit line for us. Steve and I realized that we had to plan a discussion strategy before seeing Annie the next day. The brief exchange at Tornado made abundantly clear the urgency of addressing not only the ultimatum given to her by her boss but also its direct relationship to the abuse she had withstood at the hands of her husband. This was a golden opportunity to gently dive into the rippling waters of Annie's emotions, but we were keenly aware of the possibility that belly flops might create waves. From what Annie revealed earlier, the latter scenario would not be pretty!

While we needed to be cautious about not creating the appearance of a contrived conversation, it was vital that we find a way to draw her in naturally and non-threateningly. Our hope was that the tranquility and safety of our apartment coupled with a sensitive, affirming approach from us would give impetus to a productive discussion. Trying to figure out an ice breaker was daunting. Our opening statement must steer clear of conjuring unsettling images.

This consideration provided few options. I thought to myself, *the shower at Maria's!* I mentioned this to Steve and explained my rationale. Annie had referred to it as a treat. I could go with that light-hearted reference and gradually lead her into revisiting the comedy of errors with the mailbox note and keys. It was risky but, then again, anything we might say had the potential of triggering an inflammatory response.

The dreary, depressive cloud cover and consuming rain dissipated during the night and gave birth to a new day that was sunny, brisk and invigorating. If the relationship between weather and temperament bore any veracity, we hoped Annie's disposition would be less sour and irritated than that which had been glaringly evident the prior afternoon.

She appeared right on time, threw her handbag on the dining room table and embraced each of us with a hug that was devoid of sentiment, absent of strength. Her facial expression, an open book, was tight with tension. It was obvious that her mood was unaffected by the brightness that surrounded her.

This is going to be torturous, my mind screamed as I led Annie to the terrace. Clearly, she was physically present but emotionally detached. I told her to get comfortable while I helped Steve put the finishing touches on lunch.

"Whatever," was the aloof response I heard.

We were in big trouble. She was every bit as foul as the day before. I knew we could not proceed with our anticipated strategy. I cozied up to Steve and whispered, "Change of plans … say nothing … she's a mess… let her do the talking."

We found her visually fixed on the gently rippling waters of the lagoon yet her eyes looked vacant. "Here you go, sweetie," Steve announced as he placed a dish of food in front of her. She gave a cursory glance then returned to the object of her preoccupation.

Without looking at either of us she said, "Thanks, but I'm not very hungry."

"That's okay…. If you feel like nibbling, it's there."

She cracked a partial smile and said to Steve, "Nibbling … you're so cute."

With keen instinct, Steve seized the moment and ran with it. "Your smile is lovely, Annie."

"No one ever said that to me."

"Let me be the first!"

Realizing she was blushing, she placed one hand on each cheek and lowered her head.

"I'm sorry … did I embarrass you?"

"No, it's not that. I'm not used to hearing kind words."

The momentary red glow that had brightened Annie's face drained quickly and was replaced by a pale, sickly expression. With quivering lips and eyes welled up with tears, she attempted to speak but was unable to articulate what she was thinking. As if a horror movie were replaying in her mind, she let out a scream, then the flood gates opened wide. She repeatedly pounded the table with a tightly clenched fist and gasped, "That son of a bitch … son of a bitch … son of a …"

Steve reached across the table and grabbed her hand, now redder than had been her face. "Let it out, sweetie … let it all go." She tried to pull away from Steve's grip, but he held her hand in place with greater resolve. The more she wailed, the louder became the echo that bounded off of the walls. The imagery caused her to descend, once again, to the doors of emotional hell, a place long resisted but in need of embrace. Repression and displacement had comprised her armor of self-preservation until now but in this moment of gut-wrenching purging, Annie could not hide from herself.

"Why?" she sobbed. "Why did he do this to me? I was a good wife and mom … I lived for my family."

"Sometimes there are just no answers to why bad things happen to good people." This was the only thought that seemed an appropriate response. I hoped that Annie would not find my analysis a cliché, and realize the sad reality of the expression.

"Nobody is perfect but I did my best to make our home a happy one."

"I'm sure you did, honey, but remember … you were the victim. Don't try to figure out what more you could have done or what you think might have caused your husband to become ill."

"Ill?" she questioned. "He wasn't sick." As soon as Annie said this, she realized that I was not referring to a physical malady but to a condition more covert and insidious … emotional dysfunction.

"Yeah, I guess he *was* sick, but how did that happen? I had no clue. He just became a nasty bastard overnight."

"I wish I could answer that question," I said softly, then took her other hand in mine.

As Steve and I engaged her in more conversation, tears subsided, eye contact increased and her voice became more steady.

"Try eating," Steve said as he moved her plate closer.

"Maybe just a little."

"A little is better than nothing."

"You guys haven't touched your food!"

"We've been waiting for you so we could all eat together."

Annie picked up her sandwich and labored to chew a few small bites. All was quiet but not uncomfortable. We wanted nothing to distract her from the task at hand. Once she got past the first swallows, it seemed that her appetite had returned and she knew that she could hold down the food.

"When I got here, I felt sick to my stomach ... I was afraid to eat anything. I would have been so embarrassed if I made a mess."

"Not to worry," Steve joked, "that's why they make paper towels and spray cleaner."

A full blown laugh from Annie ... that's what Steve's comment caused and was the turning point of the afternoon. For the remainder of our visit, we focused Annie on thinking about the future. She had a plan but was anxious about when and how she would accomplish it. Money was the key to all she needed to do. Not only did she have to save for an airline ticket, she had to search out and retain an attorney.

In her absence, Annie's family assured her they would begin working on her ticket to freedom. Annie and the children would stay at the home of her cousin until she was financially able and emotionally strong enough to get out on her own.

"What do you guys think about all this?"

"It sounds like you have given careful thought to what you want," Steve assured her.

"… And what I don't want!"

"This is good. So many women go back because they believe they are not worthy of more in life … or … because they are afraid to make a move. You are a strong woman, Annie."

"I wish I felt strong."

"Everything you've said proves it."

"I'm so glad I met you two."

"So are we!"

Annie then made reference to the many and varied personalities she had encountered at Tornado. This gave us an opening to discuss our observations of her behavior. She did not know what displacement meant or that her acting out was a symptom of an emotional imbalance that sent her into a rage for no apparent reason. We used examples in our own lives to make the concept more concrete and, hopefully, allow her to make a connection to herself.

"I guess I have been a bitch at work … you say you have seen it, too?"

"You are not a bitch, Annie," Steve quickly interjected. "Honey, you are in pain. People react to it in different ways. Do you understand why you have been lashing out at work?"

"I think so."

"That is why your boss had a talk with you. Obviously, he likes you or he would have fired you on the spot."

"I guess I owe him an apology."

"Not an apology but some explanation … whatever you feel comfortable telling him."

"Why not an apology?"

"Because you did nothing intentional. You reacted to your emotions in the only way you were able."

"It makes more sense now."

As difficult as it might be for her, we encouraged Annie to deal with customers in ways more cordial and less confrontational. Then, I took a leap of faith.

"Look at their faces … listen to their voices. Keep telling yourself that they are not your husband."

"I'm really gonna try … I can't lose this job."

"We know you can do it. When we are at Tornado, just look at us and remember our time together today."

"What would I have done if I didn't meet you?"

"It's not important. You did meet us … that's what matters … We are happy that you spent time with us today."

"So am I! Don't think it would have been too cool to fall apart at McDonalds."

"This conversation might not have happened."

"You're probably right."

By her own admission, this was the very first time Annie was able to look at the face of the past and stare into the eyes of the monster of abuse. She allowed herself to become vulnerable enough to express deep-rooted pain. Like a parasite, the agony of mental and physical torture had eaten away at the essence of her womanhood, the core of her emotional stability and the substance that nourished a sense of worthiness.

The strategy Steve and I agreed might be the best way to get her to open up as well as the reasoning we thought would dictate the course of conversation were clearly irrelevant. The design of the afternoon was in place before Annie's arrival. Once again, purpose and plan were the unseen, unspoken directors of the moment. We could only hope that our lunch gathering had given Annie a measure of strength, increased resolve and a greater understanding that she, not the pain, was in control.

Years before meeting Steve, I was accepted into a program of theological studies which led to my ordination to the Diaconate in the Roman Catholic Church. Father Michael, the Director of Formation, frequently used an expression which became the cornerstone of one of my early books, the autobiographical *Crossroads … Journey to Wholeness*. He said, "Sometimes, you have to go through the pain to get to the peace." How simple a statement this is!

On closer analysis, however, the words pain and peace, used in the context of a single sentence, emerge as arch rivals in a process that seeks a definitive end. I reflected upon the wisdom of this profound statement quite often during the days and weeks following Annie's visit with us. I would not have shared these words of wisdom with her had they occurred to me, because she was not ready to listen to such a declaration nor was she capable of grasping their fullness of meaning in her life. Nonetheless, they bore a direct relationship to her predicament and were like the perfect fit of gloves on hands that sought relief from the harshness of nature's elements.

In one way, she knew what that comfortable fit felt like. Doctors, nurses and therapists made possible the healing of a physical malady. In that process, Annie was not a primary decision-maker but a follower of prescription. Indeed, she already had experienced one level of the interplay between pain and peace. Now, she was on her own, cast in the role of ship's captain responsible for setting the course, aligning the sails and setting out into the unpredictable waters of life's next phase. Others, like Maria and we, could be present to her with understanding ears and listening hearts, but it was the emotionally fractured Annie who would be the ultimate decider of direction.

Changes in Annie's demeanor at work were gradual but noticeable. She was not ready to smile or engage in conversation that required lengthy eye contact with customers, but her approach was definitely more tolerant. She began to extend a greeting when serving cocktail seekers with a tonal quality no longer resembling that of a barking dog. She moved about with greater ease and comfort, her body language much less tense and stiff.

We could see that these efforts were conscious, deliberate and initially laborious, so we were sure to affirm her whenever the opportunity presented itself. As time passed, it was evident that Annie was becoming more and more spontaneous as she interacted with those looking for a hiatus from daily routine as well as the many who comprised the tourist trade. The ponderous process of moving from pain to peace was clearly in progress.

As the holiday season approached, Steve and I became unsettled. We would be traveling to New York to be with our families and Maria planned to celebrate Christmas with her family in another area of the island. Despite

Maria's repeated invitation to Annie, she declined the opportunity to be with people who knew and loved her.

When asked why she refused, Annie told us, "It's my work schedule … a busy time … I'm just not up to being around a lot of people." Her reasoning made sense but did not ease the concern that nagged at us. We three, the figurative anchors of Annie's ship, would be far away from her as she faced this first Christmas without her children.

Once again, Maria came to the rescue. Annie had become further acquainted with the 'key lady,' Lourdes Rivera. The elderly woman had taken a liking to Annie so Maria's request that Lourdes keep an eye on her friend was met with enthusiastic agreement.

Surrounded by Lourdes' small family, all strangers to Annie, she celebrated Christmas Day. It was easier for her to be with this group. They knew nothing of her background or the reasons for which she was on the island. In contrast, Maria's family had known Annie since she was a child. They knew she was married and had two children. Questions, no doubt, would have been asked … questions that Annie did not want to answer with lies.

Steve and I were fifteen hundred miles away, yet we held Annie close to our hearts. We prayed that sadness would not consume her and cause a regression, but that the spirit of the day, embodied in peace, hope and love, might strengthen her. We returned to the island filled with tentative confidence that we would find Annie in a good emotional place.

When we walked through the doors of Tornado early that afternoon, we were astounded by what we observed. Annie was laughing as she conversed with customers. In her hair was nestled a single beautiful white flower. Her blouse was illuminated by a blinking Santa Claus pin.

"What the heck is going on?" I mumbled to Steve.

"I guess we're going to find out!"

As soon as Annie caught sight of us, she lifted the arm of the counter and walked in our direction. "Merry Christmas. Did you have a good holiday in New York?"

"Yes, how about you?" we asked at the same time.

"Better than I expected. Lourdes is an incredible person! Come and sit … let me buy you a Christmas drink."

Completely dumbfounded, we trailed behind her. "Thanks, Annie, this was fun," we heard one in a group of three say as they prepared to leave.

"You're welcome. Enjoy your vacation," was her more than cordial response. We had no idea what had occurred during our ten day absence but, whatever it was, it was huge!

"Why are you looking at me like that?" she giggled as she placed drinks on the counter.

"Like what?" I came back.

"Like you don't believe it's me."

"It looks like you … what's going on?"

Apparently, Lourdes had taken Annie under her wing during Maria's absence. Each afternoon, after her shift, Annie was treated to a home-cooked meal and broke bread with Lourdes in her apartment. It was never Annie's intention to reveal anything about herself, but Lourdes opened the door one day. They were talking about family when Lourdes became teary. Unsolicited, she began to describe her abusive marriage that ended years earlier. By the time supper was ended, Annie had exposed all to Lourdes.

"She made me want to talk about it. In a strange way, it was good to know I was not the only one. She was so calm and caring … I felt safe."

She went on to tell us about Christmas Day. It was Annie's plan to remain alone before her shift began at six o'clock. Lourdes would not hear of it and badgered her into accepting an invitation to dinner. "I'm so glad she kept after me … it was really a wonderful day."

Dinner was planned for two o'clock, but Annie appeared hours earlier in order to help Lourdes with preparations. She presented the hostess with perfume, a bouquet of flowers and a box of candy, tokens of her appreciation for the kindness she had been shown. Lourdes moved toward the beautifully decorated Christmas tree that sat in front of the living room window. She lifted two gifts, handed them to Annie and said, "Everyone should have presents to open on Christmas Day."

One box contained a picture frame. In the other was a diary. "Write in this every day; it will help you. I have been doing this for years. … When you go back for your children and find a new place to live, ask someone to take a picture of the three of you. Look at the picture often; you will remember why you make the best, the only decision that allowed you to find peace and happiness."

Annie was on point when she characterized Lourdes as an incredible woman. Our efforts to help Annie paled by comparison to what the wise, motherly figure had given her. The real gifts were not those beautifully wrapped in Christmas paper but the unseen ones of compassion, understanding and encouragement born of experience. The two women had become emotional kinfolk. There was no other plausible reasoning that could explain the radical change in Annie that we were witnessing.

"Do you like my flower?"

"It's beautiful. What is it called?" Steve queried.

"Plumeria … that's what I was laughing about."

This was not the first time Steve and I were confused by a remark from Annie that came from left field. She often shifted conversational gears abruptly.

"You were laughing about the flower?"

"No, not the flower but what happened when I arrived at work."

The garden behind the apartment was filled with varieties of flora. Among them was a Plumeria bush that stood out from the rest. Before going to work, Annie went into the garden and took some cuttings. Her hands were soiled and sticky, but there was no time to wash them because she did not want to be late for work.

Upon entering Tornado, she asked the cook, "Tienes sopa en la cocina?" Within minutes, he emerged from the kitchen carrying a tray on which sat a bowl of soup. "I haven't been able to stop laughing … it feels really good!" Annie may not have realized the importance of this acknowledgment. It was a sign that another phase of healing had begun and, without question, this was a moment of transition.

Before we knew it, Holy Week and Easter were upon us. During those last few months, Annie had done an admirable job at attempting to restructure her emotional state of being and we sensed that it would not be too much longer before she made the big move. On the day before Palm Sunday, we invited her to join us for Easter dinner.

"Sure, I'd love to," she readily agreed. "What time … my shift starts at six."

"How's one o'clock?" Steve postured.

"That's perfect. I'll have time to change before work."

"We'll see you then."

"You won't be stopping in during the week?"

I explained that our tradition was to move through the days of Holy Week with quiet reflection and attendance at church services.

"Pray for me, guys."

"We do … everyday. We'll see you next Sunday at one."

"You got it!"

During that most sacred of weeks, Annie was close in mind and heart. As the agony of Christ was recounted in the Garden of Gethsemane gospel passage on Holy Thursday, we were ever aware of its relevance to her life before coming to Puerto Rico. It was impossible for us not to envision the Gethsemane moments in which she often found herself. All that comprised suffering, pain and agony heightened our awareness of the link between scripture and the human condition.

Good Friday was unlike any we had experienced in New York. From twelve until three o'clock, there was a visible slowing of life in the area. Traffic became sparse, pedestrians moved about with quiet posture and many stores were closed. Under an increasingly overcast sky, a funereal-like somberness gave testament to the sacredness of the day.

At precisely three o'clock, the time at which Christians believe Christ uttered His last words from the cross and expired, there occurred a deadening silence. It was as if time stood still. We wondered if Annie thought about how this day was also relevant to her. She had withstood repeated moments of crucifixion, one more painful and debilitating than another. We were overcome with emotion in ways different than in past years. Annie was the key to the novel perceptions and images which weighed heavily upon us.

Gethsemane and the cross … the stage was set for what we hoped would be an Easter every bit as powerful.

It was not yet daybreak when I awoke and moved about quietly so Steve would not be disturbed. I made my way through a dark apartment only to be greeted by more of the same once on the terrace. I was filled with a sense of growing anticipation as the night sky retreated and glimmers of first light appeared. Rays of sun filtered through cloud cover and beamed down to rest upon the gently moving waters of the lagoon. Within the quiet imagery of that setting, my mind replayed the events of the past week that led to this day of days.

As if with intentional design, the cloud bank that obscured the gaseous ball separated and the narrow, angular reflection of moments before became wider and wider until the bright light blanketed the expanse. The moment of resurrection had arrived. Indeed, it was Easter Sunday. Spontaneously, I began to voice the words of an ancient prayer of the Church, the Easter Proclamation called the Exultet:

> *Rejoice, heavenly powers,*
> *Sing, choirs of angels,*
> *Exalt, all creation*
> *Around God's throne.*
> *Jesus Christ, our king,*
> *Is risen.*

Immersed in reflection, I was not aware that Steve was standing beside me until I felt his hand on my shoulder. I reached up and placed mine over his. "Continue," he whispered.

> *Rejoice, oh earth,*
> *In shining splendor,*
> *Radiant in the brightness*
> *Of your king.*
> *Christ has conquered,*
> *Glory fills you,*
> *Darkness vanishes forever.*

The last line of this prayer gripped my heart and caused images to flash before me. It was a sign that the others were one with us in the hush of dawn. Steve remained close to me as I added:

> *Most holy and gracious God, we lift up to*
> *You those who have become part of the*
> *fabric of our lives. You know their pain and*
> *struggle better than we do. Be with each and*
> *all of them as they exist in every today. Help*
> *them to know Your presence and cause to*
> *heal these wounded souls for whom life is*
> *such a challenge. May we be the voice of*
> *Your understanding, the spirit of Your*
> *compassion and the heart of Your love.*
> *We make this prayer in the name of the*
> *risen Lord, Your Son, Jesus Christ. Amen.*

Steve bent down and hugged me, each one's tears wetting the other's cheek. "Happy Easter," he said, his voice barely audible.

"You, too!" I attempted to respond but the words resisted utterance.

A few minutes later Steve, almost in a tone of regret, said, "We better get moving." By the time we left for church, the table was set and food preparation was well underway. All was in readiness for Easter dinner. We hoped it would be as awesome as had been the dawning of this day of rebirth and renewal.

We were not at all surprised that Annie was the first to arrive. She looked beautiful in the tasteful black dress and heels she wore. Her hair, ordinarily wild and frizzy, flowed in loose curls that swept up on one side and were held in place with a decorative clip. Although it was rare to see her wearing make up, the touches she used enhanced the attractiveness of her appearance. That covering, however, could not hide a pensive facial expression. As curious as we were, this was not the time to make inquiry. Others were due to arrive momentarily and we did not want them to be greeted by a potentially emotional scene.

"Happy Easter," Steve said as he handed a glass of wine to her.

"The same to you. Is there anything I can do to help?"

"Just relax. Everything is under control. Excuse me while I get things ready in the kitchen."

As Steve moved away from us, our remaining four guests appeared at the door. "Make their drinks," he instructed me. "I'll carve the ham."

His request was risky because my ability to make a tasty libation was questionable. I was greatly relieved when all of them asked for beer. That, I could handle!

When Steve joined the group in the living room, Annie stood up. "I want to make a toast." All eyes were on her as she began, "I want to thank Steve and Fr..." Tears poured from her eyes making Steve and I wonder if they bore any relationship to our initial observation. "I'm okay," she assured the group after composing herself. "I want to thank ..." A pause was followed by more tears. Her lips quivering, she was unable to speak.

"It's okay, sweetie," Steve reassured her. "We'll have some pickies. Before Frank says a prayer at the table, you can try again." His ploy to get Annie to calm herself worked for the moment.

One of our friends was masterful at joke telling. As he related one after another, the ambiance in the room became light and lively. Annie smiled and giggled occasionally, but neither seemed to be spontaneous reactions but deliberate efforts to stay with the group.

Once we gathered at the table, I reminded Annie, "You can make a toast now if you still want to. I'll say a prayer after you speak."

Annie stood with her glass clutched in a shaky hand. "I'm going to do this ... I have to!"

Steve took her other hand in his. "Take your time; there's no rush." Whatever the cause of her preoccupation, it was serious enough to make three more unsuccessful attempts. "Don't worry about it, Annie. If you feel like speaking later ... we have all afternoon."

I scrapped the original prayer I had intended to offer and said one more generic and light-hearted. Annie had spilled enough tears for one day. Although the atmosphere was more subdued than anticipated, we were delighted to be surrounded by wonderful people on this most special of days.

"Let me help you," Annie piped up when I began to clear the table and make room for a bakery of desserts. Alone with her in the kitchen, she leaned toward me and whispered, "I'm sorry, Frank. I hope I didn't spoil your day."

The truth be told, it would have been better if Annie had left her distracted mood at the door, but I was not about to say this to her and risk another round of tears. Her comment, however, gave me the opportunity to try to uncover the cause of what was troubling her. "Are you all right?"

Her affirmative head nod was tentative and not at all convincing.

"Why don't you stay after the others leave so we can chat ... there should be some time before your shift begins."

"I'd like that."

As if Steve had not prepared enough food to feed a multitude, our guests brought desserts that extended from one end of the table to the other. "Everyone has to take a bag of goodies. If Steve and I keep all of this, we're going to look like two cows!" The image must have tickled Annie's funny bone because, for the very first time that afternoon, she laughed.

By four-thirty the last of our friends left, weighed down by a large bag of sweet treats. Annie wasted no time in getting to the heart of the matter. "Steve," she sighed, "I told Frank that I hoped I didn't spoil your day."

"We were glad you were with us." His response echoed mine but he seemed perplexed about what to say next. I jumped in and seized the moment.

"Annie, what's wrong? Every time you tried to speak, you became upset."

"I'm just a little emotional, that's all."

"No ... we never would have guessed!"

She got the humor in my remark and giggled. "Don't be a smart ass."

"Oh! You must be feeling better."

The silly bantering relaxed her enough to tell us what was burdening her. She took a deep breath and exhaled two words that put everything into perspective. "I'm leaving … I'm ready to go back, get my kids and do what I should have done months ago." This long-anticipated day was upon her, yet there was an uneasiness in her voice.

Annie explained how a combination of emotions had put her off balance during the last few days. She had known since Wednesday that her time on the island was short. More than ever, she was conscious of the issue she had left in the states that still needed to be resolved and brought to closure.

No wonder she was in a tail spin! Unlike her unexpected days of wandering when she arrived eight months earlier, she would not have to fend for herself when she returned home. Her cousin, Samantha, had generously offered to let Annie and the children live with her for as long as was necessary. Typical of Annie's personality, she switched gears amid these revelations.

"I think I can say the words now."

"What words?" I asked.

"The toast."

"If you don't feel up to it, don't worry. You have enough on your plate." My attempt to gently dissuade her was futile.

"No, I have to do this."

"Whenever you're ready."

We soon learned the context of her sentiments was better expressed absent of the others because we were hard-pressed to hold back our emotions.

"I want to thank you, Frank and Steve, for inviting me today. I hope you know how much your friendship has meant to me. You have helped me to look at myself differently … you made me feel like a woman again. You made me feel important and worth something. You two are among a small group of very special people I have met. I'll never forget all that you did for me. Happy Easter and love to both of you."

Annie put her hands over her face, almost as if she were embarrassed by her own sensitivity. "That was beautiful," Steve said. "We're glad you had to wait until now … you have become dear and your words mean the world to us." As Steve shared these heart-felt feelings, Annie removed her hands.

"I meant every word."

"We're sure you did!"

"There's one more thing I have to tell you. Tomorrow is the day. I have an early afternoon flight. Maria will drive me to the airport."

The reality of Annie's words hit us like a ton of bricks. This was the last time we would be with her. The probability of our crossing paths again was slim to none and made the moment of good-byes an emotional one.

"I have to pull myself together so I can work tonight."

"That's the spirit!" Steve quickly added. "You are much stronger than you think."

"I hope you're right."

My parting comment to Annie was not my own. It comprised the words of Fr. Michael. This was the perfect, the only opportunity I would ever have to share them with her.

"Annie, before you go, I want to say something to you that, long ago, was told to me by a dear priest. Take these words with you and when you hug and kiss your children again, you will know what they mean … Sometimes, you have to go through the pain to get to the peace."

"I get it … I really get it. Thanks for saying these words to me … gotta run or I'll be late."

As I closed the door, it was as if I were closing the cover of a book, a book that was unfinished. "Do you think she realizes what she's going to face?" Steve called from the kitchen.

"I don't think she has a clue," I answered without hesitation. There was so much more we wanted to know, but time became the stumbling block. Several questions came to mind, all of which could be answered by us with little more than speculation because Annie had left us with an incomplete picture.

Where was her husband during these eight months? What did he do once he learned Annie was gone and the children were with Samantha, her cousin? Had he begun any legal action against her? Was she returning to a cauldron of consequences which boiled more violently than before she left him? If we had entertained any of these questions, we would have gotten no sleep on that Easter night. There was no purpose in dissecting them because, in the final analysis, Annie was the keeper of answers and the harbor of the complete body of circumstances that surrounded her surreal journey. Annie's saga was like the finale of a television drama that emerged as a cliff hanger. The difference was that we would have no opportunity to tune in next season and find out what happened.

Jay

11

Nicky Tukats was a strange fellow. A transplant from the states years before Steve and I met him, he owned a penthouse and made sure everyone knew about it. Not only did he tout financial solvency, Nicky was one of a number of Americans who complained about everything Puerto Rican. 'Not good' or 'not good enough' were standard expressions Nicky used to characterize all that comprised day to day life. It was never wise to ask him how he was feeling because his usual response was a laundry list of irritations.

Steve and I were keenly aware that we lived in a culture where the pace was slower, some laws were unlike those by which we formerly lived and the tenacity with which work got accomplished was different; there was always 'tomorrow.' These facts of island life really got under Nicky's skin and, without question, he got under ours!

On more than one occasion, Steve suggested that, if he was so unhappy, he should consider relocating to the states where things were more to his liking. Nicky never accepted such a remark in the manner it was intended, instead taking it as an attack on his right to voice opinions. After all, when Nicky Tukats spoke, it was with the authority of the gospel! At least, this was how he perceived himself.

It was he who introduced us to Jay one afternoon during happy hour, just days after we met Annie. Nicky had heard that we were looking for someone to paint our apartment and do some minor electrical and plumbing work. He thought it important to give us vital information about Jay before meeting him. "He's an Amer-Rican, a little messed up and has a huge tool in his box." How typical of Nicky this was! We cared little about any of this irrelevant nonsense.

On a scale of one to ten, our ability to tolerate Nicky in any more than small doses was minus twenty. "We really don't give a shit about these things," I said with blatant annoyance. "Does he do good work?"

"Oh, yeah, that too," was the 'by the way' answer he offered.

A few minutes later, Jay walked into the bar with clipboard in hand. "These are the guys I told you about," he said, and without the courtesy of introducing us, Nicky turned and left. He was some piece of work!

We sat with Jay and described the tasks that needed to be accomplished. He took copious notes and asked many questions. Not withstanding Nicky's early analysis, Jay appeared focused as well as knowledgeable. He said he wanted to see the apartment in order to figure out how long the work would take to complete as well as to determine the materials he would require. Then, he'd be able to give us a written estimate.

"When are you able to stop by? I asked.

"I'm free now if you guys want to get started right away."

As we walked to our apartment, Jay brought up Nicky in conversation. It became evident to him that Tukats was not one of our favorite people. My mention of his last name caused Jay to chuckle.

"Do you know how he got the name, Tukats?"

"Isn't that his last name?"

"No, it is a nickname. He has two cats, so everyone calls him Nicky Two Cats." Heads turned as the three of us laughed uncontrollably. The image of this mousey-looking man with such a name fit well with his gossipy nature and unpredictable, sometimes eccentric behavior.

Two women were standing outside the lobby when we approached the building. While my eyesight is less than perfect, my hearing is acute. In Spanish, one made a comment to the other while eyeballing us. "I wonder what they are going to do with him upstairs."

Steve and Jay were talking to each other and did not hear the remark. That exchange came to an abrupt halt when I went on a tirade in the best Spanish I could think of. "You don't know us. Who the hell do you think you are to dare say something like that! Not all Americans are the same, so save your bullshit for someone else!"

The faces of the two became as red as cherries. If they could have crawled into a corner at that very moment, they would have done so. "Lo siento mucho, senor.", (I'm sorry, mister) the one said repeatedly when she realized that this gringo spoke her language and was completely put off by her insensitive, damning accusation.

It was not until the three of us were inside the lobby that Steve said, "What the hell was that all about?"

When I recounted the details, I had to grab Jay's arm. Obviously, he was offended and intended to go back outside and add more to my intemperate barrage. "I think they got the message," I said as we led him into the elevator.

During our ride to the eleventh floor, it occurred to me that these women may have seen us with one or another of 'the boys'. Jay was young and looked Hispanic, even though his complexion was fair. Steve and I were well aware of the stereotypical labeling that made for juicy gossip, especially in our area which was one in which there was a high concentration of gay tourists. The rule of thumb, albeit misguided, was 'Older Americans plus young Hispanics equals sex.' True, there were numbers whose behavior validated the judgment, but it made our skin crawl to think that such was a widespread, generalized notion which lumped all gay Americans into the same category. In the case of these two women at least, they heard my message loud and clear!

Jay said little as he studied the apartment and added more notes to those he already had written. After taking measurements and our pointing out the electrical and plumbing projects, he handed us a written quote. "If this is okay with you guys, I can start work tomorrow."

His price was more than fair. This, coupled with our observations of what appeared to be a very professional work ethic, sealed the deal. There was one obstacle, however. Jay did not own a car and lived in Bayamon, a city that was a distance from ours. Our vehicle was in transport from the states, so Jay would have to use public transportation if he wanted to commence work immediately.

He asked if he could leave the few tools needed in our apartment in order to ease the headache of daily travel on two buses. We thought he would have opted to wait until our car arrived so we could drive him to pick them up from his apartment. Clearly, he was hungry for work and did not want to discourage us from rethinking our acceptance of his estimate.

As much as he liked to begin work in the early morning, he reminded us about the often 'not so efficient' bus schedules.

"Don't worry, Jay, whenever you get here is fine," Steve reassured him. "We just want to get the work started!"

Jay left us excited as well as reassured that our decision to hire him was a good one. I thought of something Nicky said earlier, "He's a little messed up," and asked Steve for his take on the remark.

"He doesn't seem to be, but we know Nicky … to him, everyone is messed up!"

The next morning, Jay arrived at nine-thirty carrying two weighty tool bags. Moments before, we received a call that our car had arrived from New York and was ready for pick up. "Before you can take your car, you have to call the Tax Department. They will give you instructions." We had been given a price quote from the New York transport company, so we were somewhat confused as to why it was necessary to contact the Taxation Department.

While I spoke to a representative, Steve and Jay enjoyed a cup of coffee on the terrace. Steve saw that my face became tight and heard a distinct elevation in my tone of voice. By the time that phone conversation concluded, my blood pressure was through the ceiling! No one in New York had informed us of the myriad fees not included in the price range of eight hundred to one thousand dollars to ship the car to Puerto Rico. When all was said and done, we faced a bill that totaled two thousand eight hundred fifty dollars.

Steve became pale when I gave him the less-than-good news. "We're going to have to take care of this today. The guy on the phone rattled off four different offices we have to go to before they will release the car. Is nothing easy?"

Jay smiled and said, "Welcome to Puerto Rico!"

We apologized to him for making the long trip for nothing, but this situation needed immediate attention. "I've been there before, so I'll go with you guys if you want. I'm here now, so I might as well do something." His words were a great relief to us. Not only did he know the procedure, he spoke fluent Spanish. Although he resisted our offer to pay him for going with us, we insisted that this was a condition to our acceptance of his kind suggestion.

The transport company was a quick cab ride from our neighborhood. That was the easiest part of the day! By the time we had all the stamped, signed documents needed to give us possession of our vehicle, it was noon. We entered yet another building and got in one of a number of lines that led to a payment window. Just as we were about to move forward, the clerk yelled, "Almuerzo" (lunch) and pulled down a shade. The other three workers followed suit and left a sizeable group of very agitated people in four different lines. We were given numbers in order to assure that we would not lose our place when the windows reopened in one hour … maybe!

Needless to say, Steve handled the inconvenience much better than I. "Calm down; it looks like the veins in your neck are going to burst."

"Don't get me started!"

"Please don't … the immediate world will hear you."

Steve always believed he had no sense of humor. His comment actually calmed me and made me laugh. He was right, there was nothing we could do to change a situation that was not worth my getting bent out of shape. At ten minutes past one, the security guard opened the door and allowed all of us to re-enter. I had anticipated a free-for-all, but things proceeded in a relatively orderly fashion, and we resumed our position in line.

Once our clerk got reorganized, we were out of there in less than two minutes. All she needed to do was to accept our check and stamp one of the documents. Cars were lined up in a parking area. Once we located ours, we had to find someone to drive it to the inspection area. Only one person was permitted to inspect the car along with an employee. If there was any damage, that was the time to report it. Once outside the gate, tough luck! Since Steve's name was on the paperwork, he was the lucky one. Jay and I stood about thirty feet away from the location and heard him speaking to the worker as he pointed to the rear bumper.

"What's wrong?" I yelled to Steve.

"The rear bumper is damaged." With that, the worker waved us on and we saw what Steve had been talking about. The bumper was not only dented in a number of places, there were deep gouges all across it. That two minutes at the payment window was too good to be true. We were required to fill out more paperwork and go to another office to file a claim. Luckily, pictures of the car had been taken at the transport company in New York. The claims person to whom we spoke attempted to insinuate that perhaps the damage had occurred prior to shipping.

"That is impossible!" I said with deliberate emphasis.

"How do I know, for sure, that the responsibility is not yours?"

"I'm telling you, the car was in perfect condition."

"You have to do better than that!"

I reveled in the moment I presented several Polaroid photos of the vehicle. Each was dated and initialed by the New York customer service representative. A second set was taken and maintained in our contract folder. That information made my argument airtight. Our car would be repaired at the expense of the Puerto Rico-based company. We were given a list of approved body shops from which to choose, but that would be kept for another day. Steve and I were completely out of gas and wanted to get out of there as fast as possible.

We returned to the site inspector and gave him a copy of the claim form. He countersigned it and handed the car keys to Steve. It was late afternoon when we finally pulled into our parking lot. Beverages were sorely needed! Since it was close to supper time, we invited Jay to join us for a bite to eat and told him we would be happy to drive him to Bayamon later that evening. The day had been harrowing, but it was not yet ended.

Jay had been given more than a glimpse of our personalities, especially mine, but we knew little about him. That was all about to change.

Jay lived in what we would call a walk-in apartment, the first floor of a multi-storied house. Before coming upon it, we seemed to have driven a circuitous route in and out of numbers of very narrow side streets, none of which was well-lighted. Loose dogs were about the only sign of life we saw. Quickly, we realized that he did not live in a very desirable neighborhood.

"Jay, we cannot thank you enough for being with us today," Steve said appreciatively as he handed him some money.

"I told you this was not necessary."

"… And we told you it was! Take it, please."

"Thanks, guys."

"Do you have anything else in the house that you'll need for work?"

"Just a few things."

"We'll take them now."

"Why don't you park and come in for a minute."

Three blocks later, we found a spot, then trailed behind him to the house. As we walked, I commented, "It's very quiet here."

Matter of factly, he said his neighbors never talk. Steve and I had no idea what he meant until he gave us the punch line. "There is a cemetery behind the houses."

The darkness made us uneasy, especially since dogs maintained squatter's rights wherever we looked. Now, we had to deal with the unsettling eeriness of knowing that a graveyard was a little too close for comfort. Neither the darkness, dogs nor cemetery mattered much, once we saw the literal hovel in which Jay lived. Steve and I were taken aback as he gave us a ten second tour of the interior. Lights hung from the ceiling on exposed wires. Within a very few minutes, we were sweating profusely; there was no air conditioning.

We heard a God-awful noise in the kitchen area. "Oh, that's the refrigerator. It doesn't work well and the freezer doesn't work at all." Apparently, Jay had become accustomed to the sporadic gasps of the compressor.

Water trickled from the sink faucet. "Feel this ... that's the cold water." It was lukewarm. "There is no hot water at all."

We observed fly paper and rodent traps everywhere as we made our way to a door that led to a back sitting area. "The cemetery ... it's not visible, is it?" I stammered.

This was the first moment of laughter from Jay. "No, there is a large wall ... you won't see anything." The yard was sizeable, probably the best part of all we had seen so far. A table with an umbrella stood in the center. Plants and flowers, although not well cared for, dotted the perimeter.

"Let me get the other tools for you. Stay out here; I'll be right back." As soon as Jay was out of sight, Steve and I looked at each other with the exact same thought. The place was deplorable and the conditions under which Jay 'existed' were below sub-standard.

"Are you thinking what I'm thinking?" Steve whispered.

"Yes! He can't stay here, sweat to death every night, travel on two buses and expect to have any energy to work … this is really horrific!" Our sofa bed had been used by others in need of a retreat from reality. Clearly, Jay desperately needed one, too.

Jay plopped a bag down on the pavement and asked if we wanted to sit for a few minutes. "I'd offer you something to drink, but there is only bottled water in the fridge and I don't know how cold it is."

"That's okay," I answered. "We can wait until we get home … speaking of home, Steve and I thought that rather than traveling such a distance every day, why don't you throw some clothes in a bag and stay at our apartment for as long as the job takes to complete. We have a sofa bed … we're sure you'll be comfortable."

Tears welled in his eyes and were accompanied by a shaky voice when he spoke. "That is awesome. I don't believe it … I'm finally going to get away from this hell hole for a while. The only reason I stay here is because the rent is cheap. I get work in your neighborhood, usually through Nicky, but that doesn't happen all the time … thank you so much, guys!"

At that moment, we did not realize Jay's acceptance of our offer would be the catalyst that would change his life forever.

By eight-thirty each morning, the breakfast dishes were washed and put away, and Jay was on the job. Unless he had a question or concern, he preferred not to converse while he worked. He was neat, meticulous and paid close attention to detail. Steve was delighted because Jay's work ethic provided a consistent calmness in the apartment. My OCD was in check and, as Steve frequently commented, "If Frank is calm, there's peace in the kingdom."

It did not take too long for us to notice how well Jay had adjusted to his new, though temporary, surroundings. That included his becoming very attached to our dog. Not part of his job description, he often volunteered to take her for a walk. Although her personality always had been aloof, she seemed to respond to him with affection. Whenever he took a break, he sat on the floor and played with her. Peaches became a very happy camper.

About one week into the project, Steve met Michelle D'Andrea, a neighbor, at the lobby entrance. She asked if he knew of anyone who painted and did other odd jobs. Steve told her about Jay and invited her to come to the apartment to meet him.

"I can do that right now, if it's all right with you." That introduction opened another door for Jay. While Michelle maintained an apartment in our building, she also owned two studios that were in another location close by. "They are unoccupied and in desperate need of face lifts," was her vivid description.

Jay explained that he was not available until the work at our place was completed but was eager to see them. He also informed her that he did not live in the neighborhood and that we were allowing him to stay with us.

"That's great. If you agree to take on the work, you can stay in one of the studio apartments." Her words were like manna from heaven!

Jay's excitement at hearing her offer was quite evident. "When can I see the apartments?" Jay asked with enthusiasm.

As Michelle began to respond, I interrupted her. "If you have a few minutes, Jay can go with you right now."

"Perfect! I'm leaving tomorrow and won't return for three weeks … if I can get everything in place today, it will be a huge relief."

Steve told Jay that he should take as long as needed with Michelle. "The work will be here when you get back."

About two hours later, the two returned. We knew all had gone well because there was laughter in the hallway as they walked from the elevator. Michelle mentioned how thorough Jay had been when taking notes in each of the studios and that she was impressed by the fact that he asked many questions just to be sure he understood her expectations.

"When do you plan to rent them?" Steve asked her.

"There is a large amount of work to do. I told Jay not to rush. Whenever he finishes one of the apartments, I'll rent it. Then, he can stay in the other while he gets it ready."

Steve and I sensed that Jay wanted to say something but seemed reticent to speak, so I pulled it out of him.

"Jay, did you want to say something?"

"Yeah … but … forget it … it's probably not possible."

"Just say what's on your mind. Michelle is here, so now is the time to ask any other questions or tell her any concerns you have."

His speech bordered stuttering as he admitted how much he liked the studios and how great it would be if he could rent one of them, but he did not think he could afford to live in our neighborhood.

"How much rent do you pay now, Jay?"

"Four hundred fifty dollars a month to live in a place where hardly anything works."

"What do you mean?"

"Ask the guys; they have seen it."

Michelle looked at us with an expression of confused inquiry.

"You describe it, Frank. You're much better with details than I am," Steve said with a slight chuckle.

I provided Michelle with a mental tour of what caused her complexion to grow pale. She then asked our opinion of Jay. It was an uncomfortable moment for him as he stood and listened to us relate our observations of his work as well as our gut feelings about his personality. His face became red as he tried to look anywhere but at us.

Then she directed herself to him. "Four hundred a month with the understanding that you'll take care of both apartments … forward rents to me, do repairs … things like that. What do you think?"

"It sounds too good to be true."

"If you don't want to give me an answer now…"

"Yes! Yes!" Jay blurted before Michelle could finish her sentence.

"Oh … first, last and security … forget all that since the guys spoke so well of you … I'm not here too often, so it is very important that I have responsible renters in my apartments."

Michelle handed Steve a wad of cash and requested that he hold it until Jay was ready to begin work in her studios, then told him to be sure he retained all purchase receipts.

"I'm glad I bumped into you, Steve."

"I am, too, but Jay looks even happier … funny how things happen sometimes!"

"Yeah, what a coincidence!"

"Frank calls it purpose and plan … there's a reason for everything … I believe that we are where we're supposed to be at any given time … this was meant to happen today."

"I think you're right," Michelle said with a tone that validated Steve's statement.

Michelle gave Jay two sets of keys. They exchanged cell phone numbers, shook hands and she moved toward the door.

"Call me anytime, Jay, if you have any questions. The three of you can ask around if anyone is interested in renting the second studio. I want to do this by recommendation only."

"We'll do that," Jay assured her.

After Michelle left, he came to us and hugged us so tightly he almost squeezed the breath out of us. "This is awesome," he repeated several times.

"Yes, it is," we responded together. Jay had been with us a short time and already had started to glimpse clear signs that his life was changing for the better.

We had met Jay on August 13th and by month's end, the work in our apartment was just about completed. All that remained to be done was the installation of two new ceiling fans; that could be done at any time. It was more important that Jay vacate his apartment in Bayamon before September's rent was due so he could roll up his sleeves and dig into Michelle's apartments. A single trip accomplished the task of packing up clothing and one small box of personal possessions. Since he had no lease, there was no problem when he informed the owner that he was moving out.

During the ride from Bayamon to our neighborhood, I asked him about the framed photographs he had packed. "Are they your parents and brother?"

His tone became solemn. "No, I'll tell you about them when we get to your apartment." My benign inquiry caused a look of concern on Steve's face and made me wonder if I had just opened a Pandora's box.

After dinner, Jay went to the box and removed three photographs. He brought them out to the terrace and set them on the table. "You wanted to know about these people," he sighed wistfully. For the next few hours, Steve and I were given an inside look at what had been Jay's life. Almost as if the details were ingrained in his consciousness, he shared recollections with precise chronology and vivid imagery. He began by explaining that the people in the photos were not his parents and brother but the family who raised him.

That commentary set the stage for taking us back to the beginning. He was born in Puerto Rico, had one sister and one brother. His mother was a kind, loving, very humble woman with whom Jay had a close relationship. His father's personality, however, caused him to have feelings of anger and resentment from an early age. His dad was a cruel man for whom 'machismo' was an essential component of manhood. Jay was a sensitive child and, apparently, his lack of overt boyishness irritated his father.

Verbal followed by physical abuse caused great emotional distress in the household. His mother was at a loss to do anything to correct the situation because, from all indications, she lived in fear of her bullish husband. We could see a visible change in Jay's face as he spoke in a markedly elevated tone of voice that all but spewed hatred for his father. There came a time when things so deteriorated that he had to get away from it all.

The people in the photographs were the family with whom Jay spent his teenage years … in California. That was about as far away from his father as he could get. He had thoughts of returning one day but when his mom passed away, that possibility was quickly abandoned. His life on the west coast was far better than on the island. While he had never been very close to his sister or brother when they were children, Jay got along well with the 'foster' family's son, a few years his junior.

For personal reasons, he and the family parted ways when Jay had passed his eighteenth birthday. He returned to the island, but not to his father's house. He found emotional support from his mom's parents and one of her sisters with whom he always had enjoyed a wonderful relationship. He made reference to living in Hawaii for a time but did not elaborate on when that occurred or for how long he remained there.

Abundantly clear to Steve and me was the reality that Jay had never established roots and had missed out on absorbing the essence of what comprised a normal, healthy family dynamic. He paused for a few moments and studied the photos as if he were looking right through them. Whatever images were flashing through his mind, they caused tears to glide down his cheeks.

"We can stop if you want to," Steve said with a tone of great sensitivity.

"No … I'm okay. That's pretty much the whole picture. I haven't talked about any of this in a long time … guess it just got to me … it's just that I've been on my own for a long time … I never really felt like I belonged to anyone."

Jay's last comment pierced our hearts and rendered us unable to listen to any more of the unsettling description. When I suggested that he put the photographs away, Jay could see the sadness evident on our faces and offered an apology because he thought he had upset us.

Steve looked directly into his glassy eyes. "There is no need to apologize. Your story did make us sad, but look at you now. Consider the changes that have occurred in a few short weeks. That is huge!" As Jay wiped the wetness from his face, a smile appeared. He said nothing, but it was evident that Steve's affirmation touched him.

This had been an interesting evening, to say the least, but there was more to come on the new road of Jay's travels. He would experience validation in ways unknown in the past. A new, more positive self-image was in sight. All he had to do was to recognize and embrace it with confidence.

Michelle called Jay to inform him that she was returning to Puerto Rico on October 5th. That was just days away and the news sent Jay into a literal panic. He was adamant that some of the work in 'his' studio would be completed prior to her reappearance, so during those first few days of the new month he worked between ten and twelve hours daily. The young man was on a mission! It was important to him that Michelle see visible progress when she walked into the apartment.

Steve and I had driven him there with his clothing, tool bags and special box, so we fully understood the necessity of his having to work long hours. The studio, though in infinitely better condition than had been his place in Bayamon, was in need of much attention. Michelle was absolutely on point when she remarked that face lifts were needed.

Of the two, Jay had chosen the one in need of less fixing up, but that wasn't saying much! Unlike the other, his contained walls that created a separation between the living area and bedroom. It was a nice touch that gave an impression of a small one bedroom dwelling. He had accomplished a great deal of work within a few days. Except for the bathroom, the place was painted. He was in the process of replacing all of the electrical outlets in the studio, so there were unsightly holes in the walls from which hung loose wires. He was concerned that she might not think enough had been done.

"Did Michelle not tell you there was no rush?" I reminded him before it appeared as though he was starting to hyperventilate. "Calm down … you're getting crazy for no reason. Jay, under no circumstances can you let Michelle see you so wired." This was the first time either of us had ever spoken to him with an emphatic tone.

He did not accept the comment well. He pouted like a little kid and threw things around. Another piece of his personality had just been revealed. His coping skills were poor. A situation that was not serious had caused him to become unraveled. Apparently, he heard castigation in my voice and recoiled from it with a childish outburst.

Steve and I became very alarmed. God forbid he should ever display such behavior in front of Michelle! She was a strong-willed, opinionated, in-your-face woman. How would Jay handle a not-so-sensitively stated criticism from her? I had cautioned him; that was all I could do. Before we left, each of us received a reluctant hug.

Steve never was one to put salt in the wound but felt that it was necessary to reemphasize my concern and ended with a few additional positive words. "Jay, you've done a great job. Michelle is going to be thrilled."

"Thank you for saying that," he came back while looking at me as if to hammer home a point — it's not what you say but how you say it that matters. Perhaps I had been somewhat short with him, but I was addressing an adult!

In the final analysis, Jay had worried for no reason. When Michelle stopped by to see us and collect receipts for the materials he had purchased, she was obviously pleased with his progress. In a very diplomatic manner, Steve brought up the incident at the studio. He focused more on Jay's determination, diligence and sense of responsibility but managed to include how unsettled he had become by my remark. "He wants so to please you," Steve said.

"I really want him to relax and take his time … he doesn't need to get upset about anything … I'll talk to him," she said.

Steve was not sure how to field her last comment and concluded the conversation, "That might be a good idea. He really needs to hear how well he is doing. I know you'll handle things well with him."

Michelle thanked us, again, for connecting her with Jay. "I'll be here for two weeks. I'm sure we'll see each other."

"Stop by any time," Steve offered.

I wasn't sure how I felt about their brief exchange. I never had been a hand-holder and found the strategy-like conversation unsettling. I, for one, had no intention of walking on eggshells if something needed to be said to Jay at any time he might be doing work for us. The truth be told, my guard was up. Steve and I had played good cop, bad cop when our kids were young. The thought of having to role play with a young man sickened me.

Later that afternoon, Jay appeared at our door carrying one of his tool bags. I was in the bedroom but could hear Steve talking to him. When I came out, I was greeted with a broad smile and a more endearing hug. Needless to say, I was confused. Jay apologized for his reaction and said that Michelle had spoken to him. After briefly summarizing their conversation he said, "Michelle told me that you guys really care about me and that I should listen to your advice, no matter what it is."

Before I could say anything, Steve answered, "Yes, Jay, we do care about you and we would never give you bad advice." That was that and the situation was put to rest.

Jay asked where the fans were. Since he had finished his work at the studio and it was still relatively early, he wanted to complete the last leg of his work with us.

"Can you stay for dinner?" Steve asked.

"Sure. You are such a great cook!"

It was fine with me that the two seemed to be members of a mutual admiration society, but I was not quite ready to join the ranks. During the course of our meal, Jay mentioned that, while Michelle was at the studio, the air conditioner died. She called and ordered a new one but delivery and installation would not occur for three days.

"You can sleep here," Steve quickly responded. Jay looked at me sheepishly.

"Is that okay with you, Frank?"

"Sure, Peaches loves to see you." His question was an obvious acknowledgment that he was aware of my irritation with his stunt. My answer, while not directly addressing his concern, let him know that he was welcome.

The new air conditioner was installed, *five* days later. During that time, an unexpected issue occurred with our dog. One morning, Steve noticed a large jump protruding from her left flank. It was not there the day before. We immediately took her to our veterinarian who made an immediate diagnosis. She had a cancer called Mast Cell Malignancy. It was common in Cocker Spaniels; the median age of dogs who developed it was eight. That was exactly her age. We were quite distressed because she had been with us since she was a pup of twelve weeks.

As sad and worried as we were, Jay was a wreck. Once the surgery was completed and we brought her home, Jay visited each and every day. Within weeks, the situation went from bad to worse. Another lump developed and a second, more radical surgery needed to be performed. Neither of us was emotionally prepared for the outcome. She had been in Stage 2 the first time. Now, the diagnosis was Stage 4. The odds of survival were less than twenty-five percent and the time span was, at most, six months.

We were teary but Jay was hysterical when we told him that we had decided not to allow the vet to do any follow up treatment. It was he who planted the seed of doubt when he postured, "What about if the treatment works?" It's ironic that our vet posed the same question. We finally agreed to injections which, hopefully, would kill any stray cells not removed during surgery.

Following a protocol that lasted for several weeks, Dr. Hernandez told us that he felt confident the treatments had worked. Although recuperation was slow, we could see steady improvement day by day. The state of her health gave rise to another concern. We already had booked our holiday trip to New York. Peaches always had traveled with us, but that wasn't going to be the case this time. We knew of no place at which to board her and she was too fragile to be sedated in a cage that sat in the belly of an airplane for more than three hours.

This came up in conversation with Jay one day. "I'll take care of her," he announced without hesitation and added, "If you don't mind, I'll stay here with her so she'll be comfortable in her own home." Our dilemma was resolved.

The weeks must have sprouted wings because they flew by and before we knew it, the holiday season knocked at our door. Jay was settled, more or less, in his new surroundings. He had worked diligently and progress in the second studio apartment was noticeable. He was anxious to ready it for occupancy since Michelle was in possession of the names of two prospective renters who had been recommended by him. This was our first Thanksgiving as residents of the island.

What might have been the advent of a sad day of separation from our families became one we looked forward to with excitement. Danny, Maria and Frances (my son, daughter-in-law and granddaughter) were coming from New York to spend the holiday with us. Maria's dad, John, planned to travel with them in order to attend to family business. We were fairly certain that Jay had no place to go, so we extended an invitation which he readily accepted.

More than Steve, I was concerned about how the social dynamic would play out on that day. During the past months, we had observed Jay at happy hour. When I thought about the prospect of his being with my family on Thanksgiving Day, different scenarios flashed through my mind. If he happened to be in a good mood, he would display a charming, endearing personality. If there was the slightest chance he thought others found him amusing, the campy side of him might pop out. My greatest fear was that if he drank to excess and any one of us made a comment or voiced an opinion with which he took umbrage, the result might be a nasty, belligerent altercation. The odds were one in three that he would put his best foot forward and maintain a semblance of decorum. Steve was infinitely more confident than I.

A few days before my family arrived, I wanted to speak to Jay about my concerns. Remembering how he flew off the handle at the studio weeks earlier, Steve offered to do the deed for me. He realized that if I attended to this task myself, my choice of words might not come out the right way and Jay, no doubt, would have decided to remain alone on the holiday. That would have upset us greatly. My diplomatic Steve took the lead and had a little pow-wow with Jay on Tuesday afternoon. He was all smiles when he returned from happy hour. I was not sure whether this was prompted by a successful conversation or by a number of 'beverages'!

"Jay promised to be on his best behavior," he proudly announced.

"That's all he said?"

"What more did you want him to say?" Steve elaborated a bit, probably just to shut me up. I listened to his words with tentative confidence and would have no choice but to assume a posture of 'wait and see'.

"Happy Turkey Day, Gampa and Uncle Steve," were the first greetings of the holiday. Who better to announce them than my precious pumpkin, Frances, who had not yet reached her third birthday. No fancy breakfast that morning; there was much to do before we sat down to enjoy the feast. Everyone pitched in and made the prep work much less cumbersome than we remembered it being in New York.

Late that morning, Danny and John took Frances for a walk. Maria remained behind to help Steve in the kitchen and I began the process of setting the holiday table. I heard Steve yell, "Oh shit! We forgot to buy turnips." Off they went to the supermarket. Not long after, Jay arrived. He was in an upbeat mood and full of smiles. This was a good thing, but could he hold it together for an entire day?

Jay was in the bathroom when the entire group returned at the same time. Steve's ranting in the hallway was quite audible, "Seven freaking dollars for a turnip … that's outrageous."

Maria entered the apartment with teary laughter as he continued voicing his annoyance … "He's been complaining about this since we checked out," she attempted to verbalize.

Danny took out his video camera and egged Steve on. "Tell us what happened at the supermarket." Steve's look of extreme irritation became a belly laugh and sent the rest of us into hysterics.

Just then, Jay emerged from the bathroom. The camera directly on him, he pranced to the dining room doorway, threw his hands up in the air and, in nothing less than the extreme of a queenish voice announced, "Hi! I'm the handyman."

"Go on," Danny encouraged him. He put on quite a show and they all loved it! So much for maintaining decorum! I realized at that moment, the day was going to unfold as it would and not as I envisioned it should.

Little Frances was taken with Jay's dramatics and giggled every time he said something. Danny and Maria thought he was a ton of fun. Even Maria's dad, a straight-as-a-pin kind of guy, found humor in the antics of the moment. Absent of showmanship, it was time to confront the reality of the day, the reason for which we were together and gathered around the table.

As if shifting car gears, Jay became noticeably quiet. Given what we knew about his history, we were concerned not only about how the significance of this holiday would affect him, but also how he would react to being in a family setting. From the onset of the meal, there were moments when he seemed detached from all of us. As he listened to the prayer I offered, the words family, love, unity, grace and blessings brought tears to his eyes. We wondered if they were prompted by a warm sense of belonging, of being a part of, or by the stark reminder that they were missing in his life.

More than once, we watched as he scrutinized affectionate exchanges among Danny, Maria and our irresistible cutie pie, Frances. His facial expression gave testament that this witnessing of familial closeness was alien to him. Jay was cordial but guarded when he spoke to John, a strong, vocal, macho Puerto Rican man. There were moments when his face became as red as it had been that night he described the deeply-rooted disdain he harbored toward his own dad.

Then there was the relationship of thirteen years which Steve and I relished. We joked with each other, spoke with respect to one another and were unashamedly demonstrative in expressing our mutual affection. Time and time again, Jay felt the tranquility in our home and the atmosphere of warmth and welcome that pervaded it. We were aware that he never had a relationship of duration and had once told us, "I want what you guys have."

That was a very tall order where Jay was concerned because, from all we had seen and heard during these past months, it was abundantly clear that he was ill-equipped to conform to the expectations of commitment.

The basic tools of communication, compromise and healthy coping skills, the cornerstone of our life together, were missing links in his. At the end of the day, Jay extended a warm 'thank you' and tight embrace to each of us. We could only hope he thought it was a better decision to be with us than to have remained alone and not be moved to recollections that churned his emotions.

Friday was to be a beach day. We were still stuffed from the day before, so movement was slow and sluggish. By the time we set foot on the sand, it was eleven-thirty. Although the weather was agreeable and we had the benefit of an ocean breeze, this was the time of day when the sun's rays began to increase in intensity. At one-thirty, I suggested that we retreat to the deck of Tornado for some refreshments as well as relief from the uncomfortable heat. Since the hour was early, we were the only ones in the bar. This was a good thing! We did not want to deal with brassy queens or any of 'the boys' who, no doubt, would have approached us. Although none appeared, Jay did and we were given a more in-depth view of his theatrics. He stepped on the stage and, as music blasted from mammoth speakers, he flailed about to the beat of a pulsing rhythm.

Maria had majored in Psychology and was a scrupulous analyzer of behavior. Not intending to be judgmental but with genuine sincerity she said, "He's a great guy but he has issues."

I did not want to give too specific a response and betray the confidence he had placed in Steve and me, but I knew my daughter-in-law would prod and poke until she got an answer. "Yes, he has some issues. His life has not been a walk in the park, but he's trying so hard to better himself."

Just then, Jay stepped off the stage dripping in sweat. He plopped down and immediately engaged Danny and Maria in conversation.

Our little one was becoming restless. Holding her hand, we walked around and came to the stairs that led to the upper quarters. Ascending on each side were gorgeous poinsettias that led to a winter background at the top. This became a photo op for Frances. Assuming a number of different poses, she relished the attention and hammed it up.

Jay thought the whole thing was great. Why wouldn't he? He knew well what it meant to be the center of attention amid a captive audience. The difference was that the affected behavior of the little one was a product of childhood's innocence. His was clearly a compensation for recollections of its unhappiness.

Since Steve had prepared enough food the day before to feed an army, we invited Jay to join us for left-overs. While he was more subdued than earlier, he managed to find ways to make our stomachs ache from laughter. I nonchalantly mentioned to him that Saturday was going to be a family day and hoped he got the message. Steve and I wanted some alone time with the kiddies before their return to New York on Sunday.

Not yet seven o'clock, I was alone on the terrace the next morning. From behind me, I heard a sleepy, squeaky voice. "Hi, Gampa." I hoisted Frances up, sat her on my lap and we looked out at the lagoon. For one so young, she was quite verbal. Not only did she speak in complete, well-formed sentences, she obviously had inherited her mom's acute power of observation.

Imbued with the expanse before her, she pointed to it and said, "Look, Gampa, someone is in the water." I was aghast when I realized what she was looking at. A dead body had drifted to our end of the lagoon. Immediately, I brought her inside and closed the terrace doors. "That is a person, right?" I tried to dissuade her by saying it was probably a towel or sheet that had fallen in. "No, no, Gampa, I'm right!" Maria came out from the bedroom and Frances made the announcement, "Mommy, there is a person in the water!"

Maria went out to view for herself what she thought would be a swimmer. "Maybe he is learning how to float," she said.

"Mommy … he looks dead!" Clearly, the explanations we offered did not cut the mustard with Frances.

Steve was in the bathroom when Danny appeared, looking as if he would have loved more sleep. Steve came and stood next to him and they were given the news as well. "Daddy, Uncle Steve, someone is dead in the water."

Maria picked up Frances and moved to the kitchen. "Help mommy make coffee."

I slowly opened one of the sliding doors so the little miss would remain undistracted while Danny and Steve viewed the scene. By that time, there were a number of police cars and an ambulance at the site.

Maria was busy in the kitchen and did not notice that Frances was not with her until she heard, "I told you so … I told you so." What a little sneak she was! We had no idea she had been standing behind us.

"Go to mommy," Danny said abruptly then closed the door.

She was persistent and began to tap on the glass. "I want to see more." The longer we ignored her, the more perturbed she became. Gentle tapping turned into loud knocking. She was really beside herself and looked so cute when she pouted, but that did not last for long.

"Show Grandpa and Uncle Steve how you dance." Danny's shrewd maneuver worked. Steve moved aside the coffee table and I put in a CD. Not only did she spin around with deliberate movement and precise rhythm, she sang along as Cher belted out, 'Do you believe ...'. The remainder of that day was uneventful ... thank God! The only task left was to pack suitcases in preparation for an early flight on Sunday morning.

The five days my family spent with us were ones we'll never forget. Whether he realized it or not, Jay played an important role in making for a memorable holiday. His affable nature, non-offensive zaniness and a surprising ability to touch the hearts of Danny, Maria and little Frances were his gifts to them. They were smitten by the better part of who Jay was. In return, their presence afforded him a greater insight into the essence of family and celebration. More importantly, maybe for the first time in his life, he grasped that Thanksgiving is not only an isolated day each year but also a deeply rooted emotion that contributed to life's fullness.

During the next weeks, we readied ourselves for the holiday trip to New York. If ever there was a time we wished it possible to have remained on the island, this was the year. As much as we looked forward to being surrounded by loved ones and friends, our hearts were heavy when we thought about 'the boys of the street,' Annie and now Jay. Of all of them, Emily was the strongest, but we'd miss her nonetheless.

It was impossible for us to unpack the suitcases of our emotions or to snap our fingers and make all of them go away. That would have made it much easier to enjoy Christmas. That was not the reality however. All we could do was to pray that they would find some measure of happiness, no matter how small, and for that one day unlike all others, their burdens might be lightened. We decorated our apartment because Jay was going to be staying with Peaches. We did not want this festive time of year to go unnoticed or unfelt by him.

He stopped by the day before our flight to pick up keys and go over a list of reminders we had prepared. Most important was the pooch's medication schedule. She had progressed well during the months following the two cancer surgeries but it was essential that our vet's protocol be followed. The refrigerator was well stocked with food and the cabinets with snacks.

"The girl will be fine," Jay assured us. Then he added, "We're going to have a great Christmas together."

We were grateful for his obvious love, but found his remark a sad commentary on the lack of friendships in his life. I went to the bedroom while Steve reviewed a list of phone numbers, just in case!

I returned with some wrapped gifts and set them beside the tree in two piles. "These are for Peaches," I said pointing to those on the left. The others are for you." Jay had shown himself to be an overly sensitive, emotional guy, so for us to observe crocodile tears from him was no surprise. Any gesture of kindness, no matter how small, usually produced this response from him.

So he would be sure what I was about to say was meant with affection and not as an order, I smiled cheek to cheek. "DNOTC."

"What does that mean?"

"Do not open till Christmas."

That brought him back and the tears subsided. He gave each of us a huge hug while saying, "Felicidades!" We responded in kind, then he bent down and gave the pooch a kiss on her head. "See you tomorrow morning, girl."

We returned to Puerto Rico during the days between Christmas and New Year's Eve. We had learned from prior experience that cold weather did not agree with us, especially Steve. There was great truth to the notion that, after being in a given climate for a period of time, the body adjusts itself. We were definitely warm weather guys because we were freezing in New York even though some days were moderate. In December, temperatures in the forties and fifties were considered comfortable in the Big Apple. Not so for us!

Jay was at the apartment when we got there. He was unusually animated. We thought it was because he was happy to see us. "Thank you, thank you!" he yelled.

Assuming he was referring to the Christmas gifts we had left for him Steve responded, "Just a few things we thought you could use."

That was not the cause of his excitement, even though we knew he was appreciative. During our absence he became acquainted with Barbara, Rafael and "Mommy," our next door neighbors. In conversation with Barbara one day, she mentioned that her apartment rental business had grown substantially and she was looking for a full time handyman. Although we had never spoken to her about Jay, she had passed by several times, in route to her apartment and observed him working in ours. Apparently, she had been pleased with what she saw and hired him.

"When do you start?"

"I already started." he answered me. This was a tailor made situation for Jay because the condominiums in which she administered apartments were local and within walking distance.

Once Jay got on a roll, we did not see him too often. Unless there was a reason which brought him to Barbara's apartment, weeks could pass with no sign of him. We did speak on the phone and if he had an early day, he'd drop by for supper or meet us at Tornado for happy hour but those occasions were few and far between. Barbara kept him quite busy.

We knew that she would be more and more impressed as she became familiar with Jay's work ethic. He was punctual, thorough and exhibited a personal code of responsibility which made clear the fact that he did not shy away from any task. Barbara's personality was much like mine. Organized and methodical, she paid close attention to detail. The difference between us was that she was infinitely more refined at what Steve and I refer to as the diplomacy of criticism.

Steve and Rafael were the gentle, kindly souls in the group. Of course, they were more Jay's cup of tea! The combination of our four personalities presented Jay with a broad spectrum through which he was being well-schooled both professionally and personally. He was learning about time management and the establishing of priorities. The challenge which faced him, however, was his ability to become a multi-tasker while keeping his wits about him. It had been proven that his coping skills were not well-developed.

Although he knew the words authority, demands and expectations, the real test would be the manner in which he responded to all three at the same time. Steve and I knew, with certainty, that this was going to be his greatest struggle. Jay was not without an oasis however. With the passing of time, he became close to Barbara's mother and developed an affectionate closeness with her. How could he not? It was impossible not to love this elderly, wise woman. Clearly, she represented abuela (grandma) to Jay and gave him a quality of tenderness that helped him to remain balanced. His head was in a very good place for the first time in years!

Jay was one of our guests for Easter dinner. That was the day of the teary episode when Annie was unable to make a toast. He did better at this gathering than had been the case at Thanksgiving. There were a number of contributing factors. He knew everyone we had invited. He was well-established in his apartment and had completed work in the second of Michelle's studios. He had a full time job which greatly reduced his anxiety about how to get all of the bills paid. He appeared more self-assured and poised, and that was a good thing!

There came a time when, once again, he and Peaches would spend quality time together. In conversation with another neighbor whose name was George, he mentioned that he had purchased a home in Florida. Steve and I had never visited that state and were quite agreeable when he offered to show us photos of his home and the surrounding community.

Once we looked at them, we decided to make plans for a trip. We inquired about the proximity of hotels, but he insisted that we stay at his home. We never could have imagined or predicted the outcome of that jaunt across the ocean. We arrived in Florida on October 15, 2000 and by the time we returned to the island one week later, we had news that would change life yet again.

Given all we have explained, in detail, about our love of the island and all of the careful deliberations prior to moving there, it may seem strange that only seventeen months after picking up roots and re-establishing ourselves fifteen hundred miles away from them, we were back in the states. The causes were mentioned earlier, but more detail is needed to put our decision into clear perspective.

One of the issues that had begun to weigh heavily upon us was the emotional toll our 'ministry of the street' had taken. We were drained and felt the physical consequences acutely. We had shed buckets of tears, spent many sleepless nights and became increasingly frustrated because we were not able to do more, particularly where the 'boys' were concerned. We had emptied ourselves to the point where we were neglecting our relationship.

We always have taken pride in the firm substance of our life together, but when it began to experience emotional hiccups, it was time to have some heart to heart discussions. During one such 'love talk', I explained to Steve a concept I had learned during my spiritual formation for Diaconal Ministry. Each of us exercises what is called fundamental option, the choice to be other-oriented or self-oriented. Obviously, I missed the part of that discussion which addressed the need to maintain a balance. Our scale weighed heavily on the side of our need to help others. The dish on the opposite side just dangled and swayed freely because it was empty. We were incapable of helping 'a little' or understanding 'to some extent' and we knew if we continued in our efforts, one or both of us was going to become very ill.

Health was the second barrier to our remaining on the island. The number of physicians who were participating providers in our health insurance plans were few, very few, and not ones in the specialty areas we needed. The result was astronomical out of pocket expenses followed by embarrassingly poor reimbursement. By chance, we came upon a climate in Florida that was much like that of Puerto Rico. For Steve more than me, this was a vital necessity. We seized the moment and made a decision that would, no doubt, exact gut-wrenching emotional upset when the reality set in, and more when we closed the door to the place we called home … for the very last time.

The flight back to the island was as bumpy as what was going on inside us. The bottom line, all things considered, we knew the right decision had been made, but that did not alleviate the emotional nagging that made us feel like we were copping out, abandoning those we cared about and showing concern only about ourselves. We knew things would improve once we put a handle on the situation but, at that moment, we had no clue when that would happen.

Jay knew something was not right as soon as he saw us. We thought we could get away with the bumpy ride excuse, but it did not work. He hounded us until we relented and explained what had occurred in Florida.

"Oh, God … no!", he screamed and, of course, then came the tears.

We were not too steady ourselves and his visible distress set us off. "You'll come and visit us," Steve sobbed as he put his head on Jay's shoulders. Each of us took a few deep breaths and began to settle down. Of course, a beverage helped too!

"Do you have a lot of work to do in the house?" Jay queried.

"It needs much more than Botox or plastic surgery," I answered, hoping to lighten the moment.

"It's that bad?"

Steve, better able to envision a completed project, handled Jay's question. "When it's finished, it will be very nice. An elderly woman owned the house. When she became ill, she let it go … there's quite a bit to do, but we'll get it done. The first things we have to do are to remove carpets and get the place painted. We're hoping someone can recommend workers … other than George, we know no one."

Jay looked at us as if we were missing something. "Hello! What about me? Why don't I go with you. I can take up the rugs, paint, do some minor electrical and plumbing work and help you with anything else you need done." Jay's suggestion was quite tempting, but he did have a full time job. He could not come and go as he wished.

"What about work … how will Barbara feel about this?" I asked.

"I'll talk to her. How long do you think the work will take?"

"If we really push, three weeks should be enough to accomplish the most important jobs."

Jay felt confident that Barbara would be agreeable; we were not so sure! "Does that mean if she's okay with it, I'll be going to Florida with you?"

"I guess it does."

As much as we wanted to begin the process of packing boxes, it was an impractical idea. We had to show the apartment to prospective buyers and were aware that the visual appeal that created a first impression was very important. On December 9th, a contract of sale was signed, but we did not rush to begin preparations because Christmas was around the corner. We decorated, as usual, because we needed to be surrounded by a little festiveness.

Once the holidays passed, we had until January 18th to get it all together. We did everything without too much stress because we knew the drill. It had been less than eighteen months since we packed up our life, so the myriad details of process and procedure were fresh in our minds.

Jay worked things out with Barbara and would be with us as we began yet another chapter in our journey together. In a strange way, he represented a link to all the others who had become part of the fabric of our lives. This made the transition far less emotionally daunting than it might have been. Jay was the figurative vessel which carried each and all of them across the ocean, far from the sand and surf of our Isla Del Encanto.

To say that those first weeks in the Florida home was a supreme test of endurance is to understate the degree of anxiety and tension which we experienced. Almost from the beginning, Jay and I butted heads about when and how to do the mountain of work we faced. He wanted to sleep in each morning and follow a less structured daily time frame. He had the impression that the sequence of projects would be his decision. Wrong on both counts!

He must have made a deliberate effort to keep the lid on his behavior when working for Barbara because it literally flew off the pot while he was with us. Argument after argument, one tantrum after another, Jay and I became like oil and vinegar. He displayed an arrogance which we never had witnessed on the island. When it popped out, it was ugly and enraged me all the more. Steve spent day after day in the role of peace keeper. His efforts, while noble, were an abysmal failure. The morning of his birthday was the icing on the cake. Jay bitterly opposed having to give the living and dining room ceilings another coat of paint and said so with belligerent resistance. I exploded, causing Steve to storm out of the house while yelling, "Happy fucking birthday!" Jay stopped in his tracks, shocked by this uncharacteristic outburst. Without another word, he mixed the paint and climbed the waiting ladder.

Steve returned two hours later. He looked directly at Jay with extreme irritation. "I ate my birthday breakfast alone because I had to get away from this constant fighting. If it continues, I'm going to a hotel until the work is finished." Without apology, Jay turned and continued painting.

That became the quietest day thus far and the remaining three until Jay's departure followed suit. On my part, there was no sadness in his leaving because he had literally plucked my last nerve. Steve, on the other hand, displayed predictable warmth when saying goodbye to him. About a week later George, having returned from Puerto Rico, stopped by our house.

"I saw Jay at the bar."

"What about it?" I asked with an intemperate tone.

"He's telling everyone that you guys did not pay him for the work he did for you."

"Did you believe him?"

"Of course not, but there were some who did."

Knowing that George made frequent trips, I gave him an unedited account of what had occurred from the first day we stepped into our new home. I was sure that this information would be carried across the ocean and eventually get back to Jay. It was incredible to think that he, no matter how bent out of shape, would have the audacity to conjure such a lie. That was the last straw, so we thought!

Well over a year later, I heard a knock at the door one afternoon. It was Jay. My first impulse was to slam the door in his face, but that would have made my reaction as childish as his had been. He looked contrite and struggled to find words. Obviously, he had come for a reason, so I invited him inside. He was quick to compliment the renovations which gave our home a completely new appearance.

At that moment, Steve was resting. "We have company," I whispered, not wanting to startle him.

"Who is it?"

"Jay."

"You're kidding!"

"Would I kid about something like that?"

Steve roused himself quickly and, together, we returned to the living room. Thinking he was the same soft touch, Jay embraced Steve with a hug. Without reaction, Steve stood like a statue and Jay felt the chill in the air. While he made no mention of what George had reported to us, everything about his behavior clearly indicated that he knew we were aware of his slanderous misrepresentation.

"What brings you to Florida?" Steve asked with detached concern.

"I live here now. I'm renting a two bedroom house."

"Good for you," he responded with a sarcastic edge.

It was a very awkward situation for all of us. It probably would have been wiser for us to confront Jay, but that, in all likelihood would have caused another battle to ensue. I did not want to risk Steve's becoming upset for the sake of principle. We had a few cocktails and chatted about 'bread and butter' nonsense. There wasn't anything of substance left to discuss with him.

"I want you guys to see my place," he said as if he had been with us yesterday and all was well in paradise. The 'beverages' obviously tempered our agitated dispositions because we accepted his invitation.

As much as I still wanted to read him the riot act, Steve was more rational. "It's over and done with … let it go."

That was a clear message that nothing was to be brought up when we visited him the next afternoon. Jay was so proud as he took us on a tour of his ample home. He had made great strides since his days in Bayamon. For that, we were happy. He made each of us a drink, placed a platter of cheese and crackers on the coffee table and sat on a chair across from where we were seated on the couch.

"What's been going on in your life?" Steve asked. For the remainder of that visit Jay told us about Tom, his boyfriend. In his early forties, a few years older than Jay, Tom owned a construction company. Apparently, he had done very well because he was already semi-retired and spent time traveling between Florida and New York where his two grown sons lived. His wife had died at an early age and he had raised them alone.

"He's a little stubborn and tries to boss me around, but this is my house and no one is going to tell me what to do!" Was he stating a declaration of independence or reminding me of my unyielding posture in the past?

Steve caught the innuendo and shot me a look with eyes that said, "Don't say a word!"

Tom was to arrive back in Florida within the next few days. Jay was anxious for us to meet him and said he'd call us to make a date.

From the first moment we met Tom a week later, we were uneasy. A hunky, good-looking guy, it was immediately evident that he was self-absorbed and possessed a dominant personality. Jay moved about as if he were a guest in his own home, a blatant contradiction to his remark days earlier. His left cheek looked swollen and discolored.

Realizing there was no ice in the house, Tom offered to get some from a nearby supermarket. That is when Steve asked Jay what had happened to his face. "We had a fist fight … it's not the first time, either." Before Tom returned, Jay gave us a condensed summary of their already tumultuous relationship.

What was that young man thinking? Clearly, he had chosen a partner who was every bit a clone of his father! Experiencing this epiphany, we watched closely the interaction of the two after Tom returned. It was cordial but not close. The conversation focused exclusively on Tom. There was not a hint of tenderness in his voice, instead it was full of a boastful arrogance which left us cold. Requests were made as statements of demand. For a relationship so new, all the signs pointed in one direction. As a couple, they already were on their way to hell in a hand basket.

On two other occasions they invited us to dinner parties at which were other friends. The routine was the same. Tom said "jump," and Jay responded, "how high?" Everyone saw that Jay was excessively tense and outwardly uncomfortable with Tom's pushiness. If we were never in Tom's company again, it would be no loss. It was intolerable for us to see Jay act like a cross between a puppet and a trained dog!

Shortly after the second gathering, Jay called us. He was crying hysterically. "Stay where you are; we'll be right there," I said frantically.

The front door was ajar and we entered unannounced. Jay was sitting on a chair with an ice pack pressed against his eye. "Sweet Jesus," I gasped. "What did he do to you?" His eye was so swollen, he could barely open it. At that very moment all the anger, frustration, stress, tension and hurt of the past meant nothing because deep within the recesses of our hearts, we never had stopped caring about Jay's well-being. He sobbed so, we thought he was going to choke on his tears. That made it difficult for us to catch every word of what was a ghastly description.

He and Tom had an all-out brawl. After Tom pummeled him, Jay told him to get out and not to return … ever. "Your fucking clothes will be on the street waiting for you."

"You cannot stay here," I said with urgency. "Pack a bag right now. We have to get you away from the house in case he returns." Jay knew, by my insistent tone, that we were not making this a matter of choice.

Within ten minutes, we had him in our car and were headed to the safety of our home. After arriving, it looked as if the swelling had worsened. His eye was completely shut. The skin around the eye orbit was black and blue. He resisted our suggestion to go to the emergency room of a nearby hospital because he had no health insurance.

We knew that excuse was bogus. He did not want to reveal the truth of the matter, implicate Tom and live in fear of worse repercussions. That was the bottom line! Jay was beside himself for most of that afternoon. In a repetitious cycle that became predictable after a short span of time, he lapsed back and forth between quiet and hysterical outbursts. It took a few hours for him to finally settle down and have an uninterrupted conversation.

"He keeps telling me he's going to change, then he does it again!"

"What does that tell you?" Steve asked pointedly.

"I love him."

"Obviously, then, you don't love yourself!" This was a very different Steve. Never, had he spoken to Jay so candidly and with no regard for his feelings. Jay needed a huge wake up call and, this time, Steve was the one who gave him a dose of tough love.

"He's not going to change," Steve continued. "This situation is going to get worse and worse."

"But he said he would try."

"Then why did you kick him out of the house?"

"I've done that before, but he knows I'll take him back."

"Listen to yourself, Jay. You sound pathetic!" Steve was on a roll and continued with a less than flattering assessment of the situation. I sat, speechless, and watched him force Jay to drink from the cup of reality.

"You don't love him, you need him. He has money and can make life easy, so you think. Is this what you call an easy life? Are you willing to let him beat you just so you can have nice things? Wake up and grow up!"

All during Steve's monologue, Jay's cell phone rang repeatedly. Following this summation by Steve, Jay answered. It was Tom. As if nothing had happened, Jay's calm, affectionate tone resumed and sickened us. Steve and I left the family room to give Jay privacy and also because listening to him was unbearable.

"If he wants to go home, let him," I said with firmness. "We have done our part, but this is it … if he wants to be with that maniac, it is his choice. We really cannot be involved with him any longer."

"You're absolutely right," Steve agreed readily.

After about twenty minutes of our overhearing one side of the conversation, Jay told us that Tom was coming to pick him up. All that needed to be said, had been said. Steve told Jay that because of his decision to return to a completely dysfunctional relationship, one that was a grave threat to his safety and well-being, we needed to separate from the situation now and forever.

"We cannot watch this go on," I added.

Unmoved by our comments Jay said, "I'll just wait outside."

As he moved to the door, I called to him. "If you remember nothing else, remember these words … after a while, there are no more victims; there are only volunteers."

Lady Peacock

12

As if they were aware that this was a special night, clusters of stars and a full moon were clearly visible in the blackness and provided an enticing setting. A cool brisk breeze whistled through the interior with modulating sounds easily imitated by one's voice. Every so often, excited gusts forced a crescendo in the overture. This imagery of nature's gift was short-lived, however, once the splintery deck rail became host to a seamless mass of onlookers that extended from one end of it to the other. The human barrier interrupted the flow and obscured the otherwise expansive view. The rest were huddled in tight formation around a make-shift stage that rose about eighteen inches above the planked floor.

Weekend shows, a relative novelty at the remodeled establishment, usually drew a sizeable crowd but this gathering was unique. Steve and I were part of the vacuum-packed can of sardines. We knew it was going to be an extraordinary event, so the decision to arrive extra early proved to be a wise one. Even at that, well over an hour before the festivities were scheduled to begin, there was a steady flow of men who, like we, wanted to stake out a prime spot.

While most of those already inside milled around in pockets of gab and gossip, we scoped out a table for two very close to the focal point. Steve claimed it while I negotiated a path to the bar. Not two, not three, but four bartenders scurried about in an attempt to keep pace with drink orders that were being thrown at them from every direction. By the time I held a filled glass in each hand, the number of show goers had multiplied substantially and presented an even greater challenge for the return trip. I moved slowly, deliberately, as body parts rubbed against me while I pressed through a thick sea of human flesh.

All at once, a path opened when numbers of those engrossed in chit-chat realized the hour was at hand. They scrambled to the few remaining, unoccupied tables. Tough luck for those who were less agile; it was SRO!

Nine o'clock … show time. The lights dimmed, a gradual hush came over the place, then there was a pause. That's when the remaining talking and laughter became more and more muffled, like sounds traveling farther and farther away from a point of origin. Then, dead silence.

Muted strains of an instrumental selection filtered from the speakers as the spotlight beamed across center stage to its destination and illuminated the staircase and balcony-like platform at its top. The melodic tones became more audible but not so loud as to rob the headliner of an introduction long anticipated. A deep, resonant celebrity-like voice became partner to the music that already had mesmerized more than one hundred gay men. "And now … for the very first time on the stage of Tornado … put your hands together for the diva of drag … Lady Peacock."

There was an explosion of applause as she came out form the shadows and stood at the head of the long staircase. She did not move immediately, but remained in that position as if to revel in this moment of glory. The long train of her blue, sequined gown trailed steps behind her when she eventually began a slow descent.

She savored every move, every second of an entrance she thought would never be resurrected but remain at rest within the memories of decades long gone. But, here she was, Lady Peacock, stepping onto a stage once again, repeating the act that was the greatest joy in her life. We knew her and when her gaze caught us sitting directly in front of her, she blew a kiss as if to tell us, "I'm so glad you're here."

Steve and I were not great fans of drag shows, but to watch her circulate about the perimeter with graceful gait, exuding an almost euphoric expression, made us proud to be part of the excitement. She moved to the center and extended her arms forward. One could hear a pin drop as Act I commenced. It comprised pop and show tunes that culminated with the only logical choice from the sound track of La Cage, "I Am What I Am." What a great closer before intermission! It was the quintessence of affirmation to all whose eyes were riveted to hers.

We were floored by her command of the stage, the impeccable timing of her lip-sync and the flow of her rhythmically perfect movements. We could not wait for the second act to begin. What was to have been a ten minute break lasted more than twenty so that those in need of refills had time to get seated again.

As the second act began, Lady Peacock stood in darkness on the stage. The harmonious strains of an operatic aria permeated the house and ushered the audience back to silence. The ambiance became one of church-like solemnity. The spotlight focused narrowly upon her face, then widened to reveal the entire stage. Her gaze was intense, upward, a clear reflection of the mood she was intent on establishing.

An aria? An opera? This was a stark transition from the more upbeat repertoire of Act I. Even that had been risky, because audiences had become accustomed to the fun and frolic of past performances by drag queens and an array of male strippers whose quality of entertainment ranged from mediocre to dastardly. There were a few who had been able to "wow" a crowd but no one, not the best of them, could hold a candle to the overpowering presence and theatrical polish of the Lady. That was abundantly clear in the uproarious approval she had received thus far.

Of all the operatic pieces to tackle during a premiere performance, "Sempre Libera" (A Round of Pleasure) from Verdi's *La Traviata* was a courageous choice. The last movement of Act I finds the character of Violetta unhappy as she shakes the illusion of love and vows to devote her life to pleasure. Steve and I knew the erratic pace and musical complexities of this composition and became nervous about the Lady's ability to create credible characterization and make the rendition palatable in a classical style.

There was no middle ground. As she became one with Violetta in this moment of transport to a different time and place, either she would draw the audience in and nail it or lose them to boredom and it would nail her. She managed the multi-part prelude well, but there began some murmuring within the ranks. It was evident they were getting restless because this was not their cup of tea.

Oh, but Peacock knew exactly what she was doing! An abrupt turn accompanied by a spontaneous bizarre expression silenced the antsy entertainment seekers and brought them back to her. She moved toward a small table on which props were neatly arranged. As she began to sing the opening bars of the climactic, "Sempre Libera," she held the props up one by one, then ambled clumsily from one side of the stage to the other. Curiosities were aroused by her abandonment of what, just moments before, had been an austere presence.

Once all were given a glimpse of a hypodermic needle, cut straw, glassine bag that contained a white powdery substance and a bottle of Rush (a sexual stimulant), Lady Peacock knew she had everyone in the palm of her hand. Her rendition of the aria would have sent opera buffs into cardiac arrest! Instead of the expected outpouring of passionate emotion inherent in the traditional version, the diva's interpretation was clad in the extreme of comedic hilarity and exaggeration. Precise timing and the well-placed use of "aids" were the key ingredients that set the mood and tone for what emerged as an aria with a distinct yet very strange personality.

By the end of the finale, Lady Peacock was a vision of exhaustion swimming in a pool of sweat. One of her false eyelashes hung by a thread and flapped up and down with every blink. What had been meticulously applied eye make-up found its way to her cheeks. Her wig had shifted forward and hugged her forehead. The Lady was a sight to behold!

She cared little about any of what was, indeed, post show entertainment. All that mattered was the applause and accolades that filled her with an overflowing sense of self-satisfaction. This had been her night to shine and she did so … brilliantly!

In order to understand Lady Peacock's psychology, emotions and overall perceptions about life, it is necessary to revisit her past. The façade of character made real in a fictitious, female counterpart was one piece of The Lady's identity, but there was another. It was the one with which we became acquainted weeks before we knew that Lady Peacock existed.

He was Billy Joe, a gentle, non-assuming, humble guy who was pushing seventy years of age. We were introduced to him by Joe, the bartender, whose social graces usually left much to be desired. We three were Joe's only customers one afternoon, well before the start of happy hour.

Rather than sitting in our usual spot, Joe asked us to move to where his other customer was located so he would not have to walk back and forth from one end of the counter area to the other. That's how we met Billy Joe. After that day, whenever the three of us were at Tornado, we sat together.

At first, our talks were one-sided and focused exclusively on Billy Joe's inquisitiveness about us. He seemed fascinated by the details of how Steve and I came to share life together, and that it had lasted for so long. It was not that he was bent on prying into personal matters, as much as it was a matter of his being intrigued by our candor when relating descriptions that painted a portrait of who we were. There came a time when we literally had nothing else left to tell him. That's when the tables turned and we learned about the dual nature of his identity.

Billy Joe was born and raised in New York. Taller than most others of the same age, he was lean, lanky and somewhat awkward. By his own admission, he had not been blessed with a hint of good looks. He was teased, even taunted, about arms that looked like legs and hands that were grotesquely large. As he described himself I envisioned Ichabod Crane, the school master in *The Legend of Sleepy Hollow*. The two had physical attributes that were much the same. Though not a flattering comparison, it seemed an apt one.

Billy Joe was unaware of the true nature of his sexuality as a youth, but he knew he was different. That understanding became an obstacle when attempting to fit in easily with others. Not so much Steve, but I completely identified with this revelation that pulled at my heart strings. As he spoke of his background, it became obvious to us that he harbored his fair share of unpleasant recollections. I was able to commiserate fully with him because I, too, had known the pain and struggle of finding my identity while feeling like an outcast.

"While I was in high school, I became friends with two guys who were quiet … just like me. I didn't know they were gay … I didn't know I was gay! We became good friends. They came out to me first," he told us.

"So, you were comfortable with them?" I asked.

"Very! They were the ones who helped me come out … the only ones I really trusted … it was like a ton of bricks off my shoulders."

"Where did the name Lady Peacock come from?"

"The first time I dressed in drag, I was with them. One told me I looked like quite a lady and the other said I looked like a peacock because of the bright colors I wore. That was the day Lady Peacock was born."

As Billy Joe became more acquainted with and connected to his "Lady," he began to perform at parties and other social gatherings. His two friends had friends who had friends. The early events at which he entertained were the springboard from which he dove into his career as a drag queen.

Eventually, he performed at Manhattan clubs and made quite a splash. The money wasn't bad either. It was difficult for us to imagine him in a different era, when he possessed the gift of youth. Now, his face was a mass of wrinkles and he was so thin that the arms and hands description about which he had often been mocked were almost unsightly. He took that criticism, however, and used it to his advantage as he developed graceful, flowing gestures that would keep both busy and lessen the scrutiny and predictable criticism of others.

Billy Joe was well aware that age had caught up with him and joked about the wrinkles he referred to as facial canals. "When I was in my prime, the biggest struggle was to choose a razzle-dazzle gown. Now, it's the hours it takes to make myself look something like a woman, and that is no easy task!" We admired his sense of humor and uncanny ability to poke fun at himself.

"Once I learned how to laugh at myself, this queen ran with it. I made it part of Lady Peacock's personality. She wore the humor so well, I included it in some shows, not all of them, because too much of the same thing gets boring … get it?"

Steve and I never met a drag queen and knew absolutely nothing about what made a man want to dress and act like a woman. "What made you want to do drag?" I asked.

"That's a long story. Where do I begin?"

"How about at the beginning?"

"From the very first time I dressed up, I liked what I saw and how it made me feel. I have always believed that Lady Peacock is the better part of who I am."

"What makes you say that?" Steve interjected.

"I've always been much more comfortable with her than with plain old Billy Joe … I guess I was looking for approval. He got very little, but she was a hit!"

It unsettled us to think that a fictitious, female character was what he believed to be the core and essence of his identity … all because of his need to be affirmed and feel comfortable within his own skin. He was emphatic in his perception that when he acted out the part that was his female alter ego, he was surrounded by attention but when he assumed his true identity, he was ignored.

"You guys are coming to my first show … you must … you have to! Next Saturday… 9 p.m."

"Sure!" I responded for both of us in a decisive tone, even though the prospect of a drag show was not at all thrilling.

"Just watch the crowd react to Lady Peacock … they're going to adore her. After that, note how the very same people react to Billy Joe. It has happened so many times before, I'm sure it will be the same then."

"Maybe this time will be different!"

"Don't count on it, honey … just watch and you'll see what I mean … nobody wants to be bothered with a troll."

"A troll? What's that?"

"That's me… a wrinkled, saggy old queen … what nobody knows is that *this* troll has some fire left in her furnace … get it?"

The analysis of contrast between Lady Peacock and Billy Joe proved to be an accurate assessment. She was showered with praise from an audience that clamored for more of her. After the lights dimmed and the glitz and glitter of a stellar performance faded, Billy Joe re-emerged and might as well have been invisible. He was charming and funny, so what was it that made most guys recoil from interacting with him … troll or not?

It was as if they saw two separate people and were unable, or unwilling, to embrace the whole person. Maybe, the thrill of a drag show helped those in the audience escape their own deserts of reality. Perhaps they viewed Lady Peacock as an endearing, feminine presence lacking in their own lives. Billy Joe as Lady Peacock was very much like Robin Williams as Mrs. Doubtfire in the movie with the same title. Both had a profound impact when they were in character.

Whatever the case, whatever motivated the thinking of others was pure speculation on our part. Steve and I came to know Billy Joe, the total person. Although Lady Peacock was classy, sometimes sassy and always the personification of style and grace, she existed in the forum of appearance. She was an integral part, but did not define the whole of Billy Joe's persona. The mathematical theorem states it most succinctly — "The whole is equal to the sum of its parts." We understood that, but it seemed that our friend had difficulty in locking the pieces together to create a distinct, complete self-portrait. It was as if the reactions and behavior of others dictated how he perceived himself and all we had heard from him thus far validated his opinion.

As our friendship with Billy Joe grew, he became more comfortable with discussing some of the more personal aspects of his life. The first time he made any reference to a relationship was when he told us about Desi, a young Puerto Rican guy he had taken in. It was obvious that Billy Joe had feelings for him, but he stopped short of supplying details from which conclusions might be drawn about the nature of their closeness.

He had met Desi at the bar and was immediately drawn to him. Despite caveats from Joe and some close friends, he allowed himself to become vulnerable to the charm, wit and exceedingly good looks of the young man, who was thirty something years old. He knew that Desi came with baggage, but that did not dissuade him from dusting off the welcome mat.

"I was so lonely and depressed, there were times when I didn't care if I lived or died. Years ago, I had it all … money, clothes, cars, great apartments. That's all gone now and I just about get by. Desi needed a place to stay and I was desperate for company in a drab, run-down apartment." Teary-eyed, he continued to create images that left us speechless.

Despite Billy Joe's awareness of Desi's drug use, the two began to live together. The one and only condition was that Desi would seek help. Although there was no guarantee of success, he had a very strong anchor, and that was Billy Joe. Compared to 'the boys of the street' we knew, this young man did not realize that he was leaps ahead of any feeble attempts the others had made to get well. One would assume that gratitude would be forthcoming from this complete stranger who had been gifted with shelter, food, clothing and a healthy dose of tough love.

It did not take Billy Joe very long to realize that his efforts were an exercise in futility. Desi's needs smothered our friend's hopes and eventually left him with a devastating "thank you" captured in an image of smoldering embers… the remnants of very poor judgment. Billy Joe came home one afternoon only to find that his apartment had been ransacked. Desi was gone. Not only had he stolen some personal possessions and jewelry, he knew where household money was kept. Billy Joe was penniless and lost his apartment soon after.

For the first time in his life, he understood what it meant to be homeless. Not only did he sink into a state of deep depression because of the hurt Desi had caused, he was not prepared to be left with nothing and have to depend upon the kindness and sympathy of others in order to survive.

"I kept thinking … how did it all get to this point? I would have been better off by myself … I have never felt so used in my life!" Steve and I reached out and gripped his hands. That was all we were capable of doing at that moment because we were at a complete loss for words.

Close friends invited Billy Joe to stay with them until he got back on his feet. During that time period, Tornado reopened under new management and Billy Joe became acquainted with the new owner. "Lady Peacock came to the rescue," he said with the faint hint of a smile.

"Lady Peacock?" I repeated.

"Yes, Lady Peacock! Joe told me that the owner was interested in providing additional weekend entertainment. I spoke to him and he hired me on the spot."

Earlier, Joe had spoken to the new owner and put in a good word. Initially, Joe's recommendation was received with little enthusiasm because Billy Joe was decades older than the young things and strapping hunks in the lineup. Joe pushed the unique style of The Lady and convinced the boss that her presence would broaden the spectrum of entertainment for audiences in which there was a wide age range.

This was the second time that Joe stepped up to the plate on behalf of another person. The first was years earlier, when he came to Emily's assistance on the day of that dreadful beach incident. He showed himself capable of true friendship to both during times of extreme emotional upheaval. It was he who made known the circumstances that caused Billy Joe to search for a new place to live.

The boss owned a small apartment building in the area and when he heard of the plight, he offered Billy Joe the option to rent a recently vacated one bedroom unit that just happened to enjoy an ocean view. How befitting a setting for The Lady in her twilight years! While our friend always had been adept at disassociating gender roles, it was impossible for him to separate the convoluted emotions that weighed heavily upon him after the robbery.

Steve and I were of the opinion that the loss of material possessions, money and his living quarters did not cut and slice as deeply as the unspeakable hurt of abandonment he experienced at the hands of one for whom he cared so deeply. Life had become a random roll of the dice that rendered Billy Joe fragile and questioning his purpose and worth, but that was all changed now. The resurgence of Lady Peacock in combination with a new living environment were the spark plugs that tuned up a heart that had been plagued by the loud, sputtering noise of emotional discord.

During the tourist season that began in November 1999, Lady Peacock entertained a packed house each weekend. As laborious as were the evident efforts of other performers, there was little doubt in anyone's mind that the diva owned the limelight. A tremendous ego boost for her, the reality was not well-received by her stage colleagues because of the perception that their purpose was to act as openers for the headliner.

This did not bode well for the continued success of weekly entertainment or for Lady Peacock. She remained the constant in a cast that changed with increasing frequency. As discouraged players quit, she spent more and more time on stage. Eventually, she became the sole act in shows once manned by two, sometimes three other performers. Although she added more and different tunes to the first act, the operatic aria was the standard finale.

Peacock was no spring chicken! She was exhausted not only from the necessity to expend greater energy but also from the pressure of pondering what more she might do to keep the boat afloat. By April, most vacationers had left the island and audiences dwindled. The expense of a D.J. and lighting person were no longer cost-effective and the boss decided that the time had come to discontinue weekend theater.

We thought, for sure, The Lady would be devastated by his decision, but she was actually relieved. She had been encouraged to search out other places where she could put her talents to work, but the aging lady of the stage was just about out of gas. Days after the last and final show, Billy Joe joined us for lunch at our apartment. The conversation went immediately to her plans to locate new stage spots. The wisdom of her age and years of experience had taught her to recognize when enough was enough.

"Lady Peacock has hung her gowns and boxed her wigs for the last time."

"How do you feel about that?" Steve asked in a sympathetic tone.

"It was a great run, but I cannot do it anymore. Back in the day, I would have been in my glory as a solo performer. The old Lady is tired now and needs to be put to rest."

"Why do you say that?"

"Because I know that Lady Peacock will never perform again."

This was a sad commentary, but one which did not surprise us. As often as we had tried to impress upon Billy Joe that his Lady was part of who he was, the reasoning always seemed to elude him.

"Just because you are not on the stage," I interjected, "does not mean that Lady Peacock no longer exists."

"I don't get you," he came back with a perplexed look.

"Lady Peacock came from you. You gave her personality, emotion, charisma and an awesome ability to entertain people. That didn't happen by itself. She is everything she is because you are who you are. Does any of this make sense?"

Billy Joe sat in quiet posture for a few moments and gazed at the tranquil lagoon while trying to wrap his mind around what I said to him. Although he was not forthcoming with voiced agreement, he did not argue against my reasoning. Steve and I realized that it was not possible to make our vantage point his, but at least we provided, yet again, some food for thought.

After that luncheon, we saw less and less of Billy Joe. From all indications, he had embraced a more reclusive lifestyle. If we bumped into each other by happenstance, the chats were brief and of no substance. During one such street encounter during the summer, Billy Joe told us that there was a rumor circulating about the possible sale of Tornado.

Once the shows were eliminated, we saw a steady decline in patronage that was most glaring during happy hour. A group of twenty was considered a crowd. There was, however, a much bigger picture. It was more than conjecture that the newly elected governmental administration was headed by a homophobic leader. The first inkling of this was when a gay mayoral candidate running for office in our area was exposed. Needless to say, he lost the election.

A more blatant clue was the closing of gay bars and clubs in rapid succession. Tornado, Buena Vista and "The Wrinkle Room" hung on, but the owner of Tornado saw the handwriting on the wall. That last election was, among other things, the death knell for gay life in an area that traditionally had extended its arms in unprejudiced warmth and welcome. The demise of gay life in our neighborhood was accompanied by a mass exodus of countless vacationers who were loyal admirers of the "Isla Del Encanto." The new hot spot had become Fort Lauderdale, Florida.

What had been speculation became a reality. One afternoon in September, we headed to Tornado at four o'clock. The side street was quiet and the few men who stood outside were across the road in front of Buena Vista. As we neared, it was all to obvious; the large wooden doors were closed. Reluctantly, we crossed the road only to find that the number of guys seated at the counter or around tables did not exceed fifteen. Mission accomplished … the gays were gone!

The only place left was "The Wrinkle Room." For some reason, that was the only gay bar that survived the hammer of homophobia. It was there that we began to see Billy Joe a bit more often. As the holidays of 2000 neared we were well on the road to moving back to the states and, for the first time, we remained in Puerto Rico for the Christmas holidays. Billy Joe was among our guests on that special day when I took the last photograph of Steve and David the Younger. Where Annie had left off at Easter, Billy Joe filled the spot quite well. He was extremely emotional throughout the afternoon.

"I can't believe you thought enough of me to invite me to Christmas dinner. I haven't celebrated with anyone in years … and look at the others who are here. What a Christmas you have given them, too."

"We are happy to have each and all of you with us today," I said affectionately.

"Who else would be kind enough to do this?"

"I'm sure there are others."

"Where? Show me!"

That Christmas Day was the last time we socialized with Billy Joe. On a return trip to the island in June 2005, we passed each other on the avenue and spoke for a very few minutes. He did not look well and his gait had slowed considerably. His speech was labored and breathy. That brief encounter was our last. Our dear friend, Billy Joe, along with his darling diva of the stage, Lady Peacock, passed away some months later. Gone was a person for whom we had developed a warm affection and it broke our hearts to think that we never had the chance to say "Good-bye."

He left a legacy however. Our memories are the keepers of imagery that make him and the Lady present to us whenever we pause to remember. The following words not only give us closure but also celebrate how blessed we were to have known the remarkable substance of this truly special human being:

On The Stage of Forever

On the stage of forever,

A new act commenced

When last the curtains closed

To the limits of time and space.

How melancholy the emotion we feel,

That no longer can be seen and heard

Those companions ever-present,

The partners that colored your wholeness

In a unity of complemented oneness

Upon the canvas that was your life!

Though more pleasing, fulfilling, distinct,

You unrelentingly perceived as truth

More the character of fanciful frolic

Than the man less alluring in reality.

An unleashed spirit that danced

In grand spectacle unparalleled

Was welded to a heart of song

Upon this earthly, temporal platform,

But now shed brightness upon your place

In the celestial, heavenly realm.

The elusive butterfly of fellowship

Lamented with your wrenching tears

Is captured in the multitude of souls

That holds fast the inseparable euphoria

Of a repertoire unceasing, unending

That is set in a rhythm of perfection

Inside the vast theater dome

Of everlasting, blissful tranquility.

We dare not utter the trite cliché,

"Rest well, our dear, departed Billy Joe",

For to have been touched in our depths

By the bearer of the enticing Lady Peacock

Would not comprise a fervent prayer

But render ill-received the invitation

By a new and unencumbered audience

That exists in an unchanging present.

Instead, we cheer with loving affirmation,

"Take your place upon the stage of forever

And be about the business of sharing those gifts

That brought such joy to your days

And treasured delight to our senses."

F.L. Richards
©2009

Zeus

13

Whenever the first signs of the holiday season appear in stores, Steve makes a conscious effort to keep me away from them. As early as our first celebration as a couple in 1986, he learned two things about me. I was a Christmas junkie and made purchases whether needed or not. I'm sure there were times he wished it had been possible to tie my hands behind my back. Once he saw the little boy in me resurface, however, his joy at witnessing my sense of child-like wonder and excitement made the first issue unimportant.

Although our first apartment was small, we continued to accumulate holiday trinkets and the number of storage cartons increased steadily. Our having a garage did not help matters, instead it only fueled my need to add to an inventory that could well have decorated two apartments. In 1999, we did not have to wait for Christmas season to visit us. During that summer, we were forced to visit it. By then, fourteen cartons sat in the garage and the daunting task of rummaging through them began.

Our move to Puerto Rico was scheduled for August 10th, so some serious down-sizing was necessary. There were lots of tears, because everything we looked at conjured images and memories not only of our years together but also of my mom and Steve's parents who were no longer with us. When all was said and done, we had narrowed the selections to those that fit into two cartons. The remaining ones were resealed and placed back on shelves only to look forward to cold, bleak winters in darkness.

Our first decorating escapade in Puerto Rico was quite unlike the ritual of prior years. What had taken four days to accomplish in New York was completed in less than an hour, but was not without stress. We had forgotten to pack the door wreath. One of the very few items that had been a part of each Christmas since 1986, it was the bearer of many holiday memories.

Off I went on a mission to find a replacement. That early December day was unusually hot and sticky. By the time I arrived at a local variety store, I looked as if I had been in a sauna. Once inside, it was so cold I began to shiver. There was no pleasing me, and if I was unable to find what I was looking for, that would have been the icing on the cake. A lone wreath sat on a display rack but did not have a Christmas-like appearance. It was plain, but had potential. I grabbed it along with some embellishments so Steve could perform his magic and create an attractive door hanging. When I exited the store, I almost keeled over from the blast of hot air that assaulted me. We usually did not make solo trips to Tornado, but I desperately needed something cool to drink before facing the walk back to our apartment.

Another new one, I thought as I plopped on a stool. Since the reopening of the bar, employees came and went. Some lasted only a few days. One was fired after his first shift because he was caught with his hand in the cookie jar. The new hire was at the cash register unaware that I was sitting directly behind him. When he turned he said, "I'll be right with you." He came from behind the counter and walked over to one of the tables at which lunch customers were seated. When he resumed his work station, he extended his hand to shake mine.

"How ya doing?" he asked with a broad smile. "My name is Zeus."

"I'm Frank … you mean Zeus, like the Greek god?"

"That's me!" As if his response were not boastful enough, he made a complete rotation so I'd be sure to see all that encompassed the name. He was dressed in black jeans looped with a thick garrison belt. He must have worn that for effect because the jeans were beyond tight-fitting and needed no assistance in being held up. A black, ribbed muscle shirt gave definition to a well-developed upper torso. His skin was perfect, there was not a hair out of place and he owned eyes that could melt a block of ice. The crowning glory, however, was a deep, resonant voice that completed the image.

Oh, boy, everyone is going to have a field day with this one, I chuckled.

"What can I get for you?"

"Club soda with a twist of lemon."

"Are you on vacation?" he asked as he placed the thirst-quencher in front of me.

"No, we live here."

"We?"

"My partner, Steve, and I. We moved here in August."

"I have some gay friends … it's not my thing, but I'm cool with it."

"That's good to know since you're working in a gay bar!"

Robert stepped behind the counter. Pointing to my drink Zeus said, "I got this one." Robert was the bartender on duty and had been on a break. Zeus was waiting tables that day and had filled in during Robert's twenty minute absence. "I just have to clean off the tables and I'm done for today."

"Nice to have met you," I said as Zeus came from behind the counter. Within minutes, I glanced over and saw him sitting at a side table. He extended his hand in the direction of the chair across from his in a gesture of invitation to join him. Although I thought it strange that he made such an overture within minutes of having introduced himself, I picked up my glass and the cumbersome bag containing the wreath and strolled over to him.

"Can you sit for a few minutes? I don't like to drink alone."

"Sure. Thanks for asking," I answered as if this kind of situation were commonplace.

Initially, the conversation was a mix of nondescript generalities. In passing, I mentioned our upcoming trip to be with our children for Christmas. That was the wrong thing to say and caused a change in his facial expression. I was puzzled as to why my reference made his lips quiver and tears stream down his face. Then, he began to share with me the reasons for such visible emotion. What he was about to describe not only put into perspective his present condition but also shook me to my bones.

Zeus's best friend, Javier, introduced him to Diana in 1982. He was twenty-two at that time. They married in 1983, and eventually became parents to three daughters. The couple worked in the hotel industry and, although not people of great means, they extended themselves in order to provide for their family.

Diagnosed with an enlarged heart, Diana's health began to fail. She was placed on a transplant list and cautioned to have no more children. Despite the caveat of her physician, she became pregnant in 1994 and gifted Zeus with a long-time dream of his, a son. He held Diana in his arms as this new life began and hers ended.

Her death set Zeus into an emotional tail spin. Unable to deal with the loss, he left his four children in the care of neighbors and sank into an abyss of drug use. Eventually, the children were taken away by the Department of Family Services.

At that time, Javier worked for an organization called San Juan Housing Services. As soon as Zeus reappeared following his emotional breakdown, Javier introduced him to a psychiatrist who would become the key to his rehabilitation. Near the end of 1995, after two months of residential treatment, Zeus emerged a much healthier, more emotionally stable young man. He had finally dealt with Diana's passing and was on the road of recovery from drug addiction.

In order to reclaim his children, he was required to show evidence of employment. He accomplished that, but the job didn't last. Now he had the children, no job and faced the wrath of Diana's parents who blamed him for the loss of their daughter. Filled with malice, they removed every stick of furniture from the house they had purchased for the couple. Blow up mattresses became the family's nightly place of rest.

One day, he went to Walgreens to get Pampers and baby food. Filled with desperation, he attempted to shoplift the items and was caught. Fortunately for Zeus, the store manager and police were compassionate once he told them the sad tale of the past year. The manager offered him a job as long as he could prove the veracity of his story. The police drove Zeus to his home and observed, for themselves, that what he had described was the truth. They reported their findings to the store manager and Zeus began to work there.

Although life was stressful, Zeus slowly recaptured his identity. He better understood the priority of providing for the needs of his children and that it was his responsibility to keep the family afloat. This precluded any temptation to engage in activity that might place them in danger.

The period of regained balance and family normalcy came to a screeching halt in 1997. Although Zeus's name appeared on the documents which gave him title after Diana's passing, her parents, the owners of his home, were relentlessly vindictive and maneuvered to take it away from him. Their successful ploy bore grave consequences. The children went to live with Zeus's family members and he was taken in by his dear friend, Javier who realized the tightrope of emotional balance on which Zeus was walking and held him in a posture of guarded safety so he would not fall back into the all too easy escape of drug use.

I looked at my watch and realized that more than one hour had passed. I needed to excuse myself and get home not only because Steve was probably wondering what was taking so long, but also because I was on emotional overload and could not bear to hear any more of what had been a surreal recounting of this young man's journey.

"Thanks for listening to me. I haven't talked about this for a long time … hope I didn't freak you out."

"Not at all," was the blatant lie with which I responded. "Why did you decide to tell me these things?" I asked.

"Your kids … you said you were going to New York to be with them for Christmas. That made me think about the past and want to talk about it. You look a little pale. Are you sure I didn't upset you?"

"No, I'm fine, but some of what you said was difficult to hear."

"There's more," he said with a tone that made me wonder if there was unsettling description yet to be revealed.

"Another time," I quickly replied.

"I want to meet Steve," he said as I rose and shook his hand.

"I'm sure that will happen soon."

When I returned to the apartment, Steve was pacing and displayed an expression that mixed concern and annoyance. That quickly subsided when I told him about my having met Zeus. Our supper conversation was a rehashing of the details I had heard earlier. During our many years of relationship with Puerto Rico, we had heard some strange tales but this, by far, was the most gut-wrenching of them all. The wreath and decor I had bought sat in the bag for another time. Neither of us were feeling the festiveness of the season.

Steve met Zeus the next afternoon and appeared uncharacteristically comfortable. Perhaps it was due to my having laid the groundwork. Maybe it was just the endearing cordiality of the new worker. Whatever the case, that day was the beginning of yet another journey of relationship with one who knew well the face and personality of struggle.

During the next weeks we saw Zeus frequently and were impressed by his ability to make people laugh. Whether serving drinks or waiting tables, he exuded a charisma that was contagious, and that was good for business. We wanted to become better acquainted with him and extended an invitation to join us for supper sometime. He was readily agreeable and plans were made.

"What a nice place you have!" he commented as he stepped into our apartment.

"Thanks, we're very comfortable here," I responded to his compliment. "Let's go out on the terrace … we're going to eat outside."

Steve was already enjoying the cool evening breeze when we joined him.

"How ya doing, Steve?"

"I'm well … how are you?"

"I've been looking forward to this."

"I hope you're hungry," Steve chuckled.

"I'm always hungry!"

Steve excused himself and returned within minutes carrying dinner plates mounded with food. Zeus attacked his with a vengeance and was ready for seconds before either of us barely had made a dent in our meals.

"Zeus, you told me there was more to your story," I reminded him. "We'd like to hear about it."

"Are you sure?" he laughed. "You looked pretty pale that day."

"Yes, if you want to tell us more, we're ready to listen."

"Where did I leave off?"

As best I could, I provided a brief summary of what had already been discussed. His expression changed to one more serious as he continued to provide us with images of who he was.

Not long after moving in with Javier, Zeus became somewhat uncomfortable. He knew that Javier was gay but that never had been an issue. Zeus unashamedly admitted that he liked to sleep in the buff. A number of times, he awoke to find Javier fixated on him.

"I always thought he had a thing for me, but he kept it in check. He started to make comments that made me think he wanted more than friendship. I really think he began to love me. I loved him, too, but only like a brother."

"How did you handle that?" Steve asked.

"I bought myself a pair of pajamas," he laughed.

"Did the situation improve?"

"Yeah, for a while."

"A while?"

"I'll get to that."

Javier was well known in his community and became the leader of the organization for which he worked. Zeus received training and became a drug counselor for families in crisis. The salary was not great but gave him a sense of personal satisfaction, especially if his efforts were successful.

His family was well aware of the difficulties inherent in being both mom and dad to four children and knew he was trying his best to move forward. They did not insist that he take them back right away, but offered to keep them as long as it took for Zeus to become more financially solvent. The children appeared happy, well-adjusted and were repeatedly told, "Daddy is trying his best." The generous spirit of the caretakers reassured Zeus of their love for him and his children. This removed a tremendous burden from his shoulders and allowed him to continue to heal as he helped others to do the same.

Later that year, he accompanied Javier to Buffalo, New York, to attend a Habitat for Humanity conference at which he was a speaker. Zeus had no idea how his life was about to change once again. He saw a woman whom he found very attractive and attempted to strike up a conversation with her. She showed no interest in speaking to him. Instead, she focused entirely on the purpose for which she was at that conference.

Her name was Andrea, and she was currently living in Troy, New York. She was part of a group called Good Neighbors, and was intent on learning how they might be of greater assistance to those in the home community.

Zeus was a persistent bugger! By the conclusion of the conference, the two had exchanged phone numbers and a new chapter in both of their lives was about to begin. Although this was a long distance relationship, they spoke for hours at a time and realized that mutual feelings were developing.

"She sounded like she was scared. Once she told me she had been married, I understood why." He told us that she had withstood emotional and physical abuse from her husband over a span of thirty-five years.

It had not been her choice to marry him at the tender age of eighteen but a decision made by her family years earlier. He was seventeen years her senior and was the school bus driver when she was a young girl. Being completely submissive to the will of her parents resulted in a hellish life for her. Two daughters, Marisol and Marina, were the only good that came from a union that never should have happened.

Much like Annie's husband, Andrea's was prone to outbursts that resulted in physical assaults. Annie's harrowing account of being thrown out the bedroom window became lightweight when Zeus told us that Andrea's husband attempted to burn down their house while she and one of the children were inside it.

Unlike Annie, Andrea did not run but remained with this disturbed man. By the time the Buffalo conference occurred, her girls were grown and on their own. That's when she finally got the strength to get a divorce. Having Zeus in her life gave her confidence and strength.

In September of 1998, she relocated to Puerto Rico to be with her new love. Initially, she lived with Zeus in Javier's home while she searched out employment as a teacher. Her first assignment was in San Juan. It did not take long before the emotional baggage of the couple produced negative side effects.

Whenever Zeus raised his voice to her or displayed the slightest anger, Andrea recoiled and left. She went to Arroyo, stayed with a long-time friend of hers and made the trip from there to San Juan each day. Those periods of separation sometimes lasted for weeks. By the end of that school year, Andrea requested reassignment and was placed in a school in Arroyo.

Their relationship returned to one that was long distance in nature, since they saw each other only on weekends. Zeus had deep feelings for Andrea, and was not pleased with the arrangement.

As Steve and I listened to the continuing saga, we looked at each other frequently. It was as if our reactions were singular. "Do you understand why Andrea moved to Arroyo?" I asked.

"Yeah, she got a teaching job with more pay."

"Is that the only reason you can think of?"

"What else could have made her do that? We love each other and want to be together."

This comment gave us an opening to give some reactions to the complex nature of their relationship. As Steve and I gave our impressions of what emerged as a quid pro quo dialogue, Zeus became agitated. It seemed that he did not want to hear anything that was remotely negative. We likened their relationship to the building of a house and emphasized the importance of a strong foundation. From our vantage point, this was lacking in their life as a couple.

"What do you mean?" he shouted indignantly.

"Listen to yourself!" Steve came back at him.

"I know what I'm saying."

"It's not what you are saying. but how it is being said."

"Your tone of voice," I added.

"When I get pissed off, that's how I talk."

"Exactly! … Do you understand how that has affected Andrea?" I said with little concern for how he might react.

Zeus wasn't getting it, so we connected the dots for him. We wanted him to get a clear picture of our perceptions of them, individually and as a couple. He was quite angry when we used the term emotional baggage to describe what, to us, was an evident impediment in their life together.

I focused on Zeus's background and Steve gave reactions to what he understood to be Andrea's emotional fragility. He had lived through loss, drug dependence and a degree of alienation from his children. She was attempting to begin a new life but carried the deep scars of an abusive marriage.

"Every time you get angry and raise your voice to her, something clicks," I explained.

"Clicks? … what do you mean?" he answered back with a tone of complete unawareness.

"When you raise your voice to her and your face becomes as red as it is right now, she sees her ex-husband."

"No way … I'm not like him at all." Zeus banged on the table and began to babble in Spanish. I grabbed his hand.

"Let me finish," I said calmly, even though this was an extremely tense moment.

"Didn't it take some time for you to pick up the pieces of your life and get back on a steady path? It's the same for her. You had Javier's help and the professional care of a psychiatrist. She's doing this alone. When you fly off the handle, you force her to remember a very painful time in her life … that may even make her think that all men are like that … and that includes you."

It was as if these remarks punctured the balloon of irritation in which Zeus was contained, because the color left his face. My words should not have been a profound revelation, but his reaction was a clear indication of his failure to relate her tragic past with a frequent need to escape to Arroyo.

"Do you think that's really true?"

"Yes, Zeus, I do. She is not healed and what you're doing is opening the wound every time your temper gets the best of you."

Steve and I usually did not share the more personal aspects of our relationship, but he could not contain himself. "Let me add something … maybe you'll understand what we're trying to explain to you. Like you, Zeus, I fly off the handle once in a while. Frank becomes quiet and distant. His reaction always makes me realize that I should have thought before I spoke, that my reaction to a situation could have been different. We talk about it and things get back to normal. Communication is the key. You need to talk to Andrea about your feelings instead of ranting and raving about them. Each time that happens, the result is the same … she runs away to a place of safety … her friend's house in Arroyo. Does any of this make sense to you?"

Tears filled Zeus's eyes as he focused on the lagoon in quiet reflection. We remained silent and hoped that when he returned from wherever his thoughts had carried him, he would say something, anything that hinted an understanding of an obvious cause and effect situation that somewhat resembled a game of cat and mouse.

"I don't want to hurt her … I love her," was his response filled with credible emotion.

"We're sure that is true, so you know what you have to do, now, to keep Andrea close to you."

"Think before I speak."

"That's it, but it's not as easy as it sounds. It takes practice and doesn't happen overnight. After all these years with Frank, I still say things that come out the wrong way."

Steve's self-analysis was on point, but I wanted Zeus to be aware that I, too, was not exempt form situations when an intemperate remark made me wish I could have pulled back the tone with which I said it. "We all have moments when the mouth works before the brain. I just have to look at Steve's face to know that the attitude or feeling I'm trying to express has not been well-received … it's all about being aware of the other person."

As much as Zeus claimed he understood our reasoning and promised to be more conscious of Andrea's feelings, there was something in his voice that made his resolve tentative and not convincing. Just as I had left Tornado feeling emotionally drained following my introduction to Zeus, this dinner gathering was no less unsettling.

Within a span of two weeks, we had learned a great deal about his precarious background. The stage was now set for what was to become a close friendship with him. That friendship, however, would not walk a straight path of growth. The interplay of tender moments and occasions of happiness would be obscured, at times, by those which were tumultuous and severely tested our forbearance. This became the road map on which we walked.

As much as we enjoyed taking visitors to the old city, it became predictable and somewhat tedious. Although there were a number of other tourist attractions available to those who wished to explore the island, they were costly. Steve and I had seen most of them, so to go with guests on one or another of the guided tours would have been an unnecessary expense for us.

Because we were novices at negotiating highways and side roads, we never offered to drive to places that were a distance from where we lived, and family and friends did not appear too enthusiastic about bus tours which lasted four to six hours. They preferred to stay close to us and let each day unfold as it might. The result was our assuming the roles of social directors who needed to ensure for them a fun-filled vacation experience.

In passing conversation with Zeus one day shortly after having celebrated the holiday season which ushered in the year 2000, we mentioned our quandary.

"Guavate," he piped up enthusiastically. "Everybody loves to go there, especially on weekends when crowds gather for nightly music and dancing." The name sounded familiar to us. When Zeus began to describe the geography of the area and the main attraction — roast pig cooked on outdoor spits — our memories were jogged. We had been taken there by some friends eight years earlier, but our images of this place about which Zeus spoke with such excitement were vague.

Steve's brother, Hal, was the first winter visitor to enjoy all that comprised the scenic topography of Guavate. Zeus was the tour guide for our inaugural car venture outside the city limits. Having been a passenger eight years earlier was a relaxing, carefree experience when compared to the task of being behind the wheel. Much like El Yunque, the rainforest, access to the town required an ascent on narrow, winding paths which, at some locations, made passage along the two way roads an extreme challenge.

Zeus, Steve and Hal remained calm and appeared entertained by an occasional expletive that found its way out of my mouth. I was a nervous wreck, especially when it became necessary to move to the right to allow oncoming cars and trucks to pass. There was no wall, fence or any kind of barrier separating us from the view of miniaturized towns and cities which lay hundreds of feet below.

"It's on the left," Zeus announced as he pointed to the roadside restaurant.

"Thank God," I yelled. "This trip plucked my last nerve!"

The three found my comment humorous, but I was dead serious. The best I could hope for was that my stomach settled down before we ordered our lunch meals. Before eating, we crossed the road and stood in awe as we surveyed the panoramic expanse below us. The day was exceptionally clear, so images were crisp. Zeus waved us on in an attempt to get us to join him close to the edge of the road but we chose to remain in a zone of safety, feet behind him.

The distance between us did not hamper his ability to excite our interest in this unique location. Zeus really knew his stuff! Not only did he speak about the geography of the mountain region but also commented on culture and customs specific to the places he called to our attention.

This interlude allowed my stomach to settle and regain an appetite. "Let's eat," I called to Zeus, who was still engrossed in his role as tour guide.

The aromas of native cooking lured us to the spot where we saw, first hand, what a roasted pig looked like as it rolled around on an open spit. It was not a glamorous sight, but delicious nonetheless. Along with rice and beans, salad, chicken and morsillas (blood sausages), our dishes were piled high with savory treats. Having been tricked into tasting the morsillas eight years earlier thinking they were stuffed with meat and rice, I knew not to order them.

Just as Hal had thoroughly enjoyed his tour of Old San Juan with Roberto and George, this experience provided him with a vivid perspective of rural living.

During the day, there were moments when Zeus appeared distracted. I was able to speak to him alone while Steve and Hal walked around the grounds after lunch. Things were not going well with Andrea or Javier. This was one of those times when she was in retreat mode following an argument. Zeus was convinced that, despite his relationship with Andrea, Javier was unrelenting in his efforts to win more attention from the object of his affection. It almost was as if Javier reveled in the stress that caused increasingly frequent periods of separation because he had Zeus all to himself.

Weekends without Andrea were tense. Javier did not work on Saturdays and Sundays. Zeus, as yet, did not own a car. Unless he took public transportation or walked, he was a captive straight guy to the eye of a "queer" guy.

"I don't understand what his problem is," Zeus said with irritation. "I've told him over and over where I'm coming from!"

"That doesn't matter to someone like Javier. It's where he's coming from that matters to him. Don't you know that the greatest conquest for a gay man is to bed a straight guy?"

Zeus looked at me as if I had two heads. "You're kidding, right?" he said incredulously.

"No I'm not … just be on your guard … he's not going to give up so easily."

"I'll just have to kick his ass … then he'll know I mean business."

"Do that and you'll be on the street!"

"So, what should I do?"

"Keep your P.J.'s on, dress and undress in the bathroom and try to ignore his teasing."

Steve and Hal approached, so the conversation was cut short. Zeus reverted to tour mode and smiled as if all was well in his world as he continued to explain what made this remote area so intriguing.

We returned to our apartment in the latter part of the afternoon still stuffed from the scrumptious food we had enjoyed hours earlier. As the time neared for Zeus to leave, the change in his behavior was obvious. During most of the day, save passing moments of noticeable distraction, he had been relaxed, humorous and engaged in a most enjoyable trip away from the city. Now, he seemed to retreat to a place where walls were up and a posture of defensiveness shrouded whatever sense of enthusiasm he had projected.

As Steve and I rode down to the lobby with him, the reasons for his demeanor's blatant transition became clear. That was when Steve got an idea of what was going on and his observations of Zeus while in Guavate made sense.

The issue, more commonplace than not, revolved around Andrea and Javier. Zeus faced yet another weekend without her due to the ongoing stress that, more and more, was defining their relationship. Her absence placed him in the uncomfortable position of being alone with Javier. His tone of voice gave a clear indication that Zeus was neither willing nor ready to deal with either scenario.

He hinted at the possibility of staying at our place. I explained that Hal was returning to New York the next morning and once we got home from the airport, he was welcome to come back and remain with us until Javier returned to work on Monday. At that moment, we did not realize how frequent would become these weekend sleepovers or that Javier would be a proverbial cog in the wheel to Zeus's emerging friendship with us and his already tenuous relationship with "lady love."

Within an hour following the airport run, Zeus arrived at our apartment. His face was tight with tension as he described Javier's displeasure at hearing that Zeus had chosen to stay at our place rather than at his. Javier knew of us and that we were a couple. Until now, this never was an issue for the "third wheel." We could only surmise that Javier's voiced disapproval was rooted in jealousy and that we, somehow, were a threat to his agenda.

Not long after Zeus attacked the breakfast Steve had prepared for him, his cell phone rang; it was Javier. Moments of civil conversation mixed with those in which our friend's voice became elevated. Since Zeus spoke to him in Spanish, it was difficult to understand what was being said. I did, however, manage to piece the unpleasant bantering together contextually and was taken aback by what I heard.

Javier was convinced that Zeus was with us for fun and games and threatened to make Andrea aware of his belief that there was a sexual layer to our friendship with Zeus. Steve's look of disbelief mimicked mine as I shared with him what had been overheard by me. How misguided and off base was Javier! The expression, "Hell hath no fury like a woman scorned," flashed through my mind. In this case, the male gender was an apt substitute that characterized his evident feelings of rejection.

Having heard enough nonsense, Zeus abruptly ended the phone conversation. "Did you understand any of that, Frank?" he asked.

"I got enough to know that Javier has some serious issues."

"I told you … now you understand why I didn't want to stay there for the weekend."

"The situation seems to be getting worse, not only between the two of you but also between Andrea and you … what's going on?"

Zeus was well aware that his girlfriend did not like any type of emotional outburst. Her witnessing of an escalation in the tension between the two men was another cause for a retreat to Arroyo. Zeus was certain that Javier staged moments of tension because he knew that Andrea would not tolerate them, especially when Zeus retaliated with marked anger.

"You know exactly what's going on," Steve said rather emphatically, "so it's up to you to change things."

"I get that, but I'm stuck at Javier's place for now. I can't afford an apartment and Andrea is not ready for us to live together."

"That shouldn't surprise you, Zeus."

"What do you mean?"

"She's trying to bury the past and you are allowing it to remain alive. It's hard enough for her to deal with your anger. Now, she's confronted with more than occasional arguments between Javier and you. Something has to change!"

Zeus was a smart guy. He knew that the entire situation was a mess, but seemed incapable of taking a stand and risk being thrown out by Javier. The need for self-preservation was dictating behavior that pushed Andrea away more and more. The phone rang again, but Zeus did not answer it. The message left by Javier was no less inflammatory than had been their earlier conversation.

Getting no satisfaction, the misguided friend continued to leave message after message which Zeus translated for us. One was more disgusting and vulgar than another as Javier vividly described whatever sick fantasy he was imagining. After a dozen unsuccessful attempts to spoil Zeus's weekend, the calls ceased.

"This is nuts ... I have to make things better with Andrea and get away from Javier before I kick his ass!"

"Don't just talk about it, do it!" I said. "You've faced worse situations than this and you've handled them. If you really love her, do whatever it takes to keep her."

"Sometime, I want you guys to meet her. I know you're going to like her."

"We'll have to plan something soon ... and bring Javier, too. Maybe if he meets us, he'll let go of his sick notions about our friendship."

Both Zeus and Steve looked at me as if I were crazy but as I further explained my rationale for wanting to see the triangle in action, both of them became agreeable to what was initially thought to be a preposterous suggestion.

Zeus had some homework to do before a dinner gathering could occur. Even if with disingenuous sentiment, he had to get back on good terms with Javier. More challenging was the need to convince Andrea to return to San Juan to be with him. Steve and I did not envy his position and hoped he would be able to succeed without allowing the nemesis of his short fuse to make the plan explode.

It took about two weeks for the "happy threesome" to get back on an even keel before a dinner date was planned. Zeus told us that Andrea and Javier were eager to meet us. That may have been true, but there was little doubt in our minds that Javier's reasons for agreeing to this up close and personal encounter were far different in nature than Andrea's sincere desire to get to know us.

By now, it is evident that Steve and I have a great affection for Andrea. We liked her from the moment Zeus introduced us to her on the night of our dinner gathering. Meeting Javier, however, was strange and bore witness to all that Zeus had said about him. From the moment he observed Zeus hug us, his facial expression became stoic. Each was an embrace of greeting, but the redness of Javier's complexion clearly viewed it as something more.

For one involved in work where good public relations and people skills were essential, it was not easy to engage him in conversation. While it was necessary for Zeus to translate so that Andrea could be part of it, Javier spoke fluent English and had no excuse for his apparent detachment from the chit-chat. Uncharacteristically, Steve and I were on the same page as we discreetly observed his body language and posture. Even as we ate supper, the displeasure visible on Javier's face was clearer and more decisive than any words he might have contributed. The few comments or responses he did offer revealed a definite edge of annoyance.

When Steve began to clear the table, Zeus rose to help him. They were already in the kitchen when Javier tapped his finger on the table to get Andrea's attention. Once she acknowledged him, he pursed his lips and bobbed his head as if to say, "Look at them."

That was the moment it became abundantly evident that the relationship between the "love birds" was in danger. Without question, Javier was on a mission to sabotage its progress and chose the method of using insidious, unspoken innuendo to plant seeds of doubt in her mind. He seemed intent on convincing Andrea that our friendship with Zeus was one with benefits.

I said nothing because I knew there would have been an explosion. We had already witnessed Zeus's anger in the past, so my decision to remain silent was both prudent and wise. Knowing I was putting salt in the wound, I waited until we regrouped for coffee and dessert before launching a counter attack.

"Steve, don't they make a cute couple?" I asked enthusiastically.

"Yes, they do. They seem well suited for each other," was his perfect response.

"Don't you think they are wonderful together, Javier?" I jabbed pointedly while staring into his eyes.

"Oh, yeah!" he responded in a most sarcastic tone.

Steve caught my drift and played into the bantering with precision. Javier practically choked on a piece of cake when I said to Andrea, "Zeus loves you very much."

That was when she uttered her first words in English that evening. "I love him, too … mucho!"

By this time, the interloper was squirming in his chair and announced that it was time to leave. Despite Zeus's objection because the hour was still early, they had traveled with Javier in his car and his decision was final.

Javier offered a perfunctory, "Thank you," that was accompanied by a weak hand shake. The other two hugged us tightly while smiling broadly. The contrast was stark. Javier couldn't wait to get them out of our apartment and was feet ahead of them as the three walked to the elevator.

"I'll call you guys tomorrow," Zeus said.

"Please do," I came back with the most affected speech I could muster.

Javier turned and shot a look of sheer disgust. Whatever had been his plan that evening, it did not succeed. Instead, the tables were turned and, without question, we had plucked his last nerve. Unlike so many visits from others that left us in various states of emotional upset, this one resulted in nothing but laughter once I described Javier's table antics to Steve. His response summed it up quite well. "I'm not surprised. He is some piece of work!"

The next morning, our phone rang before eight o'clock. As soon as I heard Zeus's voice, I knew that Andrea had made him aware of Javier's ploy.

"I saw the whole thing."

"Why didn't you tell me?" he shouted back with irritation.

"Listen to yourself! Last night was no time for a war. You know how Andrea reacts to outbursts."

"We gotta get away from him and find our own place before I do something I'm gonna regret."

"That's a very wise idea … and do it soon … he definitely wants to put a wedge between you."

"Gotta go … he just walked out of the bedroom."

Post haste, the couple was able to physically separate from Javier by finding an apartment in Rio Piedras. Their stay there was short, and then they moved to Santurce. Zeus characterized the transient nature of their living conditions as moving from one roach motel to another. Though an unsightly image, we were hard pressed to believe that either place could have been worse than Jay's hovel in Bayamon.

Despite a change in geography, Andrea seemed to crave Javier's friendship. Knowing his propensity for stirring the cauldron, it seemed odd that she continued to associate with the very person whom Zeus had come to disdain. Steve and I tried to analyze her reasoning and came up with a few plausible explanations. The two were on a par in terms of education. Javier, by virtue of his work, was articulate. He was not prone to outbursts.

While there was logic in this reasoning, something else occurred to us. Just maybe, she wanted Javier to be her eyes and ears during the week when she was teaching in Arroyo. Although a possibility, this notion left us questioning the trust component. If this was true, there was little hope that they would survive the inevitable emotional hiccups that were sure to occur.

While he appeared motivated and his efforts were commendable, Zeus found difficulty in maintaining employment for any length of time. Within months, he was hired by two security guard agencies and, before we knew it, he was unemployed again. His seeming inability to hold on to a job was stressful for Andrea. This was fodder for Javier, who took full advantage of every opportunity to speak negatively about the irresponsible work ethic of his supposed best friend. It was not unreasonable for Andrea to voice concerns about her love's potential as a partner bread winner, but she was confiding in the very person who, with baited breath, waited for a break up to occur.

This is how the year 2000, progressed. It was highlighted by continued unpredictability, the ongoing delusional behavior of Javier and an increased awareness, on our part, that notable strides had not been made by this couple for whom we had developed a great affection. Each time Zeus visited us, whether for a few hours or days at a time, we tried to impress upon him the need for personal growth as an absolute prerequisite to his continued healing as well as any possibility of a happy future.

We were convinced that his erratic temperament needed attention first and foremost. This in control, it was likely that he would find more success in the workforce, a steady income would result and Andrea would feel a sense of shared responsibility from him. In theory, this sounded like the remedy to cure all ills. The reality, however, proved to be vastly different.

That year was truly an emotional roller coaster ride as we continued to witness the ups and downs, twists and turns of a relationship which, in all likelihood, would have been long abandoned by others in the same unsettled situation. Despite everything, and for reasons we did not grasp, they chose to remain together and attempt to make it work. By the time Steve and I moved to Florida the next January, we had become close to Zeus separate and apart from our feelings for this couple who seemed to experience more frequent periods of crisis than calm.

On more than one occasion, Zeus told us that we were his guardian angels. Although we were always touched by his sincere emotion, we never believed we were deserving of such flattery. Given his track record during the past year, the essence of such a characterization escaped our understanding. It did not seem as though we had made a noticeable dent in the obvious defensive armor he wore. Clearly, his past remained a weight upon his shoulders. There was more inside the deep recesses of his emotions yet unvoiced. We sensed it. We felt it. We observed it during times when he became captive to silent distraction.

Often, we were tempted to ask him where his thoughts had taken him. If and when he was ready to share them with us, that's when the time would be right. "We're just a phone call away," I said as tears glided down my cheeks on the night before we left Puerto Rico. Neither Zeus nor Steve said too much in this moment of good-byes, but we did learn that his parents lived on the west coast of Florida.

"Do you visit them?" Steve asked.

"I haven't seen them in a while," he answered with a tone of lamentation. "I really miss them."

"You never spoke about them before now."

"There's a lot I haven't spoken about."

There it was in one simple sentence. Steve and I had been correct in our assessment that there remained more gunk in Zeus's gut that needed to be released.

"We have some big projects to do in our house, but when the work is done let's see if we can help you to get to see your mom and dad," Steve said with great affection.

"You would do that for me?"

There were no more words, just tears, as we three embraced each other in a bittersweet moment. Steve's compassionate sensitivity shone as a bright light of reassurance that a change in geography would not affect our friendship. At that moment, we did not realize that the road on which we were about to place our feet would be more unpredictable, indeed precarious, than had been our past journey with Zeus.

By the time the holiday season of 2001 arrived, Steve and I were recuperated from living in dust and debris as project after project was completed in our new home. It had seemed like an interminable process during which contractors and teams of workers turned our living space into a war zone. All was quiet now and we were able to experience what it felt like to be owners, not just captive bystanders.

All of the Christmas boxes which had been at rest in our New York garage for the past two years were with us once again, and the multi-day task of decorating resumed. During those long, tiresome months of our home's facelift, we spoke to Zeus now and then. We were pleased to learn that he was living with Andrea at her home in Arroyo and that a long overdue distancing from Javier finally had happened. He was working and, for the first time, we sensed that he was truly happy and at peace.

One morning during mid December, he called to extend the greetings of the season. "I want to come to see you guys for Christmas," he announced with an animated voice.

"Oh, I don't know," I answered quickly.

"You're still doing work in your house?"

"That's not the issue." Despite my explanation that it was rather late to make an airline reservation which, no doubt, would be very costly, he persisted. After leading me along as he pretended to be perturbed by my reasoning, he let me in on what had been an intentional decision to tease me.

"I'm at my parents' house in Florida … about two hours away from where you live."

"No way!" I yelled so loudly, Steve ran into the kitchen thinking something was wrong. I handed him the phone and his face lit up like a Christmas tree. By the conclusion of that phone conversation, plans were made for Zeus to visit us.

There were a few days between then and his arrival to stock up on food so his always ravenous appetite would be satisfied during his stay. The words of Lourdes Rivera, the woman who befriended Annie and invited her to Christmas dinner in Maria's absence, rang loudly in our ears … "Everyone should have gifts to open on Christmas." Although it was an unexpected last minute shopping venture, we made a number of purchases so that when Zeus saw our home for the first time, he'd know that Santa had made an early stop.

Steve and I paced back and forth inside the small Greyhound bus terminal with excited anticipation. It was as if we had not seen Zeus in years, when in fact it had been only eleven months. Of course, tears flowed, but they were happy ones for a change. He looked wonderful and his voice gave a clear indication that life had been good to him. He was most complimentary as he toured our home and stopped short as he gazed at our Christmas tree.

"Santa said to be sure to wish you a Merry Christmas," I said matter-of-factly.

"Santa … what?" he asked.

"Yeah, Santa made an early stop." I pointed to the gifts that lay beneath the tree.

"Oh! He brought you guys your gifts early."

"No, Zeus, he brought them for you."

"My God… these are all for me?"

"You must have been a very good boy!"

What should have been a moment of humorous exchange became a deeply emotional one. He cupped one of his hands over his mouth as if he were incredulous of the sight before him. We had seen his tears on other occasions, but this was full blown sobbing.

We settled him down and told him to sit on the rattan rocker adjacent to the tree. One by one, we handed him gifts. He became like a little boy as he ripped each open and reacted every bit the part. While there was nothing in any of the boxes that had extreme tangible value, there was an invisible presence in each which gave them immeasurable value — our deep affection for him.

He returned to his parents' home to celebrate Christmas Day and then made a second bus trip to Ft. Lauderdale so he could join in the festivities of our "Second Day of Christmas" holiday gathering. He met our neighbors and friends, all of whom were smitten with his vivacious personality. His visits with us made this special time of year all the more meaningful. Zeus had no way of knowing that his presence in our home lightened a burden Steve and I carried. He was our link to Puerto Rico and eased the emotional churning that came from thinking about those we had left behind.

The next time we saw Zeus was Easter of 2003. It had taken a year and a half to get schedules organized so Andrea could accompany him to Florida. She had not changed at all and still possessed a spark that made her so attractive. Zeus, however, did not project the same sense of happy fulfillment we had witnessed during his Christmas visits with us. While we spent hours chatting with Andrea in the best Spanish possible, Zeus remained in the guest room watching television. He was not working again and Andrea was becoming impatient. One afternoon as the three of us sat on the patio enjoying cocktails, he decided to join us.

I made a passing reference about work and he exploded like a volcano. "I know what I have to do … don't preach to me."

I was taken aback by this inappropriate outburst and Steve's jaw dropped. Apparently, Andrea got the gist of what he blurted and went on a tirade in Spanish. As best as I was able to catch, besides the substance of what was her obvious displeasure with his behavior, was her chiding him for his lack of manners in someone else's home. He stormed inside slamming the sliding glass patio door behind him.

We sat speechless and just looked at each other. This was the moment we learned that Andrea spoke some English, but had always been embarrassed because she feared that she would be laughed at. She felt at ease with us and made a noble attempt to communicate in our language. Her use of it was not poor at all!

Having had to piece together conversations with Roberto years earlier, I had become adept at summarizing the context of a discussion. Zeus's personality, his inclination to explosive behavior and an unpredictable inability to remain employed were getting under her skin. She was growing more and more impatient with the frustration of dealing with this most annoying threesome. She was adamant when she commented that her girls were grown and she did not want to be his mother. She excused herself and went into the house. She did not return to the patio.

After nearly twenty minutes, I went inside to find out what was going on. Her suitcase was on the bed and she was packing. "I no want to stay with him," she said when she noticed I was standing in the doorway.

The offensive tone used by Zeus earlier was replaced by a calmer one as he attempted to stop her.

"You have to convince her to stay," I said as softly as I was able, even though I was still quite annoyed at his childishness.

"I'm trying."

I left them alone and returned to the patio to let Steve know what was happening inside. "He knows how she gets when he raises his voice. What the hell is wrong with him?" was Steve's on-point analysis.

Just then, they came out and sat with us. "I'm sorry, Frank. I shouldn't talk to you like that."

"It's okay ... forget it."

Clearly, this apology was a condition to Andrea's agreeing to stay for the rest of the week. The remaining days of their visit were pleasant but, the truth be told, we were not sad when it came to an end. What we had thought to be steady growth in their relationship had proven otherwise during this somewhat unsettling time together.

Andrea sent us a beautifully written thank you letter in which she expressed what a wonderful time she had while at our home. She apologized for the incident which she hoped did not spoil the visit. She also informed us that she and Zeus were not living together and that he had returned to San Juan. At that moment, she was not sure whether he was working and living on his own or if he had returned to Javier's apartment.

The tone of her writing almost sounded as if she and Zeus had parted ways, but we could not confirm if that was true because of the vague language she used. It seemed that a cooling off period was needed.

During the remaining months of 2003, we did speak to Zeus, but those phone conversations were infrequent and brief. At some point, he had returned to Javier's place. We were puzzled as to why his manner with us was short and his tone was one of irritation. Something was definitely wrong. Either he was annoyed because he had no other choice but to return to his "friend's" apartment or a steadily eroding relationship with Andrea had begun to weigh heavily upon him. Perhaps it was a combination of the two that resulted in a marked change in his personality.

We always received a beautiful Christmas card and note from Andrea and, at times when they were not together during the holiday season, Zeus always called us. We received her card, but there was no call from him. We called his cell phone only to find out that service had been discontinued. Thinking he might be visiting his parents in Florida, we entertained the idea of calling their home. They were elderly and we did not want to cause them to become upset in the event that he was not there, so we scrapped the idea.

As much as we did not want to call Andrea, she was the only one who might know how we could contact him. She was happy to hear from us but was quick to add that she and Zeus were at odds and she did not want to talk about it. What a surprise! She gave us his new cell phone number and as soon as we concluded our conversation with her, we called him. Given the complexion of past phone contacts, I was cautious about what I said and made a concerted effort to keep the conversation light and lively. He actually sounded excited when I told him we would be coming to Puerto Rico and wanted to see him.

"My guardian angels are coming to see me," he said with a serious tone.

"Why do you always say that?" I asked.

"Because it's true … we'll talk when I see you."

I shared that tidbit with Steve. Neither of us could imagine the meaning of his statement, but we were about to find out.

"Flight attendants, prepare for landing," the captain announced as we gazed out the window and saw "our" island below on that bright morning of January 9, 2004. Our excitement was indescribable when we landed and the sound of applause filled our ears. This always had been a defining moment, one that exuded joy because of a safe return home.

Barbara was waiting for us outside the condominium in which we would be staying, Las Olas del Mar. It was an imposing structure that was set back from the avenue and hugged the beach. She was quite busy that day. Her apartment rental enterprise was flourishing and the winter months were hectic. There would be time during our vacation, however, to visit with her, Rafael and "Mommy," because she extended a dinner invitation to join them midweek. That was when she would have time to catch her breath.

The studio apartment was large and ample, a comfortable setting for what we were sure would be a perfect week. After unpacking, we made a list of items we needed to purchase and headed for the supermarket. Having stocked the apartment with necessities, we took our first walk along the avenue in three years. I mentioned to Steve that something felt strange. "Me, too," he answered. Perhaps it was psychological, but we both felt like outsiders. Given the intimate connection with the island which was ingrained in us, this was a strange reaction. Despite that initial realization, we were determined to embrace this place we loved with every bit as much fervor as when we were residents.

The next morning, we arose early so we could enjoy some beach time before Zeus arrived at noon. He knew the building's location and would wait at the security window. While Steve soaked up the rays, I sat under a nearby palm tree. Its proximity to Steve's beach towel allowed for conversation. Unlike past planned visits with others when a discussion strategy was developed, we decided that we would allow Zeus to direct the course of our interaction.

We got back to the apartment at eleven o'clock, took showers and began lunch preparations. As soon as I exited the elevator, I saw the back of his head. He was sitting on a bench outside the lobby entrance. I opened the door and called to him. When he stood and turned to me, my heart sank. Weight loss was obvious and partnered with a paleness which accented black bags under his eyes that made him look like a shadow of his former self. I knew, in an instant, what was wrong, but greeted him as if I hadn't observed the blatant change in his appearance.

Then and there, I decided what had to be done and hoped Steve would be agreeable. After they greeted each other, Zeus asked to use the bathroom. We moved to the far end of the kitchen where I shared my thoughts with Steve in little more than a whisper.

"We have to get him away from the island for a while before something drastic happens. He's back on drugs. If we don't help him, who will?"

"I thought the same thing as soon as I saw him."

Just then, we heard the squeaky bathroom door open and ended our momentary huddle. For the first time, we felt awkward in his presence and were unsure about how to tackle what was an extremely delicate situation. He sensed our uneasiness and broke the ice as we sat at the kitchen table. "I've been very depressed."

"What's making you so sad?" Steve responded with predictable tenderness.

"I feel like my life is going nowhere."

"Tell us what you mean."

Despite the fact that he looked like hell, Zeus was very much in touch with his emotions and provided a clear self-analysis. As he spoke, it became abundantly clear that he had come to the point where he questioned his purpose and worth. The lack of sustained employment, couple issues, continued annoyance with Javier, and the guilt of not being able to do enough for his children had formed an avalanche ready to smother him. Never, had we heard Zeus speak about himself like this.

In the past, he seemed better able to cope with issues even if there existed some uncertainty about how to resolve them. Now, it was as if his emotional gas tank was empty. Zeus became quiet as he made a sandwich. A facial gesture from Steve told me that it was time to put our plan into motion.

"Zeus, we want you to come back to Florida with us. You'll be able to relax and clear your head."

"You want what?" he asked as if my words had not penetrated his ears.

"Come home with us. You'll be comfortable and safe. We'll send you to visit your parents, too. You need them now."

"Oh, my God! You really are my guardian angels!" he sobbed.

Steve gripped his hand. "Don't worry, everything is going to be okay," he said with resolve.

Zeus reached over and grabbed my hand creating a literal physical connection among us. It took a few moments for him to settle down and begin to eat. Gradually, his facial expression became more relaxed and we saw his first smile. "Thank you … I don't know what else to say."

After lunch, Zeus came with us to the American Airlines office which, fortunately, was located on the main strip. Within a few minutes, he was holding an airline ticket in his hand. It was not our intention to let him be its keeper for the rest of the week. We just wanted him to feel the tangible reality of our concern and affection for him. We hoped that this paper life-preserver would encourage and motivate him to gain back some strength during the five days that remained until our return home.

Before he left us that afternoon, he told us he was staying at Javier's apartment. Zeus had not told him we were coming to the island and had no intention of mentioning anything about Florida. Zeus owed Javier no explanation and given the jealous one's poor attitude and behavior, less was definitely more in this case.

Although it was an enjoyable week, it took on a different complexion once we connected with Zeus. We were able to spend a lovely evening with Barbara, Rafael and "Mommy," and enjoyed a lunch date with Don, our retired teacher friend, but we were distracted by the physical and emotional condition of Zeus. Our hearts were heavy, yet we were filled with hope that our decision, on his behalf, would have positive results. This was the very first time in all the years we had traveled, that the thought of leaving the island was viewed with more anticipation than had been the excitement of arriving there.

Three weeks was the time frame during which Zeus would be able to relax, reflect and regroup. The first sign of improvement was the gradual regaining of an appetite we remembered as always being voracious. Within days, his complexion looked infinitely healthier, the puffy discoloration under his eyes was barely detectable and he commented that his shorts felt a little snug.

Sleep, however, presented more of a challenge. At the onset of his visit, there were nights when his moans, sometimes yells, awakened us. The emotional issues, played out in disturbing dreams, would not be as easily remedied as the needs of his stomach. He talked with us about the subconscious "action" that often prevented him from enjoying uninterrupted rest. These bad dreams, as he characterized them, were not something new, but unpleasant scenarios that had plagued him for some time. This was new information to us because we never were aware of it in Puerto Rico. Perhaps we were more attuned now because our bedrooms were across the hall from each other.

The Andrea, Javier and job situations had been discussed to death over the years, but Zeus never seemed to talk about his children. Since he had made passing reference to them on the day we ate lunch at our condo rental, we needed him to explore what, obviously, had been painful for him to mention. The question arose in our minds, *How do we get him to talk about the kids and his relationship with them without causing an emotional flair up?* This was a tough situation which required a delicate approach.

Steve always became concerned when we spoke with others about painful issues because there were times when, unfortunately, my choice of words and the way in which I expressed myself could have been better. I assured him that my occasional "bull in a china closet" mentality would remain in check. We agreed that we would wait until after he returned from visiting his parents to broach the topic of children. By then, two weeks would have passed and judging from the progress we observed thus far, he might be more inclined to be more open about what was going on with that piece of his life.

During the week he spent with his mom and dad, we spoke to him every day. The decision to provide him with the opportunity to spend time with them proved to be a good one. His parents are very spiritual and quite involved in the church they attend. Of course, sonny boy went with them and in ways unexplainable, he found a reconnection to God. More than at any time during the almost two weeks that already had flown by, his voice was animated when describing to us the experience of going to church with them. This was a very good thing!

He returned to our home for the final week, the last days of his "retreat." We were sitting outside one afternoon when he took out his wallet and showed us some photos. They were pictures of his children. Like daddy, they were extremely good looking. We could only imagine what a beauty Diana must have been. As he told us their names and ages, his voice quivered.

"If this is too difficult for you," Steve began …

He was interrupted by Zeus, "No, it's okay." Beyond identifying them and their ages, the few additional remarks he made about them were in the past tense. He said that his house had been the hangout for his children and their friends who always told them, "You have such a cool dad."

While he spoke, my memory was jolted. He once had said to me, "Don't talk about my kids in front of Andrea." I remembered passing along that request to Steve and nothing was mentioned again by him or us. He closed the wallet and placed it in his pocket. Visible to us was the strain on his face which resulted from this very brief description. We did not push, prod or pry further because it was evident he had shared as much as he felt comfortable with revealing.

By the time the day came for him to return to the island, he looked and sounded like the old Zeus. Our good-byes were emotional ones, but for different reasons. His came from feelings of heartfelt thanks for the three weeks of "recuperation" he had been afforded. Ours resulted from concern that he would be able to hold things together once away from the safety and security of being in our home and having spent time with his parents. We asked him to call us when he arrived back on the island so we would know that all was well.

Later that day, Steve and I readied ourselves for an evening out. "Did you see my bracelet?" he asked.

"You wore it a couple of days ago … where did you put it when you took it off?"

"I laid it here," he responded as he pointed to the opened top dresser drawer in which were pairs of underwear and socks. Thinking that perhaps it had fallen between the rows of whites, I sifted through them with my hands. Since Steve always has been notorious for misplacing his glasses, I reasoned that's what happened to the bracelet. "It'll show up when you least expect it," I laughed.

At about five o'clock, the phone rang. Zeus had enjoyed a very smooth plane ride back home and was at Javier's apartment. In passing, I asked Zeus if he had seen the bracelet Steve had worn when the three of us went out days earlier. That simple inquiry produced a volcanic eruption. Zeus was literally screaming into the phone that he did not take it. No accusation had even been implied much less stated, but that's how he interpreted my question.

I was so caught off guard by his verbal tirade, it was impossible for me to say another word. "Zeus … Zeus," I repeated, but there was no response. He had hung up. I was shaking when I told Steve what had transpired. Without question, the belligerence in his tone ruffled my feathers.

Steve wanted to call him back. "Don't you dare!," I yelled at the top of my lungs, "He owes me an apology … let him do the calling after he calms down." What had been a case of miscommunication was the catalyst that severed our relationship with him for the next four years.

Because of the time and attention we had given to Zeus during our island stay in 2004, we decided to return for some uninterrupted tropical pampering in June of 2005. Having told Barbara how much we liked our accommodations the year before, she gave us the same apartment again. Ordinarily, we preferred vacationing during the winter months and had originally planned a March trip, but renovations to our kitchen took longer than expected and caused the delay in our return to the island. Nothing was going to stand in the way of a completely relaxing week … or so we thought.

Rainfall was heavier and more frequent than we remembered it being during the month of June. That, however, was not the greatest impediment we encountered. On one of the very few sunny days that week, we went to the beach close to "The Wrinkle Room," the happy hour hangout that replaced Tornado after it closed.

As usual, we stopped in for a 'beverage' after Steve basked in the sun and I moved about in search of shade. It was never an easy task to adjust our vision when entering the always dimly lit bar, but on this particular day, it took but seconds to realize that Zeus was looking directly at us as we walked in. He was seated close to the door.

Steve walked to the far end of the bar; I trailed behind. While we waited for Joey to get two ice cold beers, I said to Steve, "What the hell is he doing in a gay bar?"

Before we knew it, we heard a voice behind us. Zeus had pulled up a stool thinking there would be some chit chat. Just as he began to say something, his cell phone rang. "I'll be right back," he announced and went outside. We gulped our beers and made fast tracks out the door.

Once Tornado was no longer in operation, "The Wrinkle Room" was the only cruise spot that remained where the boogies could conduct business. Buena Vista was under new management and 'the boys' were prohibited from entering it.

While we walked back to the condo, the image of Zeus inside the bar unsettled me. "Steve, you don't think he's into …"

"Please, Frank," he interrupted, "he was just having a drink … I'm sure he's not the only straight guy who goes in there."

"Guess you're right," I said and the subject was dropped.

The next afternoon, however, would remove the question mark from my unfinished curiosity of the day before. Two consecutive days of sun, how unique! Steve reveled in the thought of getting to the beach again. Of course, I was not as eager. We had been on the sand for a little under an hour when the sky became overcast and we began to feel random drops of rain. Before we got drenched by what looked like a brewing storm, we picked up and headed for the bar. Apparently, others had the same thought because there was a larger crowd than usual for such an early hour.

We found two empty stools at the far end where the bar rounded so that anyone sitting on them had a view of the front door. We were chatting with another New York Board of Education retiree when I noticed that

Zeus and an older gentleman were sitting together at the opposite end in our direct line of vision. I remembered Steve's words to me the day before and tried not to speculate about the nature of what appeared to be cozy conversation. I forced myself to abandon my visual scrutiny and got into the mix with John and Steve as they analyzed the many ills of the education system. Although I was more curious about what was occurring at the other end of the bar, I did not want it to appear as though I were uninterested in the banter.

I felt a hand on my shoulder and turned quickly. "How ya doing?," Zeus asked.

"Fine," I answered with no emotion.

"You guys gonna be here? I'll be back in a while."

Steve heard the brief exchange but did not interrupt his conversation with John to acknowledge Zeus. As Zeus walked to the front of the bar, the older gentleman stood up. I nudged Steve so I might get his take on the situation.

After exchanging a few words, the two of them walked out of the bar together and turned left at the end of the driveway.

"So, he had a drink and spoke to the guy. Maybe they know each other and that's why they left together," Steve attempted to reason with an unconvincing tone.

"Then why did he tell me he'd be back in a while?" I countered more emphatically.

"Who knows? Anyway, it's his business."

"You're right, Steve."

Once the rain subsided, we decided to begin the healthy trek back to the condo. Even though I had lots of questions, I feared Steve's impatience and refrained from further comment.

One of our rituals that was part of every return to the island was a trip to the old city. The next day, Friday, was our last opportunity to go there. We were hopeful that the weather gods would be kind so we might continue a long-standing tradition. By nine thirty, we were boarding the bus which would deliver us there in about twenty minutes.

We stopped at a red light on the corner where a side street led to the bar. Zeus was walking in our direction on the same side of the street on which the only other buildings were a bed and breakfast inn and a multi unit condo. It had been in that direction that Zeus and his companion had walked when they left The Wrinkle Room the day before. Knowing that Steve would have become quite irritated if I attempted to dissect this most recent observation, I said nothing about what, in my mind, had become more than a strong suspicion.

Our city visit was cut short by yet more rain, but the time we spent there afforded us the opportunity to reconnect with the charm and rich history of the area. Our last dinner that evening was a special one. Andrea drove up from Arroyo and joined us at one of our favorite Italian eateries. It was then that she told us that she had broken up with Zeus and, just recently, began dating another gentleman.

We said nothing about our encounters with Zeus. There was no purpose in our putting salt in wounds that were slowly healing. The best we could gather from her admirable attempt to speak English was that his name was David, he worked in construction, was handsome and very quiet. He spoke no English at all. Her face glowed as she talked about him and their budding relationship. Never, in the more than five years since we had met her, did Andrea look so happy and content.

During the next two and a half years, Steve's health issues prevented our return to the island. Letters and phone calls became the connection to our continuing relationship with Andrea. Most of what she wrote or spoke about during phone contacts revolved around David. It became evident that she was head over heels in love with this guy and, at one point, mentioned marriage as a distinct possibility in their future plans together.

By the fall of 2007, Steve was feeling well enough to travel. By then, the protocol of nerve block injections he had been administered by a pain management specialist made him feel as if he were back in the land of the living and he shared my excitement at the prospect of getting a long overdue island fix. It was during that trip in January of 2008 that we met David and enjoyed a guided tour of the eastern coast of Puerto Rico all the way down to Andrea's home town of Arroyo. We stopped along the way and observed the beauty of small coastal towns we never knew existed.

Once in Arroyo, she proudly pointed out the school in which she taught, then we headed to her home and remained there for part of the afternoon. Andrea was a trooper! She tried her best to speak to us in English and also translate our piece of the conversation so David did not feel like he was outside the loop. Despite her evident frustration from time to time, it was an awesome day which ended with dinner at a roadside restaurant they frequented.

When we returned to our condo, it was about seven o'clock and David looked weary from hours of driving. We invited them up to the apartment so he could relax and catch his breath before their return to Arroyo. We were chatting about the day trip when, from left field, Andrea began to speak about Zeus. We were so caught off guard, a feather could have knocked us over! Between April and December 2006, he was in jail for non-payment of child support. Steve and I looked at each other but said nothing and allowed Andrea to continue this very unexpected revelation. His father traveled from Florida to get him and bring him back to the states.

I asked Andrea how long he stayed with them.

"He is there … no more Puerto Rico."

Something stirred inside me when Andrea described the jail scenario. For reasons I could not explain, I asked for his address. Once our friends left, Steve and I sat for quite a while trying to make sense of what Andrea had shared with us. Unless his own family turned against him and filed a petition, the only one who we thought could make such a claim was the custodial parent. That was impossible because Diana had passed away years before.

Thoughts raced through our minds, none of which we dared entertain seriously. Had the kids actually lived with Zeus's family? Was there another woman with whom he fathered at least one of the children? The possibility that either of these might be true left us cold. At the same time, they gave us some insight into what we always believed to have been a part of Zeus's life that was shrouded in secrecy.

About a week after our return home, we received a note from Andrea that contained an address. Now that we had it, we grappled over what to do with it. It had been four years since the bracelet episode and the severing of what we thought to have been a close friendship. We realized that a material possession bore little value in comparison to a relationship we had labored to nurture for years. We were well aware, too, that we had rejected two attempts by Zeus to speak to us at the bar during our 2005 trip to the island.

The truth be told, we had missed him very much and often wondered how he was doing. Our thinking, especially mine, became murky because of our experiences with others we attempted to help. Had I not overacted to Steve after Zeus's outburst, I know he would have called Zeus right back and, no doubt, there would have been resolution. The time had come for that to happen. We decided to write a letter to him. The address Andrea sent us was that of his parents. Ironically, the day on which the process of healing began was February 13th. It was Zeus's birthday.

"Frank, this is Zeus. I'm so sorry I spoke to you so badly. No one has ever cared about me like you guys. I never wanted our friendship to end … I've missed you and Steve so much."

"We've missed you, too! So, you got our letter."

"No, my mom just called me at my apartment and told me I had mail from Ft. Lauderdale. She said the names on the envelope were Frank and Steve. I was pretty sure I remembered your phone number, and I was right!"

"By the way, Happy Birthday!"

"You remembered!"

"We never forgot it … or you."

"This is the best birthday gift I could receive. Where's Steve? Let me talk to him."

I was happy to hand Steve the telephone because his last comment caused my flood gates to open. It was not only because I was moved by what he said but also that I realized four years of a precious friendship had been lost and we could not get them back. I listened to the way in which Steve spoke to Zeus and imagined it might have been that way if I had not been so pig-headed.

Steve asked Zeus to hold on one moment and cupped his hand over the receiver. "He wants to come for a visit."

"Great! Give me the phone." Zeus and I continued in conversation as if it had been yesterday when last we spoke. Although we were excited by the prospect of seeing him again, schedules needed to be coordinated. During the winter months, "The Brunrich Inn" was as busy as it had been during our years on the island. Zeus was now employed at Ft. Meyers Airport and worked crazy hours. After eliminating blocks of time that were not mutually convenient, we were looking at the month of June and locked in four days.

"Let us know the bus schedule when the time comes."

"No more bus … I have a car," he proudly announced.

"Wow!" I answered enthusiastically. "An apartment, a job and a car … sounds like you're doing quite well."

"Now, I am."

The exchange had been so positive and upbeat, I let his last remark go. There would be time for him to explain it if he chose to do so. Time is one of the intangible gifts of friendship. Sadly, we had allowed it to slip away like sand through an hourglass. That was never going to happen again.

"Stay in touch with us, Zeus. Before you know it, you'll be here."

"Can't wait … I love you guys."

"We love you, too. Have a great birthday."

That June morning was bright and warm. Zeus had called to let us know he was starting the trip at nine-thirty. He'd be arriving just in time for lunch, around noon. At eleven twenty five, the bell rang. Apparently, our friend was as anxious to get here as we were for his arrival. He must have flown on the highway! No one we knew ever had accomplished the tedious drive in such a short amount of time.

We never had seen him carrying excess weight, but he had gained more than a few pounds and sported a belly. His face was much fuller as well. Better this than the gaunt, sickly image that had shocked us in Puerto Rico four years earlier. When we sat at the table, Zeus was true to form. He ate with gusto! He appeared content and although he missed Andrea, his wish was that she had found happiness with David.

"It's wonderful that you feel that way," Steve commented, "Can you figure out why?"

"What do you mean?" Zeus asked.

"You seem happy with your life, so you are able to wish the same for her."

"You guys always know what to say."

"Not always!" I quickly interjected and caused the two of them to chuckle.

During our reunion, we did not get much sleep. We spent hours and hours talking about Zeus's present life and future goals. The lost four years were dead and buried so unless he had the need or desire to resurrect what we already knew was a very painful period of time in his life, nothing would be said by us.

That four day visit opened a new chapter in our relationship with him. Our joking, teasing and moments of seriousness became the script on the clean pages of what was a second beginning, and it was a very happy one.

Dressed in images of hope and promise, this saying is a reminder: "All roads lead home." Years ago, Zeus probably would have argued the truth of this statement. However, with the passing of time on his journey down many varied and unusual paths, it appears he has come to understand that the meaning of home not only refers to physical geography but also, and more importantly, to the seat of his emotions.

His impressions of self-worth, dignity and purpose have undergone a transformation. He views life with more joy because he realizes that change and growth are possible and necessary in order to embrace what it means to feel wholeness. The years of association with Javier have ended. It took Zeus a long while to figure out that Javier's understanding of friendship contradicted the very meaning and essence of the word.

It is abundantly clear that Zeus has begun to glimpse the bright lights that shine upon those who believe that courage, confidence and strong conviction are among the driving forces that make life worthwhile. We believe that he is resolute in his vow to never again walk the dark streets of ambiguity, frustration and fear. Time will tell! While there may be no guarantees in life, there is one thing about which Zeus can rest assured. Steve and I will always be here for him and count him among our closest friends.

Epilogue

Rain had been predicted for the morning hours of January 29, 2009. Luckily for Steve's son and daughter-in-law, Kirk and Theresa, that did not occur because they were scheduled to tour El Yunque, the rainforest. Since they were unfamiliar with the neighborhood, we deposited them at the pick up point, one of the large hotels on the avenue.

Unlike their evident excitement at the prospect of observing all that comprised the beauty of nature, we were filled with reticence. We had not seen it since January 2008, when it was a heap of rubble. Although we were told what to expect this time, we were not prepared to see what had occurred since then.

We walked down the avenue chatting about the enjoyable vacation we were experiencing with the kids but when we approached the side street, conversation ceased. As much as we did not want to face it, we knew that this moment must be embraced. Amid the piercing sounds of jackhammers echoing from a construction site adjacent to our destination, we walked with quiet posture. The closer we came, the louder was the cacophony that resembled an abstract, discordant musical composition. We stopped at a location about fifty yards from where the construction of a condominium was under way. Our gaze became fixed on a vacant lot surrounded by a chain-link fence.

Slowly, the noises that swirled all around us faded and we became encased in a bubble of silence. Tears welled and began to glide down our

cheeks as we looked at the barrenness. The only sign of life were a few birds that swooped down in search of something to eat then retreated just as quickly. The square was dotted with dandelions and smatterings of debris protruding from grass and weeds that had been let go for so long.

Our hearts were pierced by the reality of what lay before us. We joined hands as we entered this time of remembrance, finality, indeed, closure. Something deep within the core of my emotions surged and, one by one, each of them became present. As the images flashed before me, I shared them with Steve so he might be drawn into this experience with me.

Joe, Chris and Mike were busy making drinks. "Ah! My little chick-a-dees," Mike screamed when he saw us. Big José was on a ladder and painting. David the Elder smiled at us then resumed a trance-like stare at the bottle of beer in front of him. The Younger David bounced around the bar with that signature spring in his step. King Pin was conducting business, but stopped to wave at us. Jorge jogged up the deck steps wearing a soaking wet, white Speedo. Antonio relaxed in his usual position against the deck wall and held a bottle of beer; an empty one lay on the rail. Roberto was speaking to some tourists in need of directions to the old city. Emily flitted around the interior in her blinking sneakers while honking as loudly as ever. Annie stood close to us in silence. We felt her calmness and knew all was well. Jay approached two potential customers and blurted, "Hi! I'm the handyman." Our dear Lady Peacock stood on the stage for a gown fitting. She laughed about how tight it was at the waist and how, because of the loose fit on top, the stuffing made her "girls" look droopy. Zeus sat at a table with some customers after having served them drinks. The laughter was raucous because his sense of humor was in high gear.

Yes, all of them were right there with us in one place, at that exact same moment. That was the only way we could handle the nothingness set before us. A grave now, there was a time when a proud building stood on foundation no longer visible. It had a pulse, heartbeat and personality that dressed its indomitable spirit. Although ravaged by nature in the persona of Hurricane Georges, it reclaimed its status with an appearance of newness while maintaining the essence of its inescapable charisma. It was the place where Steve and I began a most unanticipated journey in the summer of 1987. It was our wonderful Tornado!

Still immersed in visual imagery, an indescribable feeling of melancholy gripped us as I shared aloud the transition occurring in my mind's eye. These men and women who were imbedded in the fabric of our lives, and with whom we became close in varying degrees, began to fade from view. I extended my hand as if that gesture would have kept them close to us for a bit longer. The joy of this final gathering, amid sights and sounds so familiar to us, was short lived however. Once they were gone, the bubble burst and reality confronted us again.

For the gift of these fleeting moments as well as the many years that preceded them, Steve and I are so grateful. In truth, we never considered any token of kindness, understanding and sensitivity extended to one or another of them to be extraordinary. We simply listened to and followed the whisperings of our hearts. In retrospect, maybe Steve's brother, Hal, was right when he said, "You two have the ministry of the street."

We pray that the spirits of those no longer with us are resting in the eternal light of God's presence, except for Lady Peacock who is probably performing even as these final words are written. For the others, those with whom we have maintained relationship as well as the ones with whom we have lost contact, our fervent hope is that they will find within themselves the strength to heal, grow and realize the deepest longings of their hearts.

Postscript

When, each and together, we are willing to recognize and embrace our oneness in the common heart of the human family, that is when the sacred identity in every person will be honored, justice will prevail, and peace will be a lasting gift.

About the Authors

F.L. Richards was raised and educated in New York. He earned undergraduate, graduate and post graduate degrees from Queens College, Hunter College and Pace University respectively. During his twenty eight years as an educator, he taught English at the junior high school level then went on to become assistant principal and principal of an elementary school.

He is the father of two sons, one daughter and has been blessed with four granddaughters. His passions are writing and teaching. He has found a way to combine them by offering courses in creative expression to seniors in his home community.

Richards is a member of the Academy of American Poets.

Steve Brunner was also raised and educated in New York. Both undergraduate and graduate degrees were earned by him at Hunter College. He taught various grades at the elementary level and during the last nine of a thirty-two year career, he provided art instruction to all grade levels.

He is the father of two sons, one daughter and the proud grandfather of a granddaughter and step-grandson. His interests include reading, gardening, theater and opera. He is also an avid supporter of animal rights.

Frank and Steve have been life partners for almost twenty-five years and currently live in Florida. Their journey together has been guided by a simple principle: "It is not important who you love but that you love … unconditionally."